AFTER THOUGHT

First paperback edition, June 2023

ISBN 979-8-9879805-0-7 (Paperback)

ISBN 979-8-9879805-1-4 (E-book)

Library of Congress Control Number: 2023905321

Book design by Nuno Moreira, NM DESIGN

Published by Nate Eckman

Austin, Texas

www.s-ly.blog

@itsnateeckman

AFTER THOUGHT

NATE ECKMAN

DEDICATION

To Peter Awn, whose love for life I wish all could have witnessed.

CALL US OBSOLETE

Ada Lawrence stood in her shower, not yet wet, and debated returning to bed for another hour of sleep. But recently, Ada's mind re-arranged itself while she slept. Upon awakening, Ada struggled to distinguish dreams from memories. After each slumber, she felt a bit more adrift, further from a reality she could fully comprehend. Ada never asked if anyone else felt the same. She buried these thoughts in hopes that her nighttime imaginings would fade into nothingness.

Refusing herself another bout of delusion, Ada plunged her body under the icy beads of water. She gasped for air, but her chest couldn't fully expand. Although Ada had started her mornings this way hundreds of times, it was never any easier—the shock any less jarring. It wasn't the pain that drew Ada into the cold, it was how the temperature eradicated everything abstract. Under the cold water all Ada's worries dissolved to a single thought: flee. She always disobeyed this instinct. Instead, Ada stood firm in the chilling water and anchored herself with a slow, steady breath. It was a breath that never came quickly, but always, eventually, she found. And once she did, she'd say to herself, this is good. Cold, but real.

When Ada exited the shower, a red light activated from above, warming the space and evaporating the few droplets of water still clinging to her skin. Ada's told that she's thirty. Her taut, poreless skin suggests an age even younger. But Ada's stern and studious face betrays any signs of youth. There are no papers to prove her age. For obsoletes, like Ada, life before living in the Stratum of Knowledge is folklore. All she could examine of her past was observable in the mirror before her. She traced the edges of her torso with her fingertips. Then Ada stared deeply into her eyes through the mirror. Her mind flashed to a scene she tried drowning in the cold water; a moment when her mother, Elena, coddled her as a toddler. This was impossible. Ada's mother had died in the war when she was one.

Then, a numbing zap faded her memory black. Ada reached for the base of her neck, and caressed her BRiDG, a tiny neural device embedded into her cerebellum. A device which everyone who survived the Second Civil War wore in promise of everlasting peace. The BRiDG was invented by Sixth Domain Industries (6Di), and was the antidote to conspiratorial thinking and misinformation. It was a piece of neural-hardware that connected the human mind to The Sphere—6Di's proprietary web—which was a sanitized, safe version of the former internet. On it were no lies. No threat of radicalization or delusionment. All that remained on The Sphere, and in each mind connected to it, was truth.

Although it was still dark outside, lights throughout Ada's apartment illuminated to mimic the sunrise, as Ada's body and hair dried. Then, Ada's BRiDG spoke, "Good morning, Ada."

"Good morning, Lily."

Ada inspected her tight jaw line and plump lips, when, in the mirror, a series of agendas unfurled. Lily spoke to what was written, "Agenda A: assist in the digitization of the Renaissance archives."

Ada, uninterested, said, "pass."

Lily commented, "a boring era, but I had to ask," then read the next option, "Agenda B: assist in the digitization of personal journals from the Stratum of Reason."

Ada smirked. "Accept."

Lily, expressing a kind of programmed joy, said, "Excellent, Ada! Agenda B contains 2,532 pages. One other person will be assigned to work beside you on Agenda B. If you reach your daily quota of one thousand items you'll both finish Agenda B by lunchtime tomorrow. Begin at your earliest convenience."

Ada hadn't cared much for removed eras in history so much as she wanted to understand her own. Whenever possible, she worked on agendas in Second Civil War history or on projects from the Stratum of Reason. Those in the Stratum of Reason were officially citizens of the Sixth Domain. They were permitted to write, given that their complete dependency on the BRiDG allowed them to factually recall the past. So, Ada chose projects from the Stratum of Reason in hopes of discovering a single word of her late mother Elena from someone still alive.

The mirror blanked. Ada asked Lily to show her "the clocks."

"Certainly," Lily exclaimed, "the time is now 5:16 a.m. You've 212K artifacts remaining before earning your citizenship. You're approximately one year ahead of the obsolete expiration date."

"And my father?"

"Byron has 950K artifacts remaining. At the current pace, he is 11 years behind the expiration date."

Those who lived inside the Stratum of Knowledge had not yet proven their dependency to the BRiDG—their minds still susceptible to misinformation. Reasons for susceptibility varied. Some, like Ada, were born into the stratum. The older folks were slow to work. Few, like Byron, lived as miners. All miners were criminals, and struggled to complete daily digitization tasks following their underground labors. All obsoletes were tasked to complete the nation's reconstruction project coined "total digitization" which promised to place a digital replica of every known artifact onto The Sphere, making them available to every living mind. Those who were forced into political retraining were called obsoletes, for each had exactly two more years until Day Zero. Two more years to finish their million-item quota. This number ensured dependency on the BRiDG. Those who failed to complete the task would be sentenced to a life in the mines.

After a great pause, Ada asked, "Lily?"

"Yes, Ada?"

But Ada couldn't dare conjure the thought aloud. She wanted to hear, as she had dozens of times before, what the public record said of her mother and when she had actually died. But she thought the question was excessive, suspicious. As if the fact were incapable of embedding itself into her mind as true and that it would target Ada as one of those dangerous minds. So instead, Ada sighed, and said, "never mind."

"Of course. Good day, and good luck, Ada."

Ada slid into her sector's assigned uniform. A, black, seersucker jumpsuit; surprisingly stylish for being attire assigned by a corporation. Ada laced her black athletic sandals around her feet. Before she departed, she affixed an ornate band around her left bicep, which indicated that she resided west of the main interstate that divided the Stratum of Knowledge into two. The band bore two yellow diamonds, signifying that she belonged to sector twenty.

After she dressed, Ada stepped into the silent hallway, where 6Di's proclivities for style extended beyond its uniforms. Even the hallway Ada paced, which bore no purpose but to guide obsoletes from their residences to the elevator, was acutely adorned with a moody blend of abstract accessories. Accessories which, in past eras, would have been reserved for those in a luxurious class. The purpose of these objects hadn't changed. They'd always acted as a symbol of success and security. Which, for a people akin to corporate slaves, didn't act as proof of their successes, but rather to mask their oppression.

When Ada arrived at the elevator, its doors immediately opened. The car, empty, was carved from a chunk of gold the size of a utility closet. Its innards rocky and imperfect as the surface of an asteroid. On her descent, Ada observed, as she did each morning, the carved subtleties with renewed curiosity. How odd, she thought, that this rock is so valued. The earliest kings surrounded themselves with gold, sanctifying their existence; and for thousands of years, gold represented stability, wealth, and prosperity. Ada, frankly, didn't understand the obsession with gold. Not outside the elevator. Certainly not while on it. It was, to her, just a rock.

Then the elevator came to a stop, which Ada hadn't expected. Only twice in the past year had her morning descent been interrupted by another passenger. But those were miners. And three months ago, all were moved to units below ground in order to most efficiently transport them from work to home. But efficiency had nothing to do with their relocation. Truth was, 6Di deemed the miners too unruly for the class of people that they were trying to curate into citizens. None would become citizens, anyways. At least that's the way their lives were designed. No one could archive one million artifacts before Day Zero and also complete daily twelve-hour shifts underground, culling raw minerals out of the earth for 6Di's insatiable material consumption. Ada's father Byron had tried for a month. Three weeks in he fell asleep underground mid-shift and lost his index finger as punishment. Famously, miners who witnessed his punishment claimed he didn't wince; not when they sawed his finger clean off nor when they cauterized the wound with a branded iron that read "6Di."

At the unexpected stop, the elevator door hissed open. The sound made Ada think of her father's hand sizzling shut. The thought so preoccupied Ada that she hadn't acknowledged her friend Natsumi. Not after the door opened, nor after she stepped aboard.

"Ada?" Natsumi wondered, "are you okay?"

"Natsumi?" Ada said, surprised, "is-is it today?"

Smiling, Natsumi replied, "Today is the day."

Still jarred by the conjured images of her father's punishment, Ada jumbled a response, "You seem so-so…calm. How are you so calm?"

"I think I'm feeling too much to express anything. I'm excited. I really am. But I'm also a little scared. Who do we know beyond these walls? What do we know? Today, for me, everything starts anew. A new home, new friends, new rules, new standards of living. It's all supposed to be better but…" Natsumi pondered her words, "There is some immeasurable value in old habits."

"Yeah," Ada said, smirking, "comfort."

They both sighed. The elevator dinged before its doors opened to the ground floor. Ada and Natsumi stepped into the lobby. Ada asked, "what are you archiving on your last day?"

"Agenda D. It's a massive project. I heard there are about seven billion more artifacts in that collection."

"How many more till you're done?" Ada asked.

"Three hundred and sixteen," Natsumi said. "I should be able to make the 3 p.m. shuttle."

Jokingly, Ada asked, "You won't forget me on the other side, will you?"

Natsumi laughed, and after a pause replied, "Never."

"I can't wait to join you."

Then there was silence. Natsumi shuffled her feet, to reposition her stance and fill the silence. When she settled again, a howl of outside air whispered into the elevator car. Noises Ada focused on to avoid the stifling sadness.

"These goodbyes never get easier," Ada confessed. "You've been a sister to me."

"And you to me."

"But no one ever comes back. And I want you to know that's okay if you don't. It's like you said. Today for you, everything starts anew."

Their stomachs knotted at the sickening thought that

this walk might be their last minutes together. Neither Ada nor Natsumi noticed the soft morning glow illuminating the horizon. Neither noticed how the surrounding towers reflected dawn, how each building appeared to burn like candles. Their heads hung low. Their eyes focused on their shadowed feet. The archive's entrance still a quarter mile away. A pace which they'd walk briskly. To warm themselves against the cold, and avoid interactions with any of the guards that lined the pathway connecting home to work.

A dozen paces later Ada asked, "But why do you think no citizen ever chooses to live in this sphere?"

"That's a query that has no answer."

Uncomfortably, Ada confided, "I know, that's why I ask."

Natsumi replied sternly, "You should be careful who you're asking that to."

"I'm asking you."

Natsumi stopped, pulled Ada's ear close to her mouth and said, "If it's not a query that has an answer, then it's not important. That's what I think." Natsumi noticed a nearby guard who was acutely observing their confrontation.

"Now look," Natsumi continued, "guards are interested in what we're doing. I'm not interested in entertaining your speculations. Not at what I know they cost. Just look at your parents. Do you want that life? I know you don't, that's why you're the first one at the archives every morning. But you know as well as I do that curiosity is reserved for those on the other side—for those who've seen enough facts to begin to discern one from the other. Maybe tomorrow I'll write what I think, so that later it can be digitized and queried. But as long as we're on this side, the world is black and white. Authorized or not. Archivable or non-existent. Do me a favor, Ada, and stop asking questions that don't have answers."

Ada felt an all too familiar zap. Her mind jolted, and questions she so clearly articulated drifted further from her mind's eye, until each letter blurred into something incomprehensible and Ada couldn't recall exactly what it was she just asked. Ada felt haunted by these thoughts and memories that no one else seemed to share, fearing that maybe she, like her father, would be sentenced to a life in the mines.

Natsumi pursed her lips into a frown and awaited a response. But Ada only mirrored Natsumi's face, subtly bobbing her head in agreement. After a brief moment, they both resumed walking. They reached the archives. Outside its entrance, above the double automatic doors, a sign read: Don't think, compute.

At this hour, the entrance of the archives was still. By noon it'd be bustling with a majority of obsoletes in 20W occupying the facility to complete their daily quotas. Though attendance to the archives was mandatory, its aura was uplifting. A structure that represented liberty, and transformation, where obsoletes eventually earned their right to citizenship. And the only known place where obsoletes and citizens coexisted. Though, interactions between the two groups were rare. That didn't matter. Just the thought of brushing shoulders with a citizen was thrilling.

The archives worked like this: citizens sorted and queued physical artifacts to be archived in the basement level. Those piles were then dispersed to their corresponding wings. To natural history, technology, philosophy, current events—wherever was most appropriate. Each morning obsoletes selected which wing they'd want to spend their day. The most desirable slots went early. Current events would have no more available slots by seven each morning. And these sign ups determined which wings, and which desks in each wing, needed objects. So, when Ada arrived at her desk each morning there was a pile of artifacts awaiting her. Depending on the object, she'd scan, photograph, or transcribe it. Whatever best represented this object in a digital sphere. And once it was replicated in The Sphere—the 6Di's proprietary web—the artifact would be elevated by pulley or vacuum into the ceiling where a citizen would ensure the information entered accurately represented the object's description. The process was often mind numbing. But Ada found it odd, mostly how history had become the means to rebuild a new society, and that its control meant preventing any future wars.

Structurally, each archival facility paid homage to the grandest libraries of previous generations. At least, that's what the elders in 20W claimed. Ada had never been in a library. No one born in the last three decades had. Libraries defied 6Di's declaration of digitization. They were poor for progress. Opulent totems of a now-gone era. Ada remembered that her father, Byron, once told her that each town used to have its own library; and that all of them were carbon copies of another. Each void of anything unique. Just colossal wastes of energy and resources. Gatekeepers to truths which, if digitized, may have prevented the Second Civil War. For, on their shelves were stories that invalidated conspiracies from the insurrectionists. But inefficient truths perpetually halted exponential progress. And in the face of a technology that promised to make available all truths to all people, libraries vanished. Now each surviving person connects to The Sphere through their BRiDG, plugging into their minds an infallible foundation of knowledge.

The BRiDG was to modern memory as water pipes were to developed nations in the early 20th century. If The Sphere was a reservoir, filled with clean, ready to ingest water—in its case, sanitized, and safe to consume information, then the BRiDG was the vehicle that delivered those truths. The BRiDG minimized mental infections—like conspiratorial thinking and proliferating falsities—and thus elevated the standards of mental health across the population through consistent consumption of clean information. This was the basis of 6Di's promise to everlasting peace. No longer would people spend their days thinking. They simply computed. Truths and facts were no longer suspect, or mysterious. With the BRiDG implanted at the base of one's cerebellum anyone could know anything verifiably true. Underlying one nation, was, at last, one mind.

This was the driving spirit behind Total Digitization. After an obsolete archived one million artifacts into The Sphere they developed what scientists called, "a neuropathic dependency" on their BRiDG. This dependency ensured all thought could be monitored and censored by 6Di, and that their brain wouldn't think a thought without first passing it through the neural pathways to which the BRiDG was affixed. This ensured every thought was fact checked in live-time, and edited if false. It ensured dangerous, delusional, thinking was a disease to people of the past. Most importantly, it was the moment when someone earned their citizenship.

Today, Natsumi would complete her neuropathic dependency and become a citizen. Ada found it hard to believe that the Natsumi she walked beside at this moment would somehow become fundamentally different from the Natsumi she would meet again in a few hours. That's how change always happens. Quietly, slowly, without any signs of demarcation. No way to distinguish the old from the new.

Toward the end of the main corridor, a hall carved out of a thirty-foot tall block of marble, Natsumi stopped and said, "this is me."

"I'll see you before three?" Ada asked.

"Meet by the shuttle."

"I'll be there." They smiled. Meekly, so as not to stir any emotions other than joy. Then they hugged, though gentler than they wished.

Ada walked to her corridor again confused by the gaudy use of gold figurines that accessorized the marble hall. Even the work-corridors were moody and extravagant. Persian rugs cordoned each workstation, atop which rested strong mahogany desks. In a few hours, light would flood through the thirty-foot-high, floor-to-ceiling windows of the outer wall, absolving the need for the soft, warm, spotlights that made the space twinkle until morning. A few night workers were finishing their shifts. Their sunken eyes craved sleep. No one was assigned a shift. Just a daily quota and a life-clock, which was the same for everyone. One thousand items per day, until one million artifacts were digitized. On April 5th, two years from now, obsoletes wouldn't be that different from an artifact. Either become a citizen, a thing inseparable from The Sphere, or nothing.

IN THE NAME OF PEACE

Alone at her desk, Ada was surprised to see a journal rise, written by a citizen named "Lionel." She'd worked this desk for years and was used to the same few names contributing content to The Sphere. Occasionally, someone new would submit works for digitization. It was opportunities like this that kept Ada returning to this desk. Before her sat a new voice, a new window into the world of what it meant to live as a citizen; another person that might hold the clue to knowing her mother.

Ada tapped twice the BRiDG at the base of her neck. Lily— her BRiDG—whispered into Ada's mind, "you are entering archive mode, do you consent to full sensory recording for the extent of this session? For yes say—"

"I consent."

Ada's eyes shone a dazzling neon, like a bioluminescent sea reef at dusk. She held the notebook against the desk before her and stilled its first page. Ada blinked twice, and the subtle sound of an aperture closing confirmed that her scan was successful: the first of one-thousand artifacts from her daily quota completed. She waited for another few seconds for her BRiDG to confirm that her picture was satisfactory, then Ada flipped to pages two and three. There were drawings, obscure renditions of a kind of landscape that Ada had never seen. Trees towered over one another. Atop another. And another. *That's impossible*, she thought, *trees can't live that close together.* Who was he to dream of such a scene? Ada, once thrilled to read a new voice from Reason, exhaled with disappointment. In her mind, Ada began a quiet diatribe, *has he forgotten the privileges he has? What it means to write at all? He wastes that privilege basking in the unreal, meanwhile the real world moves forward without a record of so many people and events.* Her anger bordered on irrationality. Despite her criticisms, Ada felt magnetized to these scenes. They were blissfully magical. Completely detached from any visual that Ada had ever known as real. She scanned each page. Careful to, as she always was, move slow enough so that she could absorb each image in her mind. To let the memories before her live beyond her BRiDG. But what Ada did not know was that the scenes Lionel illustrated were real, and existed far beyond the walls of her home in the Stratum of Knowledge.

At this hour the sun began to color the room and the guards patrolling the mezzanine became silhouettes to obsoletes below. Their presence was always a kind of silhouette. Their presence more symbolic than particular. Even their appearance, in the clearest of conditions, appeared neither fully human nor robotic. Their true identity was concealed behind impermeable black visors. Visors so dark they appeared as black holes, vacuuming every wave of light that crossed their surfaces. Obsoletes rumored that if you stared at a guard's face for too long that they could also swallow your thoughts. Only the white numerals embossed on the chests of their all-black armored suits distinguished one guard from another. Their purpose was to ensure that no obsolete wasted too much time at their work station socializing or participating in anything that wasn't digitizing. This included the prevention of theft. If any attempt was made to transport an article out of the facility, the punishment, obsoletes were told, was death. No one ever stole, though. Security was too tight. And even if someone could walk away with a book, or jewel, that item could be traced back to the same desk and same shift of that particular obsolete. In other words, theft was another name for suicide.

But life in the Stratum of Knowledge wasn't unbearable enough to entice suicide. So, instead of curtailing crime, the guards spent a majority of their time adding to an obsolete's daily quota for violation of minor infractions. Each guard was authorized to assign one hundred additional artifacts per day—often in bundles of ten—in response to obsolete misbehavior. Infractions were blamed for "delaying digitization as decreed by Sixth Domain Industries." It was a catch-all definition which punished obsoletes for extended illnesses, prolonged restroom breaks, or even extended conversations in the archive's halls. Culturally, obsoletes saw these infractions as a sanity tax. A slight attempt to regain agency in a world where there is none. Rarely would an obsolete close a shift without an addition to their daily quota.

After Ada scanned all 123 pages of Lionel's journal, she elevated it into the archival warehouse above. Where, she's told, a single physical copy of every digitized artifact is held in perpetuity. Then a second journal from the Stratum of Reason rose to her table. At this hour, the obsoletes whose eyes craved sleep were replaced by ones recovering from it. The corridor, once quiet, began to hum with the unseeable energy that emits whenever large numbers of people gather. Friendly faces walked to their workspaces. Ada interrupted her scanning at each passing to say good morning to her fellow obsoletes. And happily so. This second journal was, disappointingly, a financial journal from Oliver, her least favorite citizen to digitize. Ada found his work repulsively self-aggrandizing and trite, one of those entrepreneurial types that defined the early twenty-first century American economy. His entry was a self-help memoir titled, "How I Maximized My Impact as a Citizen and You Can Too." Ada nearly gagged at the title. Then laughed to herself at a curious thought, *Sixth Domain eradicated lies but they can't rid of stupid*.

From the corner of her eye, she saw the Simpson twins, George and Corydon, enter the corridor, and rose to greet them. They were positioned five workstations away but before Ada took a single step, Guard 40 shouted from the mezzanine, "disruption to archival activities! Five articles Ms. Lawrence!" Ada glanced at the digital board hanging above the room's doorway and saw her quota increase by five. Ada smiled, shrugged, and sat back at her station. Seated at their stations, the twins snickered at Ada's misfortune.

Oliver's bloviations were so maddening that she imagined herself ripping the journal page by page. But the destruction of original artifacts carried with it a punishment of amputation. The logic was that removing part of history from entering The Sphere would fairly equate to part of an individual entering citizenship without all of themselves. It happened once a year, an obsolete would face a part of history so hard to digest, or they'd encounter a voice so vitriol, that they believed their elimination was worth losing a set of fingers or an arm. Last year, Brian Clarke began destroying propaganda posters from the U.S. Military dispersed during the recent Civil War. Brian knew his father joined the military shortly after this campaign and assumed these posters were at fault for his father's death. For his subversion against the digitization campaign, his left arm was severed mid-shift, in the exact room where Ada now sat. To keep him alive, Brian's arm was cauterized with a blow torch. The entire room smelled of his blood and burning flesh—and the vomit of those too weak to witness his punishment. But all Brian smelled that day was ammonia, from the capsules two guards broke under his nose every time he started to faint.

The visceral displays of punishment that coincide with damaging undigitized artifacts discourage obsoletes from destroying these materials. But these acts of defiance symbolize an often forgotten truth: that as long as obsoletes are the individuals responsible for transferring information from the physical world to The Sphere, history is subject to their will. The lowly are actually the arbiters of truth. As Brian said, a week after his amputation, "some child doesn't know it, but they're never going to face the temptations of war like my father."

While scanning another page of Oliver's tales, Ada laughed to herself at the thought of her losing an arm to defy this man. How pointless it would be when, next week, or month, he'd submit another journal for entry into The Sphere.

"What has you all giggly?" a voice jokingly asked.

Ada looked to the workstation next to her, "Augusta! Good morning."

"I saw you were working the diaries again, so I wanted to see what all the hype was about."

"Oh, they're really hit or miss. I'm just, well. You know."

"Yeah, any luck?"

Ada thought about this and answered, "No. But that's okay."

"You'll learn more about her, Ada. Just don't give up. She must have been wonderful. I mean—look at you."

Augusta Edwards was kind to compliment. Perhaps because she received too many. Even here, in the Stratum of Knowledge, where every outfit and accessory was assigned, where differences between each person were genetic, Augusta's svelte aura made even her uniform appear like an entirely different set of clothes. She had a beauty that surpassed sexualizing, a presence that demanded admiration and turned her witnesses into subjects.

Augusta flashed a smile. Ada returned the gesture. But, as excited as Ada was to see Augusta she quietly resented that they shared the same assignment. There was no doubt that a majority, if not all, of the guards on duty were males, and that Augusta, being the most attractive female in all of 20W would multiply the gazes of guards for the entirety of the day. Usually Ada could count on a guard glancing her way once a minute. Today, she'd have to behave like a guard was always watching. Which meant that Ada couldn't spend time absorbing each interesting page into her memory. She'd just *Click*. Flip. *Click*. Flip.

Ada stood to take a break and asked, "Do you want anything from the cafe?"

Augusta murmured "no" as she kept her head steady during a scan, eyes luminescing toward the pages below.

Ada tapped the base of her neck to exit archival mode. Recordings of all Ada's senses ceased, but the BRiDG continued to monitor quality and validity of thoughts. According to 6Di, details of thoughts were not recorded, only a binary "safe" or "unsafe" code was observable from agents at 6Di—the latter which activated an algorithmic correction which The Sphere independently implemented. The feedback loop between mind and BRiDG was encrypted, wherein 6Di agents were able to observe the volume and type of messages sent but each message's contents were private. Privacy, Sixth Domain Industries understood, was essential to broad adoption of their technologies. A few obsoletes had speculated the security measures were a hoax. Shortly after they were sentenced to a life in the mines. The message was clear to remaining obsoletes. Trust 6Di, or perish.

As Ada walked toward the corridor's exit, she observed the void, featureless faces of the guards above. She wondered who or what was behind those masks. If they were citizens, or something else. She'd never heard of anyone becoming a guard. Then again, she didn't really know what life was like as a citizen. In mid-thought, the Simpson twins magically flanked Ada, and, in unison, asked, "What are ya starin' at, Ada?"

Ada, jolted. "Where did you two come from?"

Corydon kept staring at the ceiling while George answered. "Sorry Ada. Didn't mean ta scare ya."

"I don't see what you're lookin' at," said Corydon.

"Oh," Ada said sheepishly, "it's nothing. I just think this place is beautiful."

The twins looked up again and muttered to themselves. After

a few moments George spoke for them both and said, "Mmm, I guess our minds don' work like yours." Corydon nodded his head in agreement. George continued, "Say, did ya hear today's Natsumi's last day? We should go see her off."

"I'd love that," Ada said. "She's taking the three o'clock shuttle."

"We'll be there," said George. "I'm happy for her—finally joining her family."

"Say," Corydon wondered, "isn't your pops about up for his citizenship, Ada?"

"Corydon!"

"What George?"

"Goodness, I apologize for my brother, Ada."

"What? George, what did I say?"

"Oh, it's no problem," Ada interjected. "We can't remember everything."

"What'd I forget this time?" Corydon pleaded.

"Ya know Ada's dad's a miner. He's no time to digitize."

"Oh hell, how'd I forget that? I'm sorry Ada—really. Wait, your sister Chloe, she's not a miner too is she?"

"No, no," Ada said.

"Then why is she never here?" Corydon asked.

George looked to Ada. Ada sighed, "Chloe is…not right. She can't see anything past her own nose. Thinks everything is about her."

"Well shucks, Ada. I'm real sorry. Really."

"Thanks Corydon."

"If it's not too much for me to ask, why is your pops a miner?"

Ada observed the guards patrolling the halls, "Not now, Corydon."

The Simpson twins gazed at Guard 37 as he—it, whatever— passed across the hall. George leaned into the group and whispered, "I hope they're not a thing on the other side." Ada and Corydon nodded. And all together, they returned to their work stations, and re-entered archival mode.

The day passed slowly for Ada. She normally enjoyed intently observing each page. Committing some details to memory, storing information in her mind aside from her BRiDG. It was her version of the vocal protests that rare obsoletes took once or twice a year that resulted in amputations. It was a small demonstration of her innate freedom she still believed existed. And, it seemed, a skill she possessed that few others did. Her fellow obsoletes depended on The Sphere to know just about anything. It was, like in former eras, what phone numbers became to the modern person; a fact stored away on some digital memory stick. The BRiDG made retrieval simple for obsoletes. Because of its direct connection to people's minds, queries were as seamless as thought. Many obsoletes reported no difference between recalling a thought that they remembered on their own—like how they felt during their first kiss—and a memory recalled by their BRiDG. It all felt like thinking, or computing. Facts and knowledge that their parents or grandparents wouldn't have been able to understand, let alone access, flowed instantaneously into their minds. Most people were happier for it, they felt smarter, though some people reported unexplained feelings of loss the way you might when you can't remember what it is you forgot. Sixth Domain Industries built a slogan for this: *it's not what you know, but how.*

Without the chance to memorize her favorite artifacts through mnemonics or other mental exercises, Ada felt immeasurably bored. Her work reduced to rotely scanning pages, Ada's mind felt grossly underutilized. It seemed Ada's peers never felt the same. They appeared content with scanning artifacts into The Sphere, and simultaneously consuming entertainment from it. An often-used BRiDG feature was coined layered-reality, which projected a transparent layer of an obsolete's favorite video, site, or other visual media over their vision. This eliminated the choice between being "online" or "present." Anyone could always be both. Reality, for everyone, was dual.

Ada, seeking to escape the monotony from this day started small talk and asked, "Augusta, are you seeing anything interesting?"

Augusta beamed at Ada and said, "I see why you love this station."

"Well, don't love it too much," Ada replied, noticing that Augusta hadn't turned to a new page in the past few minutes. "The guards will think you're plotting something."

"They'd let me get away with murder," Augusta said, half smiling.

"Do you take requests?" Ada joked.

They both chuckled and returned to scanning the works at their desks. Ada was now archiving a book titled *Justice Prevails* by an amateur historian named Ruby. The work was about the long arc of justice, as exemplified by the progressive's victory in the Second Civil War. But her cursive caused all kinds of character recognition errors when digitizing. "I don't know why she writes like this," Ada muttered.

Augusta took a few more seconds to stare at the same page she'd been looking at before she looked Ada's way. Augusta peeked at Ruby's scribblings and sarcastically replied, "Oh, classy." Augusta didn't wait for Ada's response before staring back at the page on her desk.

Ada, noticing Augusta on the same page implored, "Augusta, keep the pages turning."

"Sorry, it's just—" Augusta paused.

"What?"

"This journal, it's written by someone named O. You don't think…?"

"It's Oriana? What? No," Ada replied assertively.

Oriana Vespucci was an infamous rebel in the Second Civil War. According to unofficial records, she was personally responsible for over one billion dollars of infrastructural damage at Sixth Domain Industries during the conflict. She became the leader of a now defunct militia known as the Purgers. And though she was never officially pronounced dead, she was presumed killed in a fire bombing of her militia's headquarters toward the end of the war.

"Ada," Augusta gulped, "if it's Oriana. She says she knows Elena, that Elena saved her from the fire."

Ada's face went ashen. First at a thought she feared to articulate. Then at the *zap* she felt flash in her mind. Then at the sight of half a dozen guards walking briskly towards Ada and Augusta's desk. "Augusta, just scan. I'll read it later."

But before Augusta could scan another page, another dozen guards rushed into the corridor. Each positioned themselves to blockade a window or passageway. Then, the Guard numbered 40 shouted, "All obsoletes, remain in archive mode until otherwise instructed!"

What would unfold demanded a kaleidoscopic perspective from every obsolete in this room. Or rather, what would unfold was so sensitive that 6Di required every recollection to simultaneously exist as a digital artifact; a memory subject to their manipulation. Then, the main entryway doors again flung open. A *bang* like that of a gunshot rang. In walked four members of the Memory Corps. The room practically imploded as every obsolete, including Ada, gasped.

The Memory Corps was an elite archival organization whose units preserved the archival process. Individuals varied in their technical capabilities. Translators studied dead languages and transcribed archaic texts into comprehensible and indexable facts. Preservations ensured longevity of artifacts in both physical and digital spaces. Corrections reviewed inbound artifacts, compared it to existing knowledge, and updated old records according to new information. Reconnoiters traced historical passages of information and scouted possible locations where undiscovered artifacts may lie dormant. Together, they operated as a group known as the Memory Corps, as archivists who roamed the Stratums of Reason and Knowledge in search of hidden artifacts.

Members of the Memory Corps were identified by their slick, slim-fitting uniforms. An exclusive olive-green outfit, detailed with a cream trim. On their shoulders, a faded, gold double-circle signified their commitment to each stratum. At the icon's center, was a petite, branded "6Di." Members of the Memory

Corps always wore tan- and cream-colored gloves that protected artifacts from their skin's oil. Their hips were accessorized with small gadgets that to the untrained eye could not be discerned as either tools or weapons. But, unlike all other agents of 6Di, members of the Memory Corps did not conceal any of their faces. They pierced the world with their cunning eyes. They hid behind no personas or disguises, because they were committed to revealing the truth. They worked each day to live out their motto, *Retrieve. Refine. Preserve.*

The four Memory Corps agents surrounded Augusta. The lead agent was a towering, barrel-chested man with hands the size of oars. "Augusta Edwards," the lead agent said, "I'm Agent Jeremiah Warlock with Corrections. And with me today I have Kimberley Green, with preservations; Grace Gordon, Reconnoiter; and Yoko Yamamoto as translator."

Augusta burst into a sob, fearing the punishment that awaited her, the overwhelming sense of guilt that she'd somehow done wrong.

Kimberley, a rusty brunette, with husky blue eyes and the tone of a well-traveled grandmother said, "No Augusta, you've done nothing wrong. Nothing. You just, unfortunately, happened upon an artifact you shouldn't have accessed."

Augusta signaled that she understood with an incoherent nod.

Ada continued to scan the journal before her, albeit quite awkwardly. Never halting her peripheral gaze toward the scene at Augusta's desk. Yoko looked at Ada and said, "It's okay, you can watch." Relieved, Ada placed her journal aside to observe the unfolding events. Ada did so in the same manner she observed pages she committed to memory, with an unflinching gaze.

"Are you aware of what this book is?" Kimberley asked Augusta.

Still sobbing, Augusta could only muster the wherewithal to shake her head no.

"Do you know why we're coming for it?" Again, Augusta signaled no.

"Good. Now if you've any questions about this event please don't hesitate to ask." Yoko, Grace, and Jeremiah nodded in agreement.

Grace, a raspy-voiced woman with white hair who looked like she was bred for a Nordic throne roared, "that goes for everyone in this room! If you recall any of these events and have any questions, we're here to help. Do not hesitate to notify the BRiDG that you'd like assistance."

If Ada's face was being closely observed, an onlooker would have noticed her eyes slightly squint, her lips momentarily curl, her body instinctively rejecting the kindness pouring from Grace. Something about Grace bothered Ada. Her words hung like a plane among ominous clouds.

"Why can't this artifact be accessed by obsoletes?" Ada asked.

The room's aura stiffened as every obsolete inhaled, causing a palpable displacement of air.

Jeremiah broke the tension with a hearty laugh. The rest of the room mimicked Jeremiah in nervous relief. But Ada, resolute, remained stone-faced.

Grace challenged Ada's stolidness and ordered Ada to, "stand down."

"It's just a question," Ada shrugged.

Grace towered over Ada, who was still sitting at her desk. She grasped the back of Ada's chair and whispered into Ada's ear, "And do not even questions have repercussions? Is not curiosity a force more lethal than understanding?" Though the words were ominous, Grace spoke in a nurturing tone.

Ada repositioned herself on her chair. Then, looking eye to eye, seated below Grace, Ada said, "I'd simply like to understand why this is happening. Apparently—"

"Apparently what?"

Ada decided it best to conceal that she knew this author wrote about her mother. "Nothing, sorry."

"Yes, you should feel sorry," Grace responded, "focus on how sorry you feel as you digitize through the night." Ada tilted her head back at Grace in confusion. Grace grinned, then shouted, "All guards! Empty your daily punishment allotment onto obsolete Ada K. Lawrence."

All forty guards initiated a transfer of their remaining daily quota allotments. The board above the main entrance showed Ada's daily quota increase to 3,750.

"Any more questions, Ada?" Grace snarled.

Ada clenched her jaw. Grace leaned into Ada's ear and whispered, "good girl."

Grace started toward the exit with the book Augusta was previously assigned. Jeremiah, Kimberley, and Yoko followed Grace. Yoko, the last member of the Memory Corps to exit the room, turned back into the room once under the door frame. She pulled an instrument like that of a baton from her waist belt, raised it in the air, and the same *bang* that reverberated through the corridor when they first entered again shocked the room.

Then, Yoko was gone. And everything was just as it was before the Memory Corps entered the corridor. Another diary laid before Augusta, which she coolly opened as if it were a casual task on a monotonous day. Across the room, obsoletes behaved the same. There was not a signal that anyone was processing the most recent events. Except for George and Corydon. The twins paced toward Ada, quietly arguing between themselves, seeming shaken by what had just occurred.

"Ada, George and I want to help you with your quota today," Corydon said.

"Yeah," George said, "you didn't deserve that."

"That's sweet of you both. But I can't let you."

"Welp—sure you can," Corydon said, "just send us each another thousand." Considering their request, Ada bit her lip. Obsoletes were allowed to share punishments, since those digitizations were technically work beyond the threshold for neuropathic-dependency. "You'll be here all night. No one has ever completed more than three and a half thousand in a day. Just let us—"

"Come on, Ada," George interrupted, "No one's quota is fully theirs to bear."

George was right. She pondered this irony, or was it a virtue: that the pursuit of self-realization is actually a culmination of your interactions with others. That in the end, everyone becomes who they are because of the influences that permeate their lives. Ada had prided herself, perhaps too much, on her ability to live without intervention. She believed one of her finest traits was her unrelenting individualism. But this, she was always told, would be challenged. For, if any obsolete would become a citizen, they first needed to become a thread in the tapestry of society. One interlaced with the many. And at this last thought, Ada knew that she should transfer today's punishment to George and Corydon. Her BRiDG processed the transaction. The quota board above the entrance, now read:

Ada Lawrence: 2,750

Corydon Simpson: 1,992

George Simpson: 1,823

Ada leaned over her desk, opened another page to Oliver's journal, and said, "Last one to zero picks up tonight's tab." George sped toward his workstation, his brother in close pursuit. Corydon's excitement was tempered by the thought that this tab would inevitably become his to pay.

Minutes became hours but Ada felt no time pass at all. Many obsoletes never felt time pass while digitizing. This, in part, because they roamed The Sphere, engaging with whatever content they found most stimulating. For Ada, who did not enjoy co-existing in The Sphere while there was a task at hand, would instead frequently enter the zone. That hypnotic state between body and mind where time dissolves into something incalculably abstract. Which was what she entered shortly after her interaction with the Simpson twins. The only thought that could have pulled Ada from her flow was thinking about Natsumi. But Ada hadn't thought about her, or time. It wouldn't have mattered anyway. The time was almost 4 p.m. And by this time Natsumi was well on her way to the Stratum of Knowledge.

Ada finally broke from her concentration two hours later

and saw a message from Natsumi that read, "are you still coming at three?"

"Shit!" Ada shouted.

Ada's shout caused the Simpson twins to close out of their entertainment, "what is it?" yelled George. Then, before Ada could answer, he echoed back, "Oh shit."

"Let's just go see," Ada replied. Together, the three remaining obsoletes in sector 20W ventured to the corridor that Natsumi was assigned to that day. Natsumi loved to work in the corridor of Natural History, which had walls built of fossilized bone, and a floor made of preserved paws of elephants, lions, lemurs, frogs, and other less recognizable creatures. The ceiling resembled that of a jungle canopy; and the work stations were slabs of sliced redwood trees. This was the first time that George, Corydon, and Ada had ever entered the corridor of Natural History. They stood in awe at its exoticism. Ada couldn't imagine a place more juxtaposed to the world within the Stratum of Knowledge, where natural life was a subject to the curated blocks she called home— not a setting. Staring up at the jungle canopies, Ada thought *this is just like what Lionel drew* and wondered if he once worked in this corridor and missed its sights, or if places like this existed in the Stratum of Reason.

Meanwhile, the twins scanned the room in search of Natsumi. But the only other life in this room was fossilized. Natsumi was gone. On to the other side. If they'd see her again none of them could know. That's how life progresses in the Stratum of Knowledge, each day another person departs. First they leave the space, and eventually everyone's minds. The gone are eventually forgotten.

And all who remain adapt to the ever-shrinking world. Until the day the clock hits zero, and everyone moves beyond these walls, or is condemned to live to the fullest definition of an obsolete.

Ada, Corydon, and George returned to their assigned corridor for the day. It was a tad past eight and the sun had nearly set. The floor guards departed. A few remained in the upper balconies, as they would all night, no matter if an obsolete was present or not. Though tired, Ada felt the comfort of dusk alleviate unrecognized anxiety. The sun fell like a soft blanket over her body. Ada liked darkness because it allowed her to focus. In darkness, nothing else mattered but what was before you. Which, tonight, wasn't actually the remaining artifacts on Ada's desk.

It was the mysterious connection between Oriana, Elena, and why—or rather how—they wrote anything in journals without being a citizen. Why was Grace so quick to punish Ada for asking what she thought was the only question to wonder? How come the room so quickly returned to normal operations after the final *bang*? These questions replayed in Ada's mind to no answer. The last ten artifacts took her as long to complete as the fifty before. George was already helping Corydon finish his remaining thirty. She felt no rush to finish first. She was the fastest obsolete in 20W when she wanted to be.

Corydon had just three artifacts remaining when Ada finished. Though close, none of them actually believed Corydon would not finish last. Corydon's focus was always lackluster. But what he lacked in his work ethic he made up for with his lively personality. Tonight, Ada knew, would be fun. No work to get up for tomorrow, or responsibilities to limit the extent of tonight's inhibitions.

"Corydon, I hope you're ready to go broke tonight!" Ada shouted playfully.

Corydon put aside his artifact. "Ada, you won't believe this. I exited archive mode twice."

"Corydon!" George shouted. "Three more. Let's go."

"Yes Guard 40!" Corydon shouted. All three burst into laughter, and peered above to the void, featureless faces looking in their direction. "Ya know," Corydon said, "being an obsolete feels tough, but I'm glad I'm not a guard."

"Me too brother. Now come on, let's get this party started."

"Here, give us each one," Ada requested. Together, they finished the quota for the day and together they left the corridor of Living Memory.

"What a day," Corydon exclaimed, "when's the last time all guards on duty emptied out their incentives?"

"Never to my memory," said George.

"What about you Ada? When's the last time—Ada?"

George and Corydon looked back at Ada, who stopped walking and stood staring down the hallway, mouth agape. The twins traced her gaze with their eyes and were shocked when they saw Grace, reconnoiter for the Memory Corps, bludgeoned and lifeless against the floor.

A CRIMINAL MEMORY

The bar Y2K was lively, as was usual for a Friday night. But Ada and the Simpson twins sat slumped at their table and hung onto their drinks like a detective's only clue. Tad, one of the regulars, slapped a small pouch of something powdery and white onto the table. George, barely lifting his head above his glass, mustered, "Not tonight." The other two altered neither their grip nor their gaze.

Tad picked up his pouch and snarled, "I don't know what y'all are on, but if it ain't my shit you're going to pay—dearly." Tad leaned over their table, both hands gripping its edge, "Do you understand me?"

George responded again, "It's not like that. We'd only buy from you, Tad. Just a bad day."

Tad raised his chin, sniffing for any dishonesty. After a few long seconds Tad replied, "Okay George. I trust you," he reached into his jacket and continued, "but I have stuff for bad days too." Another pouch, much like the first, was slapped onto the table.

Corydon looked at him, perturbed. "What part of 'not tonight' are you incapable of understanding?"

Tad kept it cool as he responded, "My bad, my bad. Just trying to help y'all have a good night. You know where to find me if you change your minds." Tad walked to the next table and repeated the same act, as he would all night.

Below the blaring electronic music, Corydon asked, "Is it true he hasn't digitized a single artifact?"

"Yeah," Ada said, "he's planning on living just another two years."

"No wonder he lives like that," George said.

They returned to an impermeable silence. Each of their minds silently searched for the words that could even begin to address the anxiety and fear they all felt but could not yet articulate. Finally, Ada simply asked, "None of us were apart at any time tonight—right?"

George and Corydon looked at one another. Their telepathic look affirmed to one another that neither of them had left each other's sides. As for if they and Ada were ever apart, well, that was a different story.

"They're going to burn us," Ada continued, "pin us against one another."

George interjected, "They'll interrogate us till one of us confesses. It doesn't matter who did it. Who is going to say it was them?"

The three realized that among them, one would be behind bars for murder within days. None could brave asking if they should make that choice now as a team, or let fate unfold. Ada emptied her drink into her mouth. Gone was the last thing that made any sense to her. "Well," she said, "do we want Tad's stuff for a bad day?" George and Corydon, still clinging to their drinks, wordlessly nodded.

Like a new scene in a film, Tad appeared the very next second. He placed the pouch onto the table, winked, and said,

"You'll love it. Whatever's going on between y'all will disappear after your first hit."

"What is it?" Ada asked.

"Stuff for a bad day. Just treat it like cocaine."

"What does that mean?"

"You've never done cocaine?" Tad asked. Ada shook her head. "Here," Tad said, throwing another, much smaller pouch, onto the table, "this one is on me." Then, as quickly as he appeared, Tad was gone. Off to the next table, making his rounds. George received an invoice through his BRiDG and paid it in full before the first bag's seal was broken.

Corydon opened the pouch, scooped a small spoon into the bag, and tucked the substance under his nose, "Here's to forgetting tonight," he said. Then he snorted the spoon clean. They passed the bag to one another. Each scooped, tucked, and snorted the substance into their bodies. Each blissfully faded into neural incognition until the night enveloped their bodies.

Ada woke up the next day alone, in her own bed. The quietness of a mid-morning with no agenda before or behind her comforted her consciousness. Then Ada sprung upward, remembering events from the night prior, and Grace's bludgeoned body laying atop the archive's floor. Ada's breath shortened and mouth dried. She searched for news of the murder on The Sphere. It was nearly eleven the next day, but there was no record of Grace's death. Ada wondered if Grace's body still lay at the entrance to 20W archives, decaying. *Impossible*, she thought. *The body is bagged. The perpetrator has been chosen. They'll skip interrogations and deliver a public sentencing. Today will be my last day.*

Obsoletes were not given the rights of fair trial or a chance to rebut industry accusations. If enough evidence supported a claim of an obsolete's potential actions, it was not possible to refute 6Di's claims. Allowing obsoletes that chance, the industry argued, assumed that their facts were debatable. Facts in The Sphere were absolute. Ada's only chance at remaining untouched, she believed, was if evidence remained too circumstantial. But the murder of a member of the coveted Memory Corps would not go unpunished. Someone would take the blame. And the more she thought about it, the more Ada accepted the unfair idea that such a person would be her. Everyone leaves the Stratum of Knowledge eventually. It's only the lucky that do so while still living.

Ada recalled the infamous case of Stephanie Davies, who was arrested, tried, and punished for the murder of a fellow obsolete who was killed at the same moment Stephanie was having dinner with her family. But 6Di spun together an alibi and propagated it until her family's testimony was made null. For obsoletes their stories are not their own; the life story of each is a product of the stories 6Di authorizes. Truth is between the lips of the orator.

The murder was all a ploy. What no obsolete, not even Stephanie herself, knew was that she was targeted as an *intellectual threat to communal integrity.* The blanket punishment for any obsolete who demonstrated a working memory independent of The Sphere's archives. She remembered events that 6Di believed were best buried in the past. Ada hadn't thought about that case since it happened, hadn't recalled how odd it was the woman she saw on the elevator that evening had just returned from committing, or was about to commit, murder. That's the detail that Ada believed made the conviction unjust. And it's the reason why she never tells anyone about a memory she can't first discover in the BRiDG.

Hours later, Ada still sat in her room, anchored by the anxiety of her pending arrest. She'd obsessively tuned into the news. Then, just as compulsively, turned off the broadcast. Her paranoia increased with each passing hour. Unable to bear the anticipation alone anymore, she casually messaged George and Corydon through her BRiDG, "what happened last night?" After sending, Ada realized that she couldn't remember a minute of her night after snorting Tad's bad-day cure.

Almost instantly, George replied, "Haha, noooooo clue. A good time, I hope."

Corydon, always the slow one, followed with, "I can't recall a single thing. Tad did it again!"

Ada wasted no time getting to why she actually messaged the twins, "…jokes aside, how are you two today?"

"Thirsty with a pounding headache, as expected," George replied.

"No, no, I mean…" Ada wrote. Then continued, "I mean how are you feeling about the news breaking?"

For once Corydon beat his brother to a response, "News?"

Ada felt a *zap*, and knew she had crossed the line. When Ada was young she venerated her memory. As she aged, she realized it was a characteristic that endangered her life. So, she'd keep quiet whenever tempted to ask about the welfare of a student in school who suddenly disappeared, and she'd never follow up about the outcomes of petty-crimes she witnessed on street corners. Ada learned to not discuss whatever was not in The Sphere, whatever was not authorized to be known. To date, this was Ada's most difficult memory to bury. Its images were too visceral. To bear this alone, Ada believed, would condemn her thinking. Suddenly her liberated mind began to feel like a prisoner of its own making.

But George and Corydon waited for a response, so long that George aggressively responded with a set of triple question marks.

Ada assumed the twins both searched for "breaking news." So, she did the same, and forwarded a piece about downtown 20W downsizing because so few obsoletes remain.

"I thought spaces were feeling more empty," George replied.

"How is everyone finishing their quotas so early?" Corydon asked.

Ada laughed at Corydon's response, and exhaled a sigh of relief that she just escaped a conviction of intellectual threat.

At her humblest, Ada wondered if maybe it really was dangerous for her to reason—to think beyond her BRiDG. That perhaps an imperceivable set of signals that without her BRiDG made her world senseless. As if facts were cells, and The Sphere a microscope, making sense of an otherwise chaotic world. Regardless, Ada's ability to reason categorized her as one of an innumerable number of dangerous minds. It was too dangerous for Ada to discover if anyone else's mind worked like hers. Whether Ada was alone in her ability to reason, or just like every other obsolete, she'd never know. For she was certain that whoever made it a public part of their identity would soon after perish. And Ada had much to discover about her mother until that day.

The clock read 1600 and Ada prepped for dinner with her family, as she did each weekend. But Ada hoped that her sister

Chloe would arrive early and diminish the conversation to trivial thoughts and selfish ramblings. Ada felt that she was concealing too many lies at once; found it difficult to remember which events she could openly discuss. What of the note from O, it mentioning her mother Elena, Grace's murder, and the fact that no one else seemed to remember these could be safe conversation? Ada donned a weekend uniform as she contemplated her dilemma: a pair of black, airy joggers and a black, form-fitting, ribbed a-shirt with a small, black 20W band stitched on the strap over her left breast. She pulled her hair to one side, and wrapped it gently in a hair tie. Then Ada departed her apartment and rode the elevator to the floor of the miners, to apartment -1111, home of Byron Lawrence.

Byron hunched over a bistro table in the nook of his small apartment, which perfectly fit his small body and small number of possessions. The space had no windows, which made the place feel dingy and damp. The wall paint was chipped, floor tiles cracked, and appliances were aged and rusted. This was not a space designed to support liveliness but instead self-pity and despair. And Ada's father looked the part of the residents of this space.

"Pa, stop sulking in the corner," Ada announced as she entered their room. "Where's Chloe?"

Byron, scooching upright in his chair, said, "My dear, welcome." He could hardly muster the energy to speak the words.

"My God, what are they having you do? Each week I see you, you look another ten years older."

Byron looked at his feet, reinstating an unspoken vow to silence.

"I was punished yesterday too. Not like you, I'm sure," Ada said.

Byron spoke, this time more firmly, "With your family name

you really should watch your tongue, Ada."

Ada stared into the gray kitchen, at the rusting stovetop and stained cookware. The last twenty-four hours exhausted the reserves that usually fueled her patience to sit in this disarray. Patience which would have let Ada believe that it was all right to spend this meal with her father and sister in the equivalent of a sogging box. But Ada did not possess the patience nor the will to surround herself with the oppressive iconography that defined her parents' existence. She wanted to cloud that reality with a lie. She wanted to immerse them in the grandeur of a private room, draped with suede and velvet and gold. Inhale the scents of an exotic incense, piercing cocktails and rare fish. She wanted to buy an experience that transported them to a life that could only temporarily be theirs.

"I'm taking us out to eat," Ada declared.

Byron, at first bashful, then expressed fear. He claimed his clothes were too filthy, that he felt too tired. "Besides," he wondered aloud, "who could afford it?"

Ada cut right to the point, "We have less than 104 weekends to do this together…"

Wordlessly, Byron stood and prepared himself for a night out in the square. Ada, without solicitation, said, "I'll tell Chloe we're headed to Blasé."

A trail of lights on the floor of Blasé ushered Ada and Byron to a private dining room. The walls were velvet, and under the dim ceiling spotlights appeared grainy. Each curtain absorbed so much of the dim lights that the floor appeared invisible, and the table made of fossilized bone looked as if it was floating. Against the far wall, dinner's first course awaited consumption. Next to it sat an aperitif-filled vase and a small jar of olives. The olives went untouched.

Byron was, as all people are to some extent, a product of his environment. Whatever downcast expressions he animated in his confined apartment dissipated amidst the luxuries that accessorized Blasé dining. Ada fueled that transition all the more, ensuring that their glasses never reached empty, thinking with each pour, *hopefully tonight he'll tell me more than he has before*.

She wouldn't have to wait long. Soon, her practically mute father slurred, "They're pushing us to the edge. And I don't know how much longer I can take it."

"Pops, don't say that."

"It's true. Someone's had enough of it every day. Without fail, a miner will intentionally disconnect their oxygen tank and step into a nitrous pocket," Byron took another swig of his drink, then said, "it's tempting. I wouldn't do that to you and Chloe. But —"

"But what?"

"Let's just enjoy tonight."

Ada considered digging deeper into what he meant. But Byron was obviously guarded. "Are they having you do anything new, or just the same grind day-in-day-out?"

"I can't tell anymore. They're putt'n the same weight on my back as a twenty-something male miner. Which is fair—really. Everyone should bear the same weight. It's just getting harder."

A part of the back wall spun and the empty aperitif vase was replaced with a full decanter of pre-mixed old fashioneds. A series of squares sequentially spun, removing the untouched remnants of the first course and replacing it with a second. Hummus and mezze plates.

"I haven't asked since I was young. And I want to know the whole truth. Why are you a miner?"

"I've told you," Byron said. "The same way that Stephanie Davies was blamed. Everyone else is paying for someone else's crimes."

Ada, buzzed, smirked and said, "Bullshit. No more lies. I know Oriana knew mom."

"Ada," Byron sighed.

"Were you and mom both citizens once?" Ada demanded an answer.

Byron attempted to cool the conversation, "Where did you hear that Oriana was a citizen? Look for yourself."

"I'm not asking about what's on The Sphere."

"That's all you should be asking." Byron warned.

"I know she wrote a note to be digitized. Only a citizen could do that."

"What, how do you know this?"

"I remember."

"You what?" Byron choked. "Don' go sayin' that. Do you want a life beside me, underground?"

"It's true," Ada continued, "I remember. It happened yesterday. Augusta received a journal written by Oriana. She mentioned Elena. The Memory Corps came and took the journal away. I'd remember more if I were assigned to it."

"You forget ya ever read that," Byron said. "You hear me? I said forget it. You'll ruin your life if…"

Chloe entered the room, alarmingly inebriated. "About time we eat a proper meal in this fucking family."

The topics were too serious for someone like Chloe to participate in, or keep to herself.

But Chloe felt the tension, "Damn, y'all need to relax. We're at Blasé for god's sake. Good call sis." Chloe wasted no time filling her glass to the brim with the old-fashioned mix—no ice. "So, go on…what was it we are talking about? I love a juicy story. Ada, why were your friends visited by the Memory Corps yesterday?"

"Look it up," Ada said.

"I did. What's your version?"

"You know my version doesn't matter."

"About damn time that's your response!"

"Right," Ada sighed, resigning to this truth.

Chloe tore off a slice of pita and dipped it into the bowl of garlic hummus. "I heard there was a small riot yesterday in 15E. Can you believe that? *The Mill* is reporting that Vivian herself will deliver the punishment to its leader. They're saying it could be a public execution. The first since 6Di first took control thirty years ago."

"That's all hogwash," Byron said, before polishing off his glass. "She's an awful woman. An awful, awful woman."

Vivian Polanofsky, founder of Sixth Domain Industries, had acquired as many rumors as successes. She retained the position as CEO of 6Di but was commonly called 'The Head'—for 6Di monitored all thoughts. Vivian applied theories of genetics to inanimate objects and events, and uncovered a dimension of genetic material she named a-DNA and invented a genre of science-coined naturalnetics. a-DNA proved relationships between seemingly unrelated events and demonstrated an order to every occurrence. In theory, Sixth Domain Industries was positioning themselves to forecast all possible outcomes of a given day, rank those events by probability, and inform respective parties of actions they should take to prevent or embrace particular outcomes. Destiny had become a choice.

The company single handedly escorted a new era of life on earth, whereby disease and death were diminished. Though, some was sustained. 6Di's research discovered that an amount of those atrocities was necessary to "sustain natural harmony." Which is how Vivian earned her less-spoken nickname, 'Arbiter of Evil.'

Truth is, no single person could acquirethat much power and not be mistaken as evil. Once 6Di monopolized naturalnetics, they expanded the definition of their field into health, information, communication, and media. 6Di operated at alien speed. With unmatched computing capacities and the discovery of a new science that outperformed algorithmic corporations, whatever 6Di inquired it acquired. And blazingly fast. Soon, any three-letter U.S. agency expressed interest in partnering with 6Di to avoid wide-scale catastrophes within their respective jurisdiction.

6Di's success did not come without its controversies, but division over implementing 6Di's technologies was just another chisel in the chasm dividing Americans. The country's political parties were usurped by two social movements who plainly identified as Progressivist and Purgers. The issues which separated each group from another were plentiful. On the topic of 6Di, Purgers accused 6Di of embodying Satan; playing god without any characteristics of the divine.

Whatever momentum there was in repealing 6Di's presence in American life backpedaled in the face of the Second Civil War. According to the surviving records, the Second Civil War lacked any single incident and instead was best understood as a congealing of skirmishes spread throughout the country fueled by conspiratorial thinking, conjecturing, and extremist thinking. In the aftermath of the war, 6Di was commissioned to lead the reconstruction of the broken nation. They promised to do so through the dissemination of the BRiDG, which connected each mind to The Sphere, a safe, sanitized version of the internet, where falsities decayed and the lies that set the country ablaze would die in the minds of those who survived.

So, it was odd that Byron denigrated Vivian's character with striking conviction. As if he possessed a memory of her that not even his BRiDG could override. But Byron, heeding to the advice he gave Ada moments before, softened, and asked, "I'm sorry. Let me recall the story. Do you two remember how the lines were drawn?"

Chloe, quick to query, said, "The Sphere says it was 'according to who had willingly adopted the BRiDG or not. Those who resisted were placed into the Stratum of Knowledge, where they'd discover its beauties and evolve the capabilities of mankind.'"

"Right. That's true. And as you both know your mother and I were rebels. She died in her fight for freedom. But, somehow, by an act of a power higher than Vivian, I survived the war and after the forced implementations I was granted citizenship into the Stratum of Reason."

"What?!" Chloe's volume rattled the glassware.

"It's true," Byron affirmed.

"So...how?" Ada tried to find the words to form a single question among the hundreds animating in her mind.

"I was foolish," Byron continued, "and angry. I wanted to avenge the death of your mother. We fought so hard for a BRiDG-free world. And, though I lived with the BRiDG, I was without... how do they say... neuropathic dependency." Byron took a breath, then continued, "I obeyed my instincts and abandoned attempts of the BRiDG's reprogramming. And so, at first I unknowingly, and soon intentionally, began sowing dissent."

Chloe, thrilled, asked, "you tried to sow a rebellion, after the war?"

Byron exhaled, and weaved the room's excitement with regret. "I did," Byron said. "I'm a miner because I tried to reverse people's dependency to the BRiDG. But dependency on this device in the new world is an unquestionable precept. My punishment is just." The three swigged their drinks. Byron grabbed the nearby vase and filled each emptying glass. A silence hung in the air as he awaited a response.

"Why did she let you remember all this?" Ada asked.

"As a warning, I suppose."

Chloe interjected, and said, "You idiot."

"Chloe!" Ada cried.

"No, it's okay," Byron said, "she's allowed to be angry—both of you are."

"We could have..." Chloe imagined the universe, the one where she was raised a citizen, where she wasn't a daughter of a miner, whose existence was reduced to the pounds of scarce raw materials they could extract from the earth to power 6Di industries. "We could have lived good lives! You selfish bitch!" Tears roiled to Chloe's eyes. Such pitiful, selfish blobs.

"Oh, it's all a farce," Byron said. "Even if I kept quiet—never said a word. I would have been found out. I wasn't meant to live in this new world."

"What was it like?" Ada asked, "the other side?"

Byron cracked an uncharacteristic smile and said, "It's perfect."

"You really believe that?" Chloe asked, indignantly.

"I do. It's a beautiful place. But not a place you can respect without first integrating yourself into The Sphere. I don't know if it's evolution or ignorance. But it's better that way. The only way to enter the Stratum of Reason is with a base of knowledge firmly rooted in The Sphere—in total harmony with one's BRiDG."

"So, do you think maybe—" Ada began to speculate.

"Ada, don't try to reason," Byron pleaded.

Ada fell silent. Then asked, "You said she did something to you—Vivian?"

"She did." Byron reached for his genitalia.

"I thought you said it was cancer?" Chloe asked.

"Yes," Byron said, "that's what the records show. Vivian said she'd spare me the embarrassment of making that public. But some truths poison as secrets."

Chloe felt sobered by the resounding pains and unflinching spirit of her father. Her numb-drunkenness transitioned into an unfamiliar conviction. She'd rejected her family because of its broken past, but in this moment felt immense pride in the steps and missteps that formed her heritage. Without thinking twice about this feeling, Chloe uttered, "I want to join you in the archives, Ada. To help you find clues to mom's passing."

Suspect, Ada asked, "Really?"

Chloe echoed Ada's words, without question.

"You're drunk," Ada proclaimed, "come to the Memory of the Living corridor tomorrow and prove it." Chloe polished off the remaining liquor in her glass. Slapped the glass onto the table. The glass clinked. Everyone's lips, for a moment, were sealed. Which was not to be mistaken for silence. Each mind was abuzz with the repercussions of tonight's conversation. Ada, specifically, thought of all the secrets contained in this room. All the secrets lost in their lineage. All the things that had never or will never be said. And how much everything would change once each of them is uttered aloud.

Ada gazed at her downtrodden father. Recalling these events exhausted him, but she needed to know, and so asked "How did Oriana know mom?"

Byron only shook his head in disapproval, and said, "The records say she didn't."

And soon after she said that, dinner had finished. Small talk brought the evening to a steady close. Chloe, usually one to depart early because she was double booked, stayed till the rest of her family came to a mutual goodbye. They all left a little drunk, from the liquor; and a little high, from discovering so many new bits of information at once. As for Byron, he left liberated. And with a renewed hope for the future: all because they came to terms with the past. In the tapestry of time, both interconnect.

At night, every square inch of the Stratum of Knowledge appeared predestined. Every detail master planned. No light was ever out. Traffic could not jam. Skyscrapers stood individually as marvels of architecture and as a sum seamlessly complimented one another, like snowfall. All of Vivian's and 6Di's infamous tales of injustice were concealed by the visible world. Even the lowest of the remaining people—the obsoletes—could live in a world without want, within spaces perfectly planned for their personhood. Only the faceless guards who stood at each corner symbolized the all-encompassing oppression that characterized life as an obsolete.

As Ada walked these streets, she juxtaposed her intricate surroundings with the zany drawings of Lionel. Those pictures of disorder and disarray. Which made her think about all that she remembered which still had no answers. *Who killed Grace, and why did no one seem to care? Why, each morning, did I awake feeling my mind scrambled? Was that person the same one who killed mom? How did Oriana know Elena? Was father lying about how he became a miner?* With each thought Ada felt the all too familiar *zap*, which did nothing to her memory, but triggered a sense of fear. Ada peered up at the towering pillars of light that edged her apartment building and stretched into the heavens. Then a word came to her: *home*.

The next morning Ada rose early. Her fast metabolism burned off the alcohol she drank hours before, leaving her clear-headed and hungry at the sound of her alarm. She scrambled a few eggs. Drank a short glass of electrolytes. Ada selected her usual digitization agenda. Then strolled off to work in the same darkness that she wandered through after dinner. The elevator blew past the floor her sister lived on, which was no surprise. Even if Chloe helped today, she likely wouldn't arrive early. So Ada was unsurprised to arrive at the facility and find it inhabited with a few of the usual night shifters and just as many guards. She sat at the dimly lit desk, awaited the first article to rise, and once it arrived, she scanned it into The Sphere.

The morning energy stirred like the rising sun; slow and consistent. Obsoletes took their seats. The room's volume rose. Each addition occurring inconspicuously. Whispers of yesterday's Memory Corps appearance themed the day's conversations. The Sphere had reported all there was to say. Each person's repetition of its reporting further cemented its version as truth. Augusta again sat across from Ada and asked, "Can you believe it, the Memory Corps was here yesterday, must have missed them!"

"Yeah," Ada sighed, unable to stomach the memory inside her mind.

"Think they'll come again soon?"

"Eventually."

Corydon entered the corridor, George walked a few steps behind him.

"I'm going to say hello to the twins. Want to join, Augusta?"

"I-I really shouldn't." Augusta said reservedly.

Without another word, Ada rose and walked toward Corydon. A guard, anticipating her intentions, yelled, "Back to your workstation!" Ada defiantly kept walking, receiving a punishment of one hundred more artifacts toward her daily quota.

"Corydon, it's good to see you," Ada said, at the edge of his desk. Corydon didn't acknowledge her kindness or presence.

"Corydon —"

"Oh, good morning Ada," he said a bit coldly.

"I'm just saying hello," Ada pleaded. Corydon shot her a suspicious glance. Ada felt their urgency to be left alone, so she started to walk away.

"Nothing happened that night."

Ada traced her steps back to his desk, and asked, "What?"

"I said that nothing happened."

"I know—but what makes you say that?"

"What makes us understand everything we should know."

Ada nodded. She understood. Clever too, she thought, that he would use the word *should*.

EVEN HEAVEN ALLOWS HELL

Oriana and Azophi Vespucci are never seen during the day. Their milieu prefers criminal thrills. The typical ailments of night: gambling, vandalism, theft, and substance abuse. But Oriana and Azophi don't partake in criminal activities. Their very existence is criminal. So they reside in the shadows. Out of sight and out of mind. Never taking a risk they haven't already calculated. If anyone ever sees Oriana or Azophi, it's because they want you to.

The Vespuccis were leaders of the Purgers at the height of the last Civil War. They led as technologically savvy commanders, weaponizing history, ideas, and stirring within their followers the rawest of human willpower. So, though their group was almost always outmanned and armed in each conflict, the Purgers' stealthy tactics and cunning hearts won them many battles. But in 6Di's digitization campaign, successes would not be the Purgers' legacy. They, instead, were remembered for their savagery, their vile battle tactics which labeled any Progressivist as combatant, mother or child. Moreover, the Purgers were remembered for their primal aspirations; for their plea to regress innovation and pause mankind in the technologies founded in the early twenty-first century. But as fate, or rather 6Di, would have it, their worldview was lost.

Ketchum, Idaho, is where the Purgers' executives headquartered.

It was the same mountain town where Ernest Hemingway placed a shotgun against his chest and ended his life. And it was there that the Second Civil War ended in the same manner as the Second World War: with a nuclear bomb. After the Great Bombing of Ketchum, Oriana and Azophi were believed to have turned into dust. What the records don't indicate is that Oriana and Azophi were not in Ketchum on the day of the bombing, and that after the ashes settled, Oriana and Azophi went into hiding. 6Di was quick to pronounce them dead, alongside dozens of other commanders. What the records say happened next was a complete and total surrender of the Purgers. Absent any leadership, the fragmented militias crumbled. Those who possessed a willingness to adopt the BRiDG were offered a chance at retraining themselves as obsoletes in The Sphere of Knowledge. Many refused and were executed.

The records deny that any Purgers survived the Second Civil War, and this, Vivian has kept secret. In the decades since the war ended, Vivian has dispatched guards to remote areas of both the Stratums of Knowledge and Reason in hopes of capturing the long-hidden rebels. But every time Vivian believed she had closed in on their location, they vanished, untraceable, under the cover of darkness. In The Sphere, Azophi and Oriana's records only recall their names and evil deeds. There are no surviving pictures of either Oriana or Azophi, their stories and identities virtually erased. And although Vivian continues to clandestinely hunt for their remains, the public could never know. For this would upend 6Di's omniscience. Yet still, after three decades of hiding, they live.

Before the note had appeared on Augusta's desk in the archives, Ada never imagined that Oriana knew of her mother. Elena was one of millions of Purgers. A mere "rebel." Not one who died with any accolades or prestige. But for Oriana to have known Elena, she must have been a much higher rank than Byron ever admitted, or the records shown. The records also indicated that her mother died when Ada was one. The war ended when Ada was five.

In the week following the dinner with her father and sister, Ada spent each evening researching all information she could find on the Vespuccis in The Sphere. Ada searched for any inconsistencies in the story, or hints that perhaps the Vespuccis were still alive. None existed. And each time Ada whispered to herself doubts of Oriana's death, she felt her BRiDG, Lily, *zap*. But with each zap, the power of her BRiDG weakened, until the shocks were nothing more than an audible click.

The next weekend, Ada met her father in his drab apartment. He sat asleep at his bistro table. And when Ada entered her heart swelled, because he was dressed in his dinner clothes. Byron never asked to go out. He was content with a flavorless meal in his soggy box of an apartment. To protect its remaining fragments, Byron's broken heart abandoned hope. Whether it was Ada's reminder that at most they had 103 weekends together remaining till Day Zero, or the depth of the conversation last weekend, something in him had changed.

"Pops," Ada said, nudging her father's shoulders. "Pops wake up."

"Huh?" Byron said. "Oh," Byron shifted himself upright,

"Ada, dear, I'm ready." And it wasn't much, but Ada swore she saw her father smile.

"It's just us this week."

"Where's Chloe?"

"Haven't heard from her all week. Typical." Byron nodded, his disappointment enveloping the room. Ada continued, "But we can still have a good talk, like last week. Okay?" He nodded, then they departed.

Billows was a wine bar refurbished from a bomb shelter built during the Second Civil War. Its cold, dark, concrete setting created a perfect space to preserve wines. Guests were greeted with velvet and fur jackets to prolong their stay. The only light in the space was that from lit candles. The myriad of walls created private spaces for each party. Ada was seated across from Byron, his body appearing as a wave between the flickering flames.

Ada took a sip of her red wine, then asked, "Dad, when did mom die?"

"You know this sweetie, when you were —"

"Stop," Ada interjected. "It's just me. Tell me the truth."

"It's not mine to tell."

"Tell me what you can."

Byron took a deep sigh, then said, "You remember the Day of Reckoning?"

Ada nodded her head in affirmation, as her BRiDG animated the facts about the day when all surviving Purgers were given the choice between life with the BRiDG or execution.

"Well," Byron continued, "On that day I had to choose between dying for a powerless cause, or living for another chance at life."

"Was mom dead by then?"

"Ada, your mother died in the war. You don't ever question that. Last time I saw her——" Byron's eyes welled, and he continued, "she died a brave woman. Bravest I knew, till you. But this isn't an era for the brave."

Across the restaurant, in an unseen cubby, a bottle of wine was dropped but did not break. The clunk of the glass landing against a rug, startled Ada. Her eyes widened, fists tightly clenched. She peered over her shoulder. But behind her was just a cobblestone wall.

"Sorry," Ada said, returning her attention to Byron.

Byron cocked his head, observing Ada's shaking hands. Then continued, "It was a new life for all of us after I chose the BRiDG. Imagine if you and Chloe were orphans. Imagine if I was still an addict of KL. That terrible combination of gunpowder and cocaine helped me through many sleepless nights in battle." Byron paused again, as if he were putting all these thoughts to words for the first time, "it's not the best life, but it's the best life we can have."

Ada cocked her head, incredulous. "Then why did you throw all that away, why sow a rebellion when you were mistakenly categorized a citizen?"

Byron shook his head in disbelief. "I-I—really don't know. It's all a blur, truly. I don't mean to hold things back from you. There's just so much I can't remember. All I can recall is that it all felt too serendipitous. Like a stroke of fate offering me a chance to fix my mistake. I had a lot of guilt, turning my back on the fight your mother died to protect. A lot of guilt."

"No, dad. You did the right thing. You did. You have to believe that now. The more I learn of your past, the more proud I am." Byron nodded, and for the second time tonight, and in her life, Ada saw her father's eyes well.

Then, Byron leaned across the table, and whispered in Ada's ear, "I'm sorry I couldn't give you better blood or fortune. But this is our life. Don't wish for another one. You work with the one you got. That would make your mother—and me—proud. As she always used to say, 'life's full of compromises.' But," Byron looked to make sure there were no passersby, then whispered again, "even heaven allows hell."

Ada remained unsettled by the fact that the story of her mother's past remained incomplete. "Died at war" was all she knew. Not much else. But now the story was more complex. If there was such a thing as high society in the rebel clan, Ada would be among it. But rebels are a forgotten breed. And those remaining live in such shame of their past they've either completely erased the memories or dare not speak of those ventures. But the only shame Ada felt was an ignorance of those who came before her. It made her feel detached, far from home, as if her existence were detached from all that came before and after. Just a blip. But, Ada believed, if she could trace the significance of her mother's life, Ada could better understand how her life could also matter.

Three days after the dinner, Ada was living to a rhythm of normality. Awakening early, arriving at the facility alone, completing quotas—sometimes two days' worth—so that she could expedite her path to citizenship. But each day in the archives, Ada's attention toward George and Corydon waned. Yet, still, she found herself on edge. Jumping at regular noises and sights. Besides Corydon's subtle hint that deep down he remembered Grace's murder, neither spoke of anything strange that happened that evening. But, to Ada, they had acted strange. They were no longer as boisterous or bubbly. Their personalities muted. Never enough to justify an accusation. Ada couldn't put it to words how they changed—they just were. In fact, the only unusual thing anyone in the archives talked about was seeing Chloe digitize in the same room as Ada.

As Chloe digitized more frequently, Ada found herself ending her days at the archives earlier than she ever had. But she didn't know what to do with this time except more of what she used to—drink. That's all obsoletes did, it seemed. Work and drink. Until it was unclear which it was you lived for, which one recovered you from which. But even in drunkenness, Ada thought it more of a habit than dependency. She felt more so gripped by it than hooked. Because however sweet the senseless sensation of inebriation felt it never satiated her mind like memorizing a thing no one else was able to recall. And if there was one thing Ada resented about drunkenness it was that it always temporarily stole her memory. To fall to drunkenness was to, for a moment, live like the rest of the obsoletes. Which, some days, was a welcome reprieve.

The extra time they spent together evolved Chloe and Ada's relationship. Chloe had always separated herself from her family. Even as a child, she'd tell the other children at future-citizen-care, the brand of childcare for obsoletes too young to digitize, that her parents were the quickest digitizers, or that she was orphaned, or that her family belonged to corporate. Though, not even toddlers believed the last lie. Chloe fantasized all kinds of realities besides the one she was given. Any life, besides being the offspring of a miner and deceased enemy combatant, was preferred. But as she matured, Chloe recognized how much of her growing up depended on her managing the life she was given more than wishing for a new one. She started arriving at the weekly dinners she was invited to but previously never attended. Although, her insults and scoffs accompanied her too. But as she spent more time around her father, and started to see them for who they were, and not what she was told they were, her heart softened. Chloe saw a lot of herself in Byron, minus the misfortunes.

Chloe enjoyed heading to local 20W bars with Ada after their shifts to talk through all she had missed in her years as a prodigal daughter. And although all the memories were available in her family's private drive in The Sphere, easy for Chloe to download as her own, she enjoyed Ada's recollections of each event. After a couple weeks of these stories, Chloe declared, "It's like I never missed a day."

Ada pondered this thought to the twirl of her half-full martini, and responded, "That's great." But her thoughts, as always, were more piercing than her words. She remembered an old saying her father repeated once, *the body never forgets*. An image of Grace's bludgeoned body flashed into Ada's mind. She paled.

Chloe, concerned, asked, "What's wrong?"

"Nothing, sorry. Just distracted." Ada lied, as she frantically observed every face in sight.

"Doesn't look like nothing. What did you just think of?"

Ada polished off her martini, hoping to silence the unauthorized memories that occupied her mind.

"It's just," Ada reached for a lie, "some days I wonder if we'll actually make it before Day Zero."

Chloe laughed and assuredly said, "Of course we will. We all will!"

"But you have to believe there's a possibility that we won't. That one of us will fall ill and not be able to digitize at the same rate—or at all for a while. What happens then?"

"You're not wrong, Ada. Something like that could happen. I just don't see the point in worrying about it—do you want another drink?" Ada nodded her head yes.

"I don't know. Sometimes I feel like all of 6Di is against me," Ada said.

"Nonsense. Look, we're unfortunate. But all our misfortunes were earned. There's nothing unjust about them," Chloe declared.

Ada stared at Chloe, then asked, "What do you remember of the conversation we had with dad the other night, at Blasé?"

Confused, Chloe replied, "We talked about what we always do. Before dad adopted the BRiDG he tried to sow a rebellion against 6Di, he regrets it, but continues to pay the cost, and he lives as a warning to us—to do the right thing."

"Before he adopted the BRiDG, what about after?"

"After? Well, he was a miner after that."

"That's what you remember?" Ada asked, wondering if Chloe could remember the rebellion Byron attempted after he was given the BRiDG.

"Yes, Ada. That's what was said. What are you getting at?"

"Then what caused you to finally start helping?" Ada inquired. The drinks arrived. In one gulp, Ada drank half her martini.

"Nothing changed but me. It's not like I'm doing this because I learned something new." Chloe gathered her thoughts for a moment, then said, "Maybe like you I am also a little afraid of Day Zero."

All Ada muttered back to her sister was an affirmative *huh*. Then she downed the rest of her martini. Meanwhile, Chloe hadn't taken a sip. Ada's reasons for her rapid consumption, she told herself, were medicinal. She needed these thoughts and images silenced. She wished that she could forget that her father lived on the other side, that Grace was killed without explanation, she wanted these and all other unauthorized thoughts from her mind erased. And drinking helped default her thoughts to her BRiDG. But whenever Ada drank she swore she could hear her BRiDG's frequencies. A humming inside her mind, a ringing like tinnitus. Only electrified. Occasionally, Ada swore that she heard her BRiDG—Lily—speak to her without being prompted. But the voice appeared so hollow that Ada thought it a hallucination.

The night faded to an end with rambling conversations and a trail of drinks. That night, Ada woke up during the witching hour with an unshakeable feeling that she was being watched. Ada's pitch-black room would have made that impossible. She could see nothing. So nothing, she reasoned, could see her. Ada shoved the thought out of her consciousness, and began counting aloud backwards from one hundred. The only images she saw was the visualization of numbers flashing in neon colors, as was hung above her crib when she was young. She started to doze into the thirties. She felt the last wave of sleep drowning her consciousness.

Then, Adsa felt the prick of a needle enter her arm. She slapped the vein below her bicep. Felt nothing. But saw, just a few feet from her, eyes glowing yellow like a panther's. Then she felt a new kind of wave overtake her body. Not the familiar greeting of sleep; that soft welcoming into darkness. Instead, her nervous system jarred, she felt the rush of nameless toxins infect her blood. Then, paralysis. Her body locked, mind fully awake, the panther eyes stood over Ada. "Vivian requests your presence," it said, its eyes illuminating Ada's like she was born with a pair of moons above her nose.

COME TO VIVIAN

From blackness, Ada heard the clinking of metal against glass, like a drink was being stirred. The pace and subtlety of the clinking suggested tea, or some other beverage preferred by high society. In the silences between each clinking, Ada's mind fixated on the ropes binding her wrists and ankles; the hands that grasped the tops of her shoulders. She felt no pain, and however long Ada had been apprehended outlasted her fear. Still blindfolded, the image of the floating, glowing eyes replayed in her mind. Each *clink* of the petite cup reprieved Ada of that sight.

"Lily," Ada said to herself, "where am I?"

But before Ada's BRiDG could answer, a female voice said, "Release her." And in an instant, the wraps and hands that gripped Ada had vanished. She could once again see and face four, faceless guards. Their hands entangled with the same ropes and tapestry that bound Ada's limbs and eyes. She stared curiously at the one before her, guard 40. The same guard who had commanded all obsoletes to remain in archival mode during the Memory Corps's visit. Before Ada could connect any meaning to this guard's presence, the woman said, "Welcome to my lair."

Ada turned toward the woman who sat behind a cavernous slab of coral, which doubled as her desk. The top was thinly layered with glass. So, her tea cup appeared to float when placed atop the desk. Vines of ivy arched from each side of the coral to the wall behind the woman, where branches enmeshed with bundles of electronic wires that plastered the back wall—making both the biological and technological strands inexorable from one another.

Ada forced an agreeable nod, then asked, "Are you…?"

"Yes," Vivian interjected, "I'm Vivian. It's a pleasure to meet you. Sorry it's under such," Vivian sipped her tea, "unconventional circumstances. But it has come to my attention that you are wise beyond your sphere, and I needed to see for myself if you're the one who they say you are."

"Who do they say I am?"

"My successor," Vivian plainly stated. "They say you will be my heir."

"Who are they?"

"No one can behold power indefinitely. Nor can it be passed mindlessly. Every system has its rules. Monarchies rely on familial lineage. Democracies upon popular opinion. Gravity, motion. Power is in constant motion, everywhere you look—even where you can't. The Spheres require the freest mind. The one who can know without learning and see without looking. You've caught the attention of many guards. Your BRiDG activity confirms much of their suspicions. I believe you fit the description. That you are the one who could take my place."

Ada tried to speak but the words did not materialize. Instead, she bobbed her lips, like a feeding fish.

"No need for words, Ada. Just listen." Vivian took another sip of her tea. Vivian sat flanked between two armillary spheres, that old-world instrument of galactic mapping that modeled the rotations of earth and sun.

Vivian turned to the armillary sphere on her left and asked, "Do you know what this is?"

Ada, querying through her BRiDG, recited the object's article, "This is a heliocentric armillary sphere. An early model of how the earth, sun, and moon interrelate over the span of a year. This model of our solar system was created by Copernicus, father of the stars, in 1543."

"Very good, now," Vivian asked, looking to her right, "what is this?"

Ada's query drew no results. No words queued for her to speak. None besides *object not found*. But Ada didn't admit that there were no results, she only asked if she could, "take a closer look?" Vivian nodded. Ada approached Vivian's desk and began talking aloud, "It could be some kind of—I'm not sure. The earth is in the center. Maybe an alternative theory to the stars? Maybe the way people thought the planets aligned before Copernicus?"

Vivian smiled. "I was hoping you'd say that. How do you know to think this way?"

"The same way anyone knows anything?" Ada shrugged.

"I'll tell you what this other armillary sphere is, it's ignorance disguised as truth. A view of the planets before the brave and brilliant Copernicus challenged the assumptions of cronies who believed that the earth was at the center of our solar system. This geocentric model led humans astray for centuries. An untold number of people lived believing that we were at the center of the universe, then one man came along and reversed that narrative. What he said at the time was so unfounded, so ludicrous, so heretical, that he was killed professing the truth. Can you believe that? A time in the world when someone was killed for uttering the truth?" Vivian took another sip of tea. Then reached to caress a single ivy leaf. "I can't think of a single greater purpose than to propagate the truth and eliminate lies. That's what I get to do, Ada. Soon, you will too."

"Does not doing the former negate the latter?" Ada asked, after a moment of pause.

"How do you mean?" Vivian coldly responded.

"This geocentric armillary sphere, it's not in our sphere, not accessible via BRiDG because it was a lie. It was a way of viewing the world that was wrong. So you've removed it from the past. Because it's better to forget an error than remember its virtues. But all things serve a purpose. Even our errors."

"No Ada, your mind is brilliant. But even you err. You've never lived in a world where people hold dearly to lies, where they get to profess them as truth. Copernicus gave his life to progress. His murderers stained theirs with madness. Not unlike our last Civil War. I remember—with utter horror—how atrocious it was, for people to end their life in madness. I hate to say this, Ada. Your mother was a victim of her madness. But you can change the legacy of your name."

Fearing she'd turn insolent, Ada ignored the remark about her mother, and asked, "Why do you keep it, then? Why do you remind yourself of these horrors?"

"This is the burden of our role, Ada. We must always discern between truth and lies. We must perpetuate the truth and eliminate the lies." Ada foresaw another circular argument if she again disagreed with Vivian. It was at this same time that Ada recognized she was speaking to the leader of the free and unfree worlds without reserve. *Perhaps I would be her heir*, she thought, *and a better one too*. Ada didn't know if Vivian could read her thoughts, but she shot her a snarling glance, like she could.

"We'll have plenty of time for these debates, Ada. But first, I want you to receive formal training in archival methods and the centralizing of truths. I want you to take Grace's place as a reconnoiter for my beloved Memory Corps."

"But, I'm not a citizen," Ada said.

"I can grant you that. And to your dad too."

"But…" Ada felt a wave of guilt that she attempted to articulate, "that's not fair."

"Don't be so stubborn."

"Isn't there someone else?"

"There's no one like you."

Ada thought for a moment and asked, "Do I even have a choice?"

"Let's not bring such esoteric thinking into this. You have a choice, as much as you choose which roads to travel from one place to another. Because your path is already paved for you."

"I understand," Ada cooly said, "just one more question, what is that?" Ada pointed to another armillary sphere directly behind Vivian.

"This is our world, the one I've created and you'll sustain."

At the core of this model was the Stratum of Knowledge, the place where Ada and all obsoletes resided. Beyond it, the Stratum of Reason, completely encircling knowledge like an outer layer to the earth's core. Then, a third sphere. One Ada had never heard spoken of before. One that was without boundary.

"The Stratum of Imagination," Vivian exclaimed. Then she stood, explaining, "Three stratums, all interrelated. All depending on another. No one can reason without knowledge. Nor can one imagine without reasoning. And it's The Sphere of Imagination that expands them both—which tests the limits of knowledge and reason."

"Why have I never heard of imagination?"

"No one you know has been."

"Who can go there?"

"Those who've mastered knowledge and reason."

"Why only those?" Ada asked.

"Because it's dangerous. Imagination is predicated on questions, and in the Stratum of Imagination you will question everything. Your entire being will become without foundation—baseless. If you're not careful, too strong an imagination could make you lose your mind."

Ada stared at the expansive final frontier modeled against the luminescent wall of tendrilled wires and asked, "What's it like—the Stratum of Imagination?"

"That depends on who you are, Ada." Vivian smiled. "But think about this opportunity, Ada. I know you're scared. The rumors about me are brutal. But remember Copernicus. Remember that the cost of searching for the truth commands one's life. And that means you must believe in a day when your reputation will be corrected by history. That all your sacrifices will be seen by a generation yet born. You do this for them. I do it for them. That's what it means to live before your time. Your life isn't dedicated to those who surround you today."

Ada's eyes watered in both gratitude and anger. She hadn't wanted to become a citizen on account of a bribe. *Is this how it always goes?* Ada wondered. *Are lifetime achievements really just a euphemism for unspeakable compromises?* Ada let a single tear drop to her cheek. Vivian twirled her half-empty tea cup and said, "I'll send for you tomorrow. Bring nothing but the clothes on your back. Your life starts anew when you join the Corps."

PURGE OR BE PURGED

Ada woke from a sedated sleep, which, judging by the fact the sun had risen, was at an hour much later than she usually rose. The encounter with Vivian felt more like an awful lucid dream than a memory. And if not for the fact Ada was wearing her seersucker uniform, the same one she wore when meeting Vivian, the same one she never wore to bed, she would have believed it was just a dream. At this thought, the haze of her sedated mind was eclipsed by a flood of thoughts: *What was that creature that carried me away? Did it dress me? How long has Vivian known of my autonomous mind?*

In an uncharacteristic moment of desperation Ada cried out, "Lily?"

"Yes Ada?" her BRiDG's avatar asked, "did you want your morning's agenda?"

"No. No—I want to know what you know happened last night."

"Ada, you were not in archival mode last night. So, I recorded none of your activities. As a reminder, obsoletes are encouraged, but not required, to remain in scan mode at all times. This is for the benefit of accurate record keeping."

Ada, incredulous, sat upwards and asked again, "you have no records of my whereabouts last night?"

"Only your memories, Ada. But you can recall those." Lily said, giggling.

There was a pause. Long enough for Ada to ponder if Lily were telling the truth, if she were even capable of telling the truth—or encoded to fulfill other virtues. But, rather than challenge her BRiDG, Ada asked, "Lily, what do you know about my mind?"

"Oh," Lily said, giggling, "it's marvelous. I'm the luckiest BRiDG, I tell that to all the others."

Ada was swept by an unexpected wave of bashfulness. "That's… so kind of you, Lily. I think I've the best BRiDG too."

"That makes us a dangerous duo."

Ada mustered a smile and whispered, "It sure does."

And for a moment Ada thought about the layers of that statement. The fact that her mind, active as it was, represented a direct threat to Lily's job. And Lily's job, as amiable as it appeared, actually represented an existential threat to Ada's greatest gift, her living memory. Both lived in existential tension with one another. One hand squeezing metaphorical triggers ready to take a kill shot, the other shaking hands in a titular agreement to lifelong peace. And both lived inside her skull—a place no one else would occupy.

Across the Stratum of Knowledge, pandemonium ensued in response to two stories. First: *The Daily BRiDG* reported that, "the venerable Grace, reconnoiter of HQ's Memory Corps, requested a quiet retirement from the Corps citing health concerns. Vivian reportedly accepted the resignation without question. This will cause the first replacement of a member of the Corps in over a decade. Selection is slated to begin tomorrow, and will include the finest citizens competing against one another in a series of publicized games until only one remains." This marked the first replacement of a Memory Corps member in two decades.

The second report, also published by *The Daily BRiDG*, read: "Last night, the most honorable Vivian Polanofsky confirmed meeting with Ada Lawrence, an obsolete from 20W. The details of the meeting concern matters of the Vivian Memory Trust, and so will be available upon her death. But Vivian suggested, though did not verify, that the contents of the meeting surrounded the possibility of Ms. Lawrence becoming the first obsolete to join the Memory Corps. When asked why this was being considered, or how Ms. Lawrence could evade the prerequisite of citizenship Vivian stated that, "Ada possesses the most brilliant mind in all The Spheres and has demonstrated an early propensity of neuropathic dependency." A first, for the record.

Ada found it strange that no one from her family had inquired about these stories. All Ada received was messages from strangers and forgotten acquaintances that wished her well. She assumed the best, that Byron was miles deep in the mines, hard at work. And that her sister, Chloe, had already started her shift at the archives. But these justifications could not shake Ada's deepest anxiety, that once she was gone she would quickly be forgotten.

While Ada wondered about the whereabouts of her family, Lily interrupted and said, "I have a message for you."

"What is it, Lily?"

"It is from the Memory Corps headquarters." And then, in silence, Lily exposed the following words to Ada's field of vision. *Enjoy your last day as an obsolete. You'll be picked up promptly at 7pm. Do not worry about meeting in any particular place. We will find you.*

"Any questions, Ada?" Lily asked.

"None," said Ada. But in truth she had two. *How would they find me?* And, *Have I always been tracked?*

When the message exited her vision, Ada found herself in wordless thought, surveying her room for nothing in particular. She simply observed. And, unconsciously, began breathing as if she were submerged in cold water. That slow, powerful draw of oxygen grounded Ada. But just as she felt immersed in bliss, Ada was stricken by the sight of an unfamiliar and forbidden object lying atop her entryway counter. It was a folded note. No obsolete was permitted to write, nor access writing outside The Sphere. To do so risked reversing neuropathic dependency on the BRiDG. But, Ada felt she had no choice whether to read the note or not. For, whoever risked their safety to place it here, would certainly place Ada in just as much danger if she ignored their request. Ada unfolded the paper and read: *meet at the entrance of the 20W power plant. ASAP. - O*

Ada heard footsteps outside her door, and hurriedly placed the note into her pocket. Her breath heightened. *O, as in Oriana?* The footsteps passing Ada's door faded far down the hall. Ada calmed. She removed the paper from her pocket, and intricately studied the note. She observed the paper's edges, then the script itself. *How beautiful*, Ada thought, *the written language*. It wasn't like the perfectly styled digital fonts, which gave the illusion that words were a machine's invention. No, the hand conveyed emotion, revealing the condition of its author. And this note, with its tight spacing and rigid font revealed that Oriana was both urgent and composed. A message which had never been portrayed on The Sphere. Ada tucked the paper back into her pocket. Then she made her way to the entrance of the 20W power plant.

Power plants in the Stratum of Knowledge aren't much improved from the ones of previous generations. They're massive, messy, and more inefficient than the information they process. The explanations are numerous, but the lack of energy innovation was primarily explained by the enslavement of miners, which zeroed costs for historically pricey labor. As a result, coal became more affordable than the less toxic, but more sophisticated energy sources. And, absent of any competition, 6Di let prices dictate choices. This turned power plants into living museums that the future couldn't trump. Cathedrals that towered the past over the present. Each sector had its own plant. At its peak, ten plants powered the one-hundred-mile-wide Stratum of Knowledge.

Despite the essentiality of these power plants, they remained abandoned due to their size and danger. At one square mile each, guarding the entirety of each plant would have exhausted 6Di resources. More importantly, weaponry, and the knowledge of how to create weaponry, was non-existent in the Stratum of Knowledge. The risk of sabotage was zilch. Moreover, aside from repairs, the plants operated autonomously. Except whenever a transformer would blow or a line would down. In these instances, guards would escort their least favorite miners to the damaged plant. The first miner would enter—rifles pointed to their backs. Inevitably, electricity would arc. Another wire would snap. The first miner would char. And so on and so on, until one miner was successful and the plant would again resume normal operations. It's rumored that piles of charred miners littered plants, inviting parasites, which invited critters, which invited vultures. What remains below the lines is a small ecosystem of ruin. Even a quarter mile from Sector 1's power plant, Ada smelled the familiar smell of charred flesh, the same smell that burned itself into her memory after Brian's punishment for destruction of artifacts. Fitting, in that nothing Ada was about to experience existed in the archives.

Meanwhile, approaching the plant, it wasn't clear to Ada where exactly the entrance was located. The whole structure looked porous, as if every inch was an opening. Ada wondered how Oriana could ever locate Ada. And then, why she found herself wandering forbidden grounds. Risks seemed different when she believed herself anonymous. The possibility of detaching actions from consequences became more likely. But along her way to the plant, identity disguised, Ada heard her name spoken by all kinds of strangers. Ada couldn't comprehend the meaning of her celebrity, the role this demanded her to play, and if that person was at all different than who she had been up to this day.

Nevertheless, there she stood. At the edge of the plant in a lifeless plot of land with an electrical force so intense its humming wasn't only heard, but felt. *Not barren at all,* Ada thought. *Repurposed.* Biology seized where technology thrived. As Ada stood at the plant's edge contemplating if this was always true, or just there and then, a large shadow cast itself from behind her. Ada hadn't turned halfway to greet it before she was tackled to the ground. Her face smooshed into the rocky sand.

"It's okay, Ada. Don't move," said an unrecognizable young male voice. "But I can't lie, this is going to hurt." Then before Ada could process the warning she felt a snap in her brain. As if the man delivered a concussive blow, her vision went white and hearing muted; Ada felt herself oriented a few feet from where she actually was—but she hadn't moved. Ada wondered, *is this an aneurism?* The brief, painless, disorientation was followed by an inarticulable pain that infected her every nerve. The paralyzing pain imprisoned her screams. The man behind her affirmed, "you're doing great, Ada. You're doing great." Those were the last words Ada heard before she faded from consciousness.

An unknown amount of time passed before Ada awoke deep inside the power plant. Sparks and electrical arcs traveled across thousands of wires that canopied her and a half dozen purgers.

Every person wore a helmet that fully covered their face. Each was similarly framed: robust and rigid, built to receive high-speed impact. But the designs of each helmet were custom. Idiosyncratic, save for a small "p" painted on each. Ada wondered why her vision narrowed. Until she felt her face and noticed that she too was wearing one of these full-face coverings.

As Ada grasped her hands around this covering, a woman, with a helmet designed as the ceiling of an Iranian mosque, sat before Ada and said, "it protects you from the electromagnetic field."

"Oriana?"

"Yes. Thank you for meeting me so quickly. And I'm sorry for the harsh welcome," Oriana said, holding Ada's BRiDG. "We have to take utmost precautions here, nothing can be recorded." Ada felt for her BRiDG, but only felt the hard fiberglass of a helmet. It was then, Ada realized her thinking had slowed. As if her neural pathways were clogged with mud, delaying each transmission of thought. Oriana had seen this confusion before. "You'll feel a little…stupid." A few of the helmets chuckled.

"But…why remove it?"

"When I was at 6Di, decades ago, all encryption and privacy could be overridden. It's why I left and it's why I've committed my life to fighting 6Di."

Oriana knelt in front of Ada, popped open the visor of her helmet, and revealed her eyes, as deep and sensational as jungle cenotes. Another purger, whose helmet was muraled as a dark-paletted Persian mosaic sat beside Oriana. They flipped open their visors. And the eyes of Oriana's partner, Azophi, shone fluorescent and sage. He spoke with a Shirazi accent, "Ada we've waited so long to see you again."

"Again?" Ada said, confusedly.

Azophi continued, "we've known your mother and father for a long time. You wouldn't remember this, but we even took care of you when you were young. We were all very close then." Ada sat at a loss for words, her gaze ticking across the room like a watch's second hand. "In every way," Azophi said, "you're so much like her."

"How so?" Ada asked.

"This," Oriana interjected, "I'm afraid, is a topic for another time. We've a lot to share."

Azophi nodded to Oriana, and he said, "Ada, you know some of our backstory. But you don't know all of it. Each purger is a former citizen, executive, or member of 6Di. Now we live off the grid—literally, I suppose. Except for those in the field living as spies under 6Di, none of us wear a BRiDG. It's an uncomfortable life, but pure." Azophi flashed the BRiDG strung around his neck as jewelry. An arch of electricity split through their quarters.

"Times were better when your mother was our leader."

Oriana continued, "Once she was gone, the organization never recovered. But Azophi and I have kept it afloat. We've spent decades placing guards, citizens, and obsoletes back into The Stratums. All in hopes that you'd age like your mother and lead the rebellion."

At once, Ada contemplated a thousand realities. Her thoughts were neither complete nor coherent. With each flash of thought her mind further fragmented. Ada felt her entire identity crumbling, and yet, arising within her, a renewed purpose. Alongside equal parts fear. Ada first tended to the latter. After a few silent seconds, she asked, "How can I trust you?"

Oriana smiled, and said, "follow me."

Oriana shut her visor. Ada, following her every move, did too. Oriana exited the canopy of electrified wires and led Ada through the dangerous plains of 20W's grid. Outside the canopy, the grid hummed and zapped creating a sound akin to a synthetic rainstorm. The noise was too voluminous to talk over, so Oriana pointed to a door less than a hundred meters away built into the side of a dirt mound. Ada nodded, and they both walked toward it in silence. Along the way, each snap of electricity caused Ada to flinch. But Oriana walked silent and steady. A composure Ada replicated by the time they arrived at the door. The doorway was built as an entrance to a subterranean armory used during the last Civil War. Inside the mound, ammunition was barricaded by feet of earth and preserved within the cool, dark, climate of the makeshift cave. The space was now a safe haven for printed maps, papers, and photographs.

As soon as they entered, a voice shouted, "close the door!" A silhouetted figure standing twenty feet away, stepped into view. It was a purger named Tavid, whose posture was hunched and head perpetually bobbed. He walked as a man who'd replaced calories with knowledge. His brittle, anemic body stood juxtaposed to his stoic eyes, which shone with the energy of a thousand lived lives. "The light destroys the papers," Tavid assured. Odd, Ada thought, that in these times it was light that destroyed the truth.

"Sorry, Tavid." Oriana said, "but I brought someone very special today."

Tavid, near sighted, neared Ada to recognize her face. When he was an arms-length away his face scrunched as he smiled, and said, "Ada Lawrence—welcome home."

Ada, bashful, asked, "How do you know me?"

"I know everything one could know about the Lawrences. Your mother was an exceptional woman. The bravest of leaders, rest her soul." Tavid hung his head, as if that moment was the first time he heard of Elena's death.

"That's why we're here," Oriana said. "As you can imagine, Tavid. This is all a bit confusing for Ada. I brought her here hoping that she could see something…" Oriana paused to find the right words, "something to cast away her doubt."

"Splendid," Tavid said. Then he turned, and guided Ada deeper down the cool hall, which was lit only by a lamp in Tavid's hands. As Ada progressed deeper into the Purgers' archives, she was overcome with ecstasy. Each stack represented to her a hidden history, which in sum validated the existence of an alien life. Not the interplanetary kind. But of those inhabiting a divine realm, of a grander lifeform imperceptible to those not yet blessed by revelation.

Tavid mumbled to himself with each step, rehearsing the contents of each stack he passed. He paused in front of an inconspicuous pile. One like all the others. But Tavid declared it distinct from the rest when he said, "These are your mother's papers. Or at least what we could recover. See for yourself." Tavid left and disappeared into the shadows alongside Oriana.

At first, Ada did not touch a single artifact from the pile. She believed it too precious for her hands. She worried that she would erase its contents by grasping a paper too tightly and crumbling it in her hands. But after a few moments her curiosity eclipsed her fear and Ada was shuffling through a pile of papers all regarding or authored by her mother Elena. It was the first time in Ada's life that she had seen her mother's handwriting. Which, eerily, looked exactly like Ada's. Or at least what Ada remembered her handwriting looking like one drunken evening when she dared to pen a random thought while in her room.

But it was the pictures of Elena that Ada spent the most time admiring. Mostly because each image dignified her mother's existence. She was not, as her BRiDG'd memory recalled, a lost or troubled soul. Quite the opposite. Through the images kept in the Purgers' archives Ada saw her mother as a source of strength and power. As someone whose life inspired people to action, even decades after her passing. And it was the fact that Elena had the same eyes as her daughter, that made Ada believe in that moment that she too was to live in the same way.

Oriana emerged from the shadow and stood beside Ada. "I

know you want to devour each of these pages today. But you don't have time. Not now at least. Do you believe that you descend from a great power? That you are to finish what your mother started?"

Ada, with tears welling her eyes, nodded her head. Then asked, "But, I'm going into the Memory Corps tonight."

"And that is perfect," Oriana affirmed. "There is still much to learn. Much I want to tell you. Much that you need to discover. And no better place than on the inside of 6Di. We should get you back now."

Oriana led Ada out the same way they entered the mound. Then, she escorted her to the edge of the grid, where Azophi stood alongside a few other Purgers. As they all greeted another, Oriana said to Ada, "Don't live any differently than you would have if this encounter had never happened. Keep searching for what's true, and you'll find the path to lead an offensive against 6Di." Oriana took a breath and said, "And Ada, don't say a word about this to anyone. This entire conversation could be erased once you are again on the BRiDG. But if you remember that you are to lead the Purgers in their next rebellion, simply kiss the tips of your fingers and tap it to my heart before you leave."

Before Ada could take another breath, she was apprehended by two Purgers as another reinstalled her BRiDG. The procedure, at first, was painless. Even enjoyable. At the moment of connectivity, Ada's brain fog eased. Then it nearly exploded. Zaps occurred at a rate so rapid Ada thought her mind was burning. She fell to her knees in pain, her hands gripping each side of her head. She looked upwards at the purgers who watched from under their helmets. Her vision blurred at their sight, then glitched with an image of them as fellow obsoletes. But Ada's memories surpassed the BRiDG, and she saw them as they were.

After a few torturous seconds the pain subsided and Ada stood, breathless.

Oriana placed her hand to Ada's shoulder and said, "You'll be asked to report about your time offline. The answer is that you don't remember. It's a trap. You're not supposed to remember anything that happens offline."

"I understand. But are you all in danger, now that I have these memories?"

"In no more than what we were before," Azophi said.

"What happens to those who are without record that disappear?"

"They're forgotten. Not unlike the rest," Oriana contemplated, "just sooner."

Ada nodded, and before she walked toward 20W, Ada kissed the tips of her fingers and tapped against Oriana's heart.

WELCOME TO THE CORPS

Ada wandered the Stratum of Knowledge absorbing every sensation as if it were her last, so that months or weeks from now when she began to feel homesick, Ada could close her eyes and remember this place exactly as it was. This made every color more vibrant and sound more boisterous. And soon, the intensity of each step had made Ada nauseous. She sought rest at a nearby cafe. Once seated, Ada ordered a small latte and slowly sipped it, watching passersby—with no other purpose but to sit and sip. The viewpoint from the cafe chair made every scene nostalgic. As if the present were just her favorite memories on repeat. In the white noise of a city in motion, Ada's mind maundered.

She understood news about her selection was objectively good. But none of it sat right with Ada. Instead of hope, Ada felt, congealing under her diaphragm, a paralyzing wave of guilt and anxiousness. Her stomach churned. The latte lost its flavor among her thoughts. From the spot where she sat, Ada could see the entryway to 20W's archival facility. She remembered the bloody body that was Grace's, wondered who had actually killed Grace, and if her own body would also be found maimed and mutilated. Then, two guards, whose faces were void, approached Ada and said, "Your honorable Ada Lawrence, we greet you on behalf of Sixth Domain Industries to take your candidacy at selection to become reconnoiter for Vivian's coveted Memory Corps. Please, follow us."

Ada flashed a guarded smile, concealing her confusion toward the guards' kindness. Then she stood and the guards escorted her out toward the street. Nearby obsoletes began murmuring. The energy in the cafe escalated to a palpable excitement. Then it broke with an eruption of cheers. Ada's escalation to the Memory Corps was rewriting the psyche of obsoletes from 20W. What was once the home of broken families and miners was now the town that raised a beloved member of Vivian's esteemed Memory Corps.

The guards escorted Ada toward a caravan of vehicles with emblems identifying its passengers as high-ranking members of headquarters. The vehicles were all black with a simple "6Di" printed on each side, the "i" dotted with a printed replica of Vivian's eye. Ada was ushered into the second vehicle of the caravan. There, she sat inside the vehicle's cupola; a gargantuan and ornate dome atop its center. When the caravan took to the streets, Ada saw what she believed must have been the entire district of 20W lining the sidewalks. She sat stunned, incapable of comprehending her reality.

"It's okay," Lily whispered to Ada, "just smile and wave." Her unsolicited advice snapped Ada into a robotic motion. One without much authenticity. But to most passersby Ada was just a dot atop a vehicle. When the caravan turned onto the main road, which divided the Stratum of Knowledge between east and west, there was not an inch of roadway not occupied by a fellow obsolete. The sight was too much to comprehend, but Ada continued to smile and wave. When the caravan reached mile twenty-one the crowds did not dwindle. Indeed, for the next 79 miles until the caravan arrived at the Stratum of Reason, every inch of the drive paired with hordes of obsoletes eager to witness Ada. At the wall between the stratums of knowledge and reason the crowds came to an end and the vacuum of sensation caused Ada to collapse.

Just beyond the wall that demarcated the two stratums was a purgatory. A gap between yet another wall, a kind of alley between two windowless skyscrapers. Here, the caravan unloaded. Despite the barren aesthetics, the space rattled with a frenzied energy of 6Di personnel scrambling about. Inside the vehicle, Ada felt too tired to stand. But after a few calming breaths, of the kind she would use under each cold shower, she stood and for the first time in her life stepped on soil that was not within the Stratum of Knowledge.

"Welcome," Vivian said, "your life begins today." Vivian smiled. Ada, slightly disoriented, and equally disturbed at the idea that her life would be remembered as starting today, mustered nothing but a nod. Vivian led Ada into the wall she had not yet passed through. Inside was a room, where five formidable individuals, arranged in a semi-circle, sat facing Ada. "You'll get to know each one of them soon," Vivian exclaimed. "These are the keepers of the law. Those who ultimately determine what's progress and what's not. And today, they'll swear you into your citizenship."

Ada nodded in agreement, but exhaustion trademarked her every move.

An elder gentleman stood, hair as silver as the sea's surface under moonlight, and said, "I'm Dr. Weber, Chief of Information, allow me to swear you in as citizen of 6Di, a title both deserved and not." He cleared his throat, and with that any ambient noise in the room as well. "Cross both palms over your heart, tuck your chin and repeat after me." Ada assumed the position as directed, and closed her eyes. Dr. Weber's voice suddenly carried the glory of a grand choir, "I, Ada Lawrence…"

Ada said in turn, "I, Ada Lawrence." And repeated all that followed. Her echoes reverberated like words in an unexplored cave.

Dr. Weber continued, "do hereby renounce my last name, in benefit of joining one family within the citizens of the Stratum of Reason. My renouncement of my familial name shall be documented into The Sphere. I take this oath in service to the promise of progress and perpetuity of peace. My sacrifices have evolved me into a perfect being, and, having attained neuropathic dependency I am, from this day forward, living the truest of truths. A life perfectly intertwined with my BRiDG."

Ada, unsure if she should express excitement or stoicism, favored a continuance of tactfulness. Her eyes looked straight. Lips sealed, chin parallel with the floor. She stood as she believed a brave citizen would stand. Rather, she stood mimicking the pursed energy of the Keepers of the Law. There was no celebration at the conclusion of her oath—only silence. Which for Ada, registered to nothing. No sense of devotion or resolution. For the Keepers of the Law however, the silence was to them a moment to gaze upon the one who would soon lead 6Di. Their immobile faces hinted at no conclusions to their thoughts.

Ada panned her eyes across the group. As she looked at each face, Lily spoke their names to Ada's mind. Arthur Daughtry, Economies. Billie B., Experimentations. Addison Viona, Energy. The last man, sitting snarled in his seat, registered to Ada as Lex Nabakov, Defense. His gaze chilled Ada's blood. Shocked, she locked her eyes forward—away from any of them—and gulped. Never had Ada seen eyes so void. They reminded her of the countenances of the guards, except there was no hint of mystique in Lex's eyes. Only hatred, in a form more primal than Ada knew the modern world allowed.

And so, Ada hardly heard Vivian when she said, "I think we're all warming up to you quite nicely." Vivian grinned and looked to those at her sides, but no one caught the light-hearted remark. Vivian continued, "You've a long day ahead of you tomorrow, Ada. You'll take a car the rest of the way. The driver is waiting, whenever you're ready. Your family is undergoing verification of neuropathic dependency tomorrow. They'll join you once they pass." Ada heard each of Vivian's words jumbled and delayed. So, for a few seconds she stood without motion. This caused concern among the Keepers because they believed Ada was contemplating a possibility not even they could imagine.

How could they? Their lives were of privilege and authority. Since their youth they knew their positioning in society. Except for Vivian, none who sat before Ada had ever elevated their social standing. They'd been rich citizens of the nation state that existed before the war. And they transitioned as powerful citizens of the post-war world. None knew inherited shame or primal hunger. And if they did, they could afford to forget. So though she was not the most authoritative mind in that room, she stood in there the most dangerous. This she also knew, and so decided to depart with nothing but a slight bow.

Back in the barren alley, Ada entered the passenger door of the vehicle closest to the wall she had not yet passed through. She plopped herself into the backseat, heavily exhaled, and whispered, "What the fuck."

"Huh?" the driver asked through faded glass.

"Oh, sorry. Nothing," Ada replied.

He didn't flinch, but drove Ada through a passageway in the final divide between her and the Stratum of Reason. As Ada crossed the border Lily said to her, "Welcome home." Ada smirked, less at the words than their timing.

It was now night. And through the windows Ada thought it odd that she saw nothing but darkness. A few silhouettes. Nothing identifiable. Its flatness confused Ada most. She squinted out the window, searching for something familiar. Through the glass, the driver said, "Just the countryside."

"Countryside?" Ada thought. Lily, queried a definition.

Simultaneously, her driver said, "Yeah, the countryside, it's—"

Ada interjected, "Oh, I know what it is. Well, I've heard about it. Just never been there before."

"So you don't really know the countryside," her driver said playfully. "This is the best you'll get for now," he said as he rolled down the back windows. In flooded scents of grass and brisk air congealed with the distant scent of mulch.

"Nothing like the city," Ada said.

"Nothing over here is like where you were."

And for some reason the conversation died. Overpowered by the novel scents and the sound of 70MPH air filling a cabin, perhaps. Ada focused on the vehicle's tires humming against the road. But her mind also spun: *what will happen to me if Vivian knows that I know? How much can I trust O? Where is — How?* The thoughts amplified one another, until, in her mind, Ada couldn't finish asking one question before she began another. Ada propped her head against the rear passenger-side door. The countryside wind blew in her face, silencing her thoughts until, a few moments later, she fell asleep.

There was no memory of that night. Ada awakened the next morning on a bed which she could only deduce was her own; inside a room that was equal parts tidy and lifeless. Before Ada could process her surroundings, a voice from outside her room shouted, "Get up, get up!" Ada sprang out of her bed, groggy and disoriented. The more aware she became of her surroundings, the more sterile her room appeared. This disturbed Ada. Already, she missed her quaint apartment in the Stratum of Knowledge.

Then Lily's familiar voice said, "Good morning Ada. Today's your first day of training. You'll have to get up now, I'm afraid. All the candidates must arrive at the auditorium for the opening ceremony." Her tone starkly juxtaposed the commanding voice from the hall. That voice which triggered a commotion of candidates breathlessly rushing to the auditorium. After hearing Lily's voice, Ada felt neither anxious nor calm. Rather, matter-of-fact. Yet in the silence that followed as she dressed, Ada longed to hear Lily's voice again. She wished for something that reminded her of home—the only thing that made it worth continuing.

Just then, as if Lily was reading her thoughts, Lily said softly, "Remember, she wants you here." But Ada didn't know if "she" meant Vivian, Oriana, or Elena. No matter the answer it was still true.

Ada smirked. Partially comforted. Mostly at the irony of the heeding to *remember.*

Ada donned her candidate uniform. It was a plain version of the Memory Corps's official uniform. Made of sleek, form-fitting material. Some unnamed synthetic made in a laboratory. The main difference between the uniforms worn by agents and candidates was that the latter bore no emblems. There were no patches that signified a sense of belonging. Even the sheen on each candidate's uniform suggested a degree of perfection that assumed inexperience. It was the attire of the novice, of those aspiring to become something not for purchase.

Ada joined the swarm of candidates filing down the hall. The mass of individuals, the speed at which they walked, the novelty of every sensory input, caused Ada to see no one in particular. She joined a mob of faces that eventually would register as unique. But not now. Now she was focused on also becoming an indiscernible particle of this rolling wave of bodies. Ada couldn't have told you any details of the walk, not even the hallway's color. Overwhelmed, Ada's mind was capped to its more primal parts. Those that thoughtlessly reacted to stimuli it could not articulate. Ada walked alongside hundreds of others, all murmuring rumors of the day's activities. None acknowledging that wherever they felt most comfortable was far, far behind where they stood now.

The hall met its end at a doorway. But beyond its frame was a room like Ada had never witnessed. At the base of the auditorium lay a stage, empty, encircled by rows of seats that stacked so vertiginously against one another they appeared to form a wall. Each candidate filed into each row, respectively taking the next available seat after the candidate who sat before them. It wasn't until Ada was seated that she was able to absorb surrounding details. Which was also when surrounding candidates began to orient themselves. From her peripherals, Ada witnessed a person point in her direction. The pointing woman said, "That's her." A dozen other faces looked towards Ada, who tucked her chin in hopes of concealing her face.

Before another candidate could recognize Ada, the room was called to attention from a voice so thunderous its origin could not be located. The entire auditorium of candidates stood at attention to greet the Keepers of the Law, who paraded onto the stage. Ada did not recognize the last man in the file.

He stood, wooden and taut. If not for his dimples he could have been mistaken for a militant robot. He stood at attention before the table of elders, facing the auditorium until the room fell to a hush. Then he shouted, "Candidates! It's my pleasure to welcome you to Memory Corps indoctrination. I am Instructor Diaz—lead programmer of the events you'll endure for the next ten days. Over the course of your training you'll be asked to decide where ethics lacks application, where philosophy is speculative, and reality illusory. You will make decisions that are difficult. That leaves you unsettled. We cannot afford dual-minded people in this role—people, who, if even for a second, doubt the outputs of their BRiDG." Instructor Diaz paused. He was too far to tell but Ada believed Instructor Diaz emphasized his point by staring directly at her. Diaz continued, "The Memory Corps distinguishes itself from the citizenry for their uncanny ability to form perfect neuropathic dependency to their BRiDG. This is the only way you who are chosen to protect the truths can also protect yourself from lies." Instructor Diaz took a long breath, "Over the next ten days the thousand of you will be dwindled to one." Dozens of candidates shifted in their seats and glanced toward Ada.

"As you all know there are 201 archival units. One hundred assigned to the west side of The Sphere of Knowledge, 100 to the East. And one assigned to headquarters, who works directly for Vivian and the Keepers of the Law," Diaz said, pointing to the table at his aft. "Grace's retirement delivered a sizable gap in talent to Unit Zero. Headquarters hopes to welcome the best among the brightest citizens. However, should even the best of you not meet the standards of the Keepers of the Law, the position will remain open. And we will run another indoctrination. And another. Until the one worthy of replacing Grace reveals themselves."

Diaz's evocations triggered a performative response from the audience of candidates. Many of the candidates erected their postures. Ada sat, still slightly slumped in her chair, wondering if there was any other candidate in this room that also knew Grace was no longer operational for a reason other than retirement. Ada glanced across the room, looking for anyone whose appearance wasn't that of a sycophant.

Her eyes rolled effortlessly across the crowd, when Diaz began again. "As a reconnoiter, whose duty is to locate undiscovered artifacts, your most important skill will be the ability to enmesh yourself with your surrounding environment. You must make visibility a choice, not a fact. Each day an obsolete writes is another day when we all live a little further from the truth. To discover unauthorized compositions, or to catch an obsolete in the act of writing or concealing those writings is to literally usher us into a communeural society—as Vivian and her Keepers have dreamed!" At this arousing proclamation, the obsequious audience leapt to their feet, each member competing to contribute the loudest applause. Except for Ada, who stood a second slower than the rest, and whose contributions to the raucous celebrations were a mere cordial clapping of her hands. The Keepers and Vivian repeatedly bowed their heads in humility. Each bob fueling the audience to another burst of applause. Until, after nearly a minute, Vivian raised her hand to quell the noise. Then she stood, and the room hushed to a silence so pure it mimicked night.

"It is true," Vivian cooly stated, "that a reconnoiter prevents the regression of mankind—they protect the integrity of our collective knowledge. Obsoletes have no business to think independently. And to engrave their thoughts beyond their minds is not only criminal—it's dangerous. Which is why selection begins with understanding who of you can capture an obsolete guilty of such a charge. Your first challenge begins now."

Like a rough-cut in a film, Ada, and everyone she recognized from the auditorium suddenly found themselves outside, in what looked like the Stratum of Knowledge. Masterfully designed; perfect to a fault. Obsoletes roamed about. But the visualizations were slightly transparent. And each object manifested with subtle, random twitches. A simulation perhaps. *But how?* Ada thought. Ada noticed a line in the road, and when each candidate crossed it they disappeared from her vision and into the ether. When Ada crossed the line, there was a brief glitch in her vision. A slight percussion that caused her to stumble a step. She looked back at the line but it was absent. All that remained in sight was a simulacrum of a city like home—and her unremitting thoughts that what she was in now was not real.

Ada wandered the district searching for an obsolete in possession of, or possibly practicing, written compositions. The BRiDG clued Ada to look for signs of unexplainable perspiration, clamminess, subverting eyes, hands clasped tightly over bags or body parts, ink stains on fingertips. Ada walked the streets, looking for exactly that kind of person, all the while behaving inconspicuously, draping every move in incognito. Which was natural to Ada, she'd spent her whole life concealing her truest identity; always concealing her foremost thoughts. To Ada, this wasn't an exercise, insomuch as it was another day. Then, as she was silently celebrating this thought, Ada saw a smudge of ink on the fingertip of a nearby obsolete. She didn't catch who it was. Their back was to her now. Ada stood from her table and began pursuit. The hooded figure took a left at the next block.

The quickness of Ada's initial discovery made her believe that this finding was a trap. It felt too easy. No, it was too easy. On the next block, Ada's suspect slowly walked the street, observing items for sale at various street vendors. Ada pretended to do the same. Then the suspect entered a building. Ada asked Lily for a blueprint of the building. A brief moment later, the blueprint rendered to Ada's optical nerves, overlayed to the city before her. The building only had two exits on record. The first was in eyesight. The second at the building's rear. Ada entered through the one she saw the hooded figure enter.

Inside the store hung innumerable dream-catchers, some the size of mattresses. These were common household items in The Sphere of Knowledge that hung in obsolete spaces as good omens to better days. The hanging clusters of dream catchers created an incalculable number of faux walls, corners, and mini rooms. The store was a sea of thread, viscous and unnavigable. More a place to wade than wander. Visibility never extended beyond one's arm. Ada's suspect could have been five feet from her, or already out of the store. The closeted nature of the building created for Ada a sense of claustrophobia. Feeling her breath shorten and heart rate rise, Ada headed for the exit. But before Ada could orient which direction it was, she was grabbed from behind by her neck and pulled behind another wall of threads. This person remained behind Ada, unseen. Ada prepared to fight her way out of their grip, when they released their hand from Ada's neck and flashed a tattoo on their wrist of an encircled P: a Purger. She tried to ask, "How did you—"

The purger interrupted, "Just listen." Ada, free from their grip, attempted to spin to face them. But their hands prevented her from turning to them fully. "It's best you don't see me. Just hear me. It's not your stalking that's being evaluated now, it's your loyalty. Nod your head yes if you understand." Ada's head bounced. "Good," the purger continued, "Do not attempt to discern anything. The lines between real and unreal are invisible.

Intertwined. Neither can exist separate from another here. Have no concern for justice—what feels right or wrong to you. Not here. Express your loyalty to Vivian. Now go."

"Wait," Ada said, still facing the threads before her, "I have one question."

"Quick," replied the purger.

"How can I trust you? I thought this was a simulation."

The purger said nothing, but Ada heard them kiss the tips of their fingers and reached around to place them against Ada's heart.

Before Ada could respond, the purger pushed her and caused Ada to stumble toward another wall of threads. By the time she found her footing and craned her neck toward where she just stood, the only evidence of a former purger's presence was in the swaying of a few dream catchers. Ada stormed the trail of swaying threads, hoping to catch a glimpse of this purger. Not ten seconds later the space was still. Ada was alone, with no lead, and one mysterious encounter that she couldn't even account for as real. But as Ada would soon discover, life as a citizen existed in a kind of superreality, where both simulation and actuality were one. And though at this time she could tell no difference between the two, she trusted that this encounter with the purger was real.

As if this whole evening were orchestrated, the hand of the perpetrator brushed through the dream catcher beside Ada. Between the threads, Ada saw the last damning piece of evidence she needed to turn her pursuit into an apprehension. The inked hands she followed reached for a small journal in its back pocket—the kind journalists used before their work was digitized.

Ada hastily moved to apprehend the suspect turned criminal. She still believed the obsolete was unaware of her presence, but the exit was steps away. Ada leapt for the obsolete's hand. Upon contact the person froze. Ada, grasping the inked hand, barked, "Guilty of subverting The Sphere's truths." Then she saw the face of her suspect, and gasped when she saw her old friend from 20W, Corydon.

Before another word was exchanged, two guards authorized immediate punishment for means of public education. The punishment for unauthorized compositions was bilateral amputation of hands. A role usually reserved for members of implementations but the first guard on scene implored Ada to "do the honors." The same guard handed Ada a small blowtorch. After which he summoned nearby obsoletes and shouted, "Gather outdoors for this marvelous ceremony of justice." All in proximity obeyed and gathered. All who could not attend received a breaking news notification. Which after, overrode their optical nerves and broadcasted the brutal punishment.

Ada struggled to discern this moment as training. The man before her looked every bit like Corydon. Not a rendition of someone representing him. But Ada remembered the words of the mysterious purger who implored her to believe that discernment was futile—her only task was to make Vivian happy. Ada knew just what that thing would be, so she said to Corydon, "Remove the item in your back pocket."

Corydon's eyes, filled with fear, flashed with confusion as he reached for his back pocket. When he removed the journal from his back pocket, fear vanished. Confusion took its place. It crossed Ada's mind that maybe this was not his notebook. Maybe he was framed. That the ink stains from his hands were from his duties carried out at the archives of living memory, where he digitized new documents composed by citizens. Ada believed him innocent. But she lacked evidence. Cooly, she demanded he read the first page aloud.

Corydon opened the journal and read aloud, "I killed Grace." The crowd gasped. Ada, stolid, whispered in her mind *Lily, who killed Grace?* Her feed flooded with articles never before seen. Like the death of Grace was old news, a crusted column at the bottom of a stack of old papers. Ada saw the headline of a most recent article published, "Longstanding Mystery Murder Case Reignited with Confession." Ada closed her feed. She'd piece together exactly what happened later, when she was alone and again free to think like so.

"And did you write these words?" Ada asked.

Corydon paused. His eyes said no, but his voice said, "Yes."

"Burn it," Ada commanded. A guard from implementations set the book aflame. The evidence did not matter, what had been written in private was now in The Sphere. The power was no longer in Corydon's hands. Those ashes were a symbol, a warning, to the meaning of any idea or life that interrupted The Sphere's agenda. Though his confession was now physically non-existent, Corydon witnessed it matriculate itself into the minds of everyone as the article's popularity soared to the most read artifact in The Sphere within seconds.

The surrounding faces of obsoletes that encircled Ada, Corydon, and the few guards turned livid. As if they'd discovered a prolonged betrayal. As if they'd forgotten they'd all just learned that the murder even happened. The crowd chanted for justice. One voice, rising above the rest, shouted, "Off with his hands!"

But Ada knew the truth. She knew that Corydon had no part in the murder of Grace. Ada knew he was beside her that entire night, him and George both. Why Corydon confessed to a murder that was neither publicly known nor privately his business perplexed Ada. Enough to remind her that the world she interpreted now was not real. Rather, it was reality but one contrived by a poorly written script. Yet, the experiential chasm between this and what Ada knew as real was zilch. Each a near replica of another. The glitches Ada witnessed when she first entered this stratum vanished. *What if I never leave this realm?* Ada thought, *What's to stop Vivian from perpetually imprisoning me in these illusions?*

Before Ada could contemplate the powers-at-play in this moment a guard fully extended Corydon's right arm. A second his left. Corydon stood as if strapped to a crucifix made of his enemies.

Ada's hands began to sweat. She felt a churning in her stomach. A sickening revulsion to the situation she was in. Then she recalled the warnings of her purger friend. This was just a simulation. A test. No longer about whether or not she possessed the technical capabilities to stalk a potential obsolete. But if she was capable of expressing utmost loyalty. And for whatever reason, this was exactly what the purgers asked of her too. Ada forfeited her mind to that thinking. *There is no choice*, she said to herself, as the outer zone of the flame sliced cleanly through Corydon's right wrist.

Corydon yelped. His scream originated from a place deeper than his throat or diaphragm. It was the sound of physical pain congealed with inexplicable betrayal. His eyes burned into Ada's a feeling of disbelief. Nothing between them would ever be the same. He would never be the same. Neither as capable nor trusting. Betrayal is the worst kind of pain. One that causes another to distrust their own species and commit to a hermetic life. Halfway through the severing of Corydon's right wrist he fell unconscious. The guards ordered Ada to pause until he was again awake. Corydon's wrist dangled, begging for total separation.

Ada's adrenaline rushed. She perceived nearly nothing. Not the smell of burnt flesh. Not the inhuman noises emitting from Corydon's mouth. She remained focused on delivering Corydon's punishment. Huffing, as guards attempted to bring him back to consciousness. He was alert, but barely. She continued severing his wrist. The remaining attached pieces of Corydon's right wrist disconnected in seconds. His lifeless hand dropped to the ground as a clay rock. Bits of burnt ends separated on impact, leaving a trail of blackened crumbs. The end of his arm was reduced to ash. At least there was no blood. The fire burned too hot.

The crowd erupted. Justice, or the act of it, had been served. Corydon hung dangling in the arms of the guards. His body tremored, overwhelmed with pain. His face grimaced. Against all instinct Corydon remained awake. Unconsciousness was not an escape. Ada wished that she could tell Corydon that in this instant she was also behaving against all instinct; in accordance with another power. Whether it was higher or not, she didn't know. All Ada knew was that they were both victims of the same oppression, albeit whose sufferings manifested quite differently. Both suppressed their instincts in order to appease 6Di. Training complete.

A QUEENLY PARADOX

Ada's eyes opened and she was back inside the training auditorium. Which was now half as full. Five hundred of the initial thousand candidates remained. Those who remained appeared disoriented. The sudden change stunted Ada's adrenaline. Her fast-beating heart was replaced with a sense of uneasiness and guilt. But Ada hadn't felt the same emotions wave over the remaining candidates in the room. They seemed elated. As was Vivian, standing on the stage before each remaining candidate, whose eyes glimmered and stared right at Ada.

The purger was right. The stalking test was about loyalty. Belonging to the Memory Corps required an unlikely mix of autonomy and distrust of oneself. It was to live with the knowledge of individual freedom without ever having it fully pursued. Life in the Corps required one to live divided. One must possess the knowledge of right but not the foolishness to act upon it. Because the pursuit of good may cause harm. And then, is it no longer good? In that auditorium, amidst the glee and celebration and the memories of betrayal and burnt flesh, Ada envied the simple; she longed for ignorance, the life of a typical obsolete or citizen. She wished for a simple life and coherent heritage, a past that asked nothing of her but for her to be her.

Before Ada savored her simple fantasy, Vivian spoke. "At the end of day one you have all demonstrated advanced technical aptitude and unquestionable loyalty. If I ever find the need to expand the Memory Corps, I'm certain that there will be nothing short of highly qualified citizens ready to fill those slots. But, all you that remain—you 500 candidates—you're competing for one slot. And while we reserve the right to pick none of you, I am certain that the one who will replace Grace is among you candidates." Ada again felt jealous gazes shoot from across the room. Vivian continued, "Now, feast for the night. Get to know one another. As they used to say in the States, 'the only easy day was yesterday.' Quantum's Speed!"

Candidates filed into the dining hall adorned to the likings of early universities; those exclusive institutions defined by regality and tradition. Symbolized by ornate masonry and abundant, manicured ivy. While much of society experimented with new architectural designs and materials, the most exclusive institutions retained the iconography of the past. A symbol that history itself was exclusive to elites. And there was no group more elite than the Memory Corps. Their training facilities, living spaces, and dining halls were living replicas of what encased the intelligentsia of old.

In the mahogany hall, Ada sat alone under the banners memorializing previous classes. Ada expected to sit alone. Every other candidate was a longstanding citizen, people who'd lived in the Stratum of Reason together for years. Ada thought she saw a former obsolete from 20W, but the speed at which the woman looked away after their eyes met said otherwise. This was fine with Ada, she felt exhausted and hungry and eager to head to bed. Making new friends would only complicate that evening plan. It didn't take long for Ruby and Malachi to complicate that evening plan. Ruby sat first. Eagerly, and with an unabashed grin, she beamed at Ada through with her hazy eyes. "Hi Ada!" she nearly sang, "my name's Ruby. And this is Malachi." She said, pointing to the begrudging gentleman sitting across from them both, who only showed the top of his curly, sandy-blonde hair.

"I'm Ada."

"I know!" Ruby declared, giggling. "Ya know, everyone's intimidated by you?"

Ada rushed to swallow her food, "What, how so?"

"Well...it's kind of obvious. You're the first obsolete to bypass digitization minimums before becoming a citizen. And, didn't Vivian herself say that you're her heir?"

"She mentioned it's possible. I'm sure there are lots of potential—"

"No," Malachi interrupted, "you're the only one." He peered at Ada under his curly hair with his steel-blue eyes. Reminiscent of a vagabond surfer. Ada felt her heart skip a beat. A sense of exoticism and adventure roiled through her blood. There was a beat. Too long to deny that something had happened when Ada's and Malachi's eyes met.

"Say," Ruby pondered, "what happened to your chest?"

Ada looked down at a small scar she'd never before questioned. "I-I'm not sure."

"It's curious because my mother has the same. A few others do too. No one seems to know why."

"Just one of those things, Ruby," Malachi grumbled, "like birthmarks."

"Or rashes!" Ruby happily added. "Anyways, how'd you find today's test, Ada? I'm surprised there were 500 people that volunteered who couldn't complete today's challenge. If you can even call it that."

"Why wouldn't you call it a challenge?" Ada wondered, recalling the horrors of severing her old friend's hands.

Malachi and Ruby looked at one another confusedly, "Well…it was really quite simple. I mean, the lead appeared before us in the first few minutes. Then you followed the person for an hour or so. Then you confirm they possess a journal. Then the guards took over."

"That's all you did?" Ada asked.

"Yeah, that's what we all did, silly."

"Did you do something else?" Malachi asked.

Ada paused, "No." Then more affirmatively said, "I did that too."

Thinking aloud, Ruby said, "I guess it makes sense—how easy that round was. Maybe every round will be easy for those who rely most on their BRiDG. I guess, yeah, I guess those who are at the bare minimums for neuropathic dependency struggle here. Only the finest minds here!"

Ada's jaw clenched and leg flexed at the thought that Ruby was right. That maybe what awaited her was a torturous nine days of training. And an equally unbearable life in the Stratum of Reason. A thought which in that moment felt too arduous to face and yet simultaneously infinitesimal if it meant redeeming her mother's death. Ada contemplated the possibilities of her life. Her eyes glazed into a dimension other than the present. Malachi and

Ruby looked upon Ada in panic. Silence often meant unauthorized thought. Ada came to and broke the tension, joking to Ruby, "You already sound like a master of reason." They cackled.

But what none comprehended in that moment was that it took one to know one.

Feeling trapped, Ada stood and said, "Excuse me, but I should rest. I ahh—obviously I am getting tired." She hoped to excuse her internal monologue to exhaustion.

"Oh," Ruby frowned, "You'll do just fine. You obviously have a special way with your BRiDG."

"That's one way to put it," Ada said before she sipped the last of her water. Then Ada wished them goodnight and dismissed herself from their table. As Ada walked across the dining hall there was not a set of eyes that didn't look toward her as she made her way across the hall. Ada's mind raced. *What am I doing, exposing myself? Was I really given a different test than everyone else? What does Vivian know about me? Why can't I go a second without someone watching me?* She felt vexed with her fellow candidates. That they could live without conflict and in ignorance of the games and politics happening beyond their BRiDG. Paradoxically, this fueled Ada's desire to win. Because in this moment she saw her mind as unparalleled. Not as a mind whose accolades were dependent on unlocking a device's functionalities. She didn't see herself as a medium to maximizing the impacts of 6Di. But as a symbol of free thought, one worthy of the highest power. What could avenge her mother's death better than that?

Ada returned to her dorm exhausted by the previous few days. Worse than tired, she felt trapped. That particular kind of despair reserved for those mid-career, whose fortunes and direction no longer seem a mystery. Although only at the beginning of this journey, Ada swore she could see its end. Behind the celebrity of her new circumstances was an unseen force eroding her character. Prosperity awaited those who silently fulfilled their assignment. One life awaited Ada. Its terms, in the hands of another. Lying face up on her bed Ada wondered if *a life without choice was any life at all.*

"Lily," Ada said softly.

"Yes Ada?"

Ada thought, "Can you show me today's news?"

"Of course. Great job today, by the way. Everyone is rooting for you." As Lily displayed today's news to Ada's optical nerve she added, "Especially me." Ada smirked. Then she scrolled the headlines, living vicariously through each headline. The words diminished whatever existential pressure she felt moments before. Her status as a celebrity guaranteed her an audience. And so, though Ada felt herself drawn deeper into a predestined life, absent of her agency, she found rest in her life having witnesses. Whatever life she lived, at least it would be remembered.

Never mind the fact that these memories were state sponsored, sanitized and safe for public consumption. As the headlines read:

Ada Lawrence, Overnight Citizen, A Favorite in Reconnoiter Selection.

Murder Investigation Faces Complications: Abigail, Amelia, & George Co-Conspirators?

Grace Gordon Eulogy Held in Home District 30E

Obsolete Clock Continues Ticking, While Archiving Dips to Lowest

Output in Year

> *As Number of Citizens Expand, 6Di's Executive Board Also Swells*
>
> *Coroners: George Simpson's Fingerprints Found on Grace's Body*
>
> *Vivian Polanofsky Says Citizenship, $1B, will be Awarded to Obsolete*

With Info that Convicts Grace's Murderer

The news set her mind abuzz. But Ada was operating on reserves. Too tired to emotionally comprehend the words she read, Ada's eyelids magnetized themselves shut. Her mind drifted further into a delirium that preceded sleep. But just as she took a long, steady breath before completely falling into the abyss of night—a vision of her torching the hands of her dear friend Corydon to the floor alerted her awake. Her once-steady breath turned erratic. *Who plants these thoughts in someone's mind?* Ada thought, interpreting Lily's silence as guilt.

Sleep was further from Ada now than the nearest horizon. Ada opened an unread message from Byron. It was a picture of his new home in the Stratum of Reason, the same one he was assigned a decade before. It looked quainter, more inviting—as a person does when they firmly age into their midlife. Its charm a descendant of its humble facade. Under the photo was a single message: *Proud of you, can't wait to welcome you home. Love - Pops.*

Tears welled in Ada's eyes. Selfishly, from despair. All her life's work suddenly fell into question. And Ada's mind spiraled. She counted the hours wasted, the nights spent working for a path to citizenship that was subverted, overnight, by a fate that was never hers. It had only been two days, but life in the Stratum of Reason proved too complicated. Too—paradoxically—irrational for Ada's liking. Ada preferred the world of cause and reaction.

The life where outcomes had an explanation. She longed to once again live as an obsolete. For the familiarity and habits and the comforts of the only place she had ever called home.

There was another message from Chloe. Also a picture of her assigned townhome off the cobblestone streets near the fashion district. A bit more exquisite than Byron's abode. Perfectly fitting for Chloe's personality, dignified and vogue. She wrote: finally home.

Ada's stomach flipped. She was to believe that accelerating her family into the Stratum of Reason was an act of kindness. A favor in return for Ada's service to 6Di. But this act of kindness was sheer manipulation, the first of many steps Vivian would take to entrap Ada into the Memory Corps. What made Ada believe this most was the fact that neither Chloe nor Byron had achieved neuropathic dependency. Yet, when their profiles were searched in The Sphere they had—conveniently—completed digitization requirements the day Ada began training. It was true, Vivian wasn't kindly offering Ada and her loved ones citizenship. Vivian was entangling the Lawrence's loyalties to her agenda—buying their silence. But Ada's cost would be much higher than that.

Ada lay in bed confronting a most dissatisfying elixir of confusion and wistfulness. Seeing her family so happy to find themselves home, Ada wondered if she'd ever feel the same. If her feeling constantly displaced was simply a symptom of her never feeling able to embrace her whole mind. The fact that no matter where her body resided, her mind, when liberated, would always be unauthorized. These thoughts alone were evidence of her danger. The BRiDG overrides longing for past lives. The pangs of breakups, losses, and unexpected life transitions as obsolete as polio. But Ada's gift was her curse. She thought beyond her BRiDG, beyond the spaces of the mind she ever felt Lily activate, deep into a part of her mind that remained free, roaming into thoughts she—and 6Di—would rather her not possess. Ada wondered if Lionel felt the same. His zany drawings reminiscent of a person longing for a home. Why else would someone possess themselves with a world of make believe?

Honesty is a nocturnal trait; it is silenced during the commotion of everyday life. So as Ada's eyes began fluttering in submission to sleep, she realized that this Ada going to bed was not the same one who sought sleep the night before. This Ada had committed an unthinkable act against a trusted friend. She'd severed Corydon's hands, forever changing him as much as herself. His changes were visible and disabling. Hers, invisible and enabling. *No, it wasn't real*, Ada said to herself. *It wasn't real. He's fine. I'm fine. It was only a simulation.* Still, Ada couldn't shake the fact that she felt different, more capable of doing that exact same thing again. Was there such a thing as an inconsequential act? A choice that in some way did not change the trajectory of oneself, even if those changes are unseen? Is there a division between the real and simulated? Or if a simulation was happening, wouldn't that too be classified as real? Ada's head spun beyond control. She squeezed her eyes tight, suppressing her newfound nauseousness. A sickness animating from her internal tension. This wasn't a different Ada seeking rest. This was two. One who had never amputated a friend's hands, one who had. Only one would see the morning.

When Ada awoke the next morning she was unsure which version remained. Or if both still existed. In the ice-cold shower her slow steady breath exhaled any worries. She didn't need to question which one, or if one, of her remained. This, she would discover whenever she would again be forced to choose between loyalty to a loved one or 6Di. Ada was okay with this. After all, much of her life circumstances were incongruent with her choices. Ada's plans were more frequently victims to her intuition.

Ada then departed for breakfast. Not five paces outside her door, Ada heard Ruby's bubbling voice, "Good morning sunshine, today is going to be an exciting one!"

"Ruby, how long have you been up?"

"Three hours. I like to prepare for my day on my own time. Not someone else's."

Ada scowled and addressed Ruby's previous questions, "No, I have not heard about today's test."

"It's a master exam in informationics."

"The master exam?"

"I don't think any of us is expected to pass it, not till we graduate training. It's a way to measure aptitude. There's a guy— Oliver—who's expected to win. Has spent his whole life decoding ancient hieroglyphics."

"Are you worried?" Ada asked.

"Not one bit. I've studied extraction and retrieval methods all morning once today's schedule was posted at midnight."

"They posted the schedule at midnight?"

"A punishment for those violating the eleven curfew, I suppose. Imagine it kept them up all night. It's an obscure science, you know. Some of the master archivists are said to be able to extract trapped sound waves in ions from noises made decades or centuries ago. That's how we got the auditory archives of the last president's surrender to 6Di."

Ada's posture straightened at this mystically scientific thought, "That's right. I forgot about that."

"It's amazing, truly. All the ways in which the world imprints our stories. You can see it in the chemical makeup of dirt, the depth of the trees, the eyes of fellow man. It's like we discovered writing again when we began letting these things speak for themselves."

"That's the whole idea of the BRiDG. Capture sensory data and translate it into a learned language."

Ruby smiled, "and soon it'll be our jobs to comprehend and capture those languages yet learned."

Ada returned a smile. Over the course of the next nine days candidates were tested against the most advanced sciences and archival skills. Becoming a member of the Memory Corps required an unlikely blend of technical proficiency, creative thinking, and physical prowess. The ten-day selection process was designed specifically for reconnoiters, whose reliance on physically navigating stratums in search of information hidden by nature or fellow man placed extra emphasis on defense and athleticism. After training for stalking and informationics, after which only 250 candidates remained, the candidates were subject to tests in letter unlocking; krav maga and jiu jitsu; weapons handling and close quarters combat; biometrics, connectomics and the BRiDG-brain connection; x-ray microtomography; computational imagery and visual sensory beyond the human eye.

Ada excelled in each category, making it, unsurprisingly, to the last day of the test. After each day, her reputation slightly enhanced. In part to her undeniably stellar performances witnessed by other candidates. But perhaps more so to the surge of headlines broadcast across each stratum every night.

Ada Lawrence, top contender for Grace's position, wows 6Di Executives

Closing Another Top Performing Day, Ada Lawrence Advances With Unanimous Superiority

Behind Ada Lawrence's Success, a Difficult Past

How Ada Lawrence Turned her Love for Family into a True Underdog Tale

With One Day Remaining, Ada Lawrence Eyes a Graceful Victory

She'd become a sensation across spheres. Back in 20W roads and schools were renamed in her honor. The Wing of Living Memory was renamed The Ada Reconnoiter Wing of Living Memory. Ada became an icon before she'd even been selected. It never crossed Ada's mind that she wouldn't win. Not on day one of the competition, nor on day ten, when she had to face the stiff and programmed Oliver in a final competition on *Cybernetics, The Sphere, and the Infallible Truth*—whereby the two remaining contestants had to identify a false bit of information that had made itself into The Sphere and tactfully remove it from both The Sphere and citizens' memories.

All exercise happened in a training environment, a simulated reality that was streamed live across all living members of each stratum. The competitions typically attracted mass viewership, a level which demanded even those who had not watched competitions discover themselves in conversation about them.

On the last night of competition, the watch rate was reportedly at 100%. It was believed that this was the first time in history, before the population of mankind was no more than a tribe, that all eyes were on the same person at once.

On the final night of competition Ada was first to identify the false bit of information in The Sphere. She'd recognized something afoot in the meteorological records for the previous January. She'd remembered it a bitter month. Her BRiDG (in the training exercise) recalled a moderate month. To examine the totality of artifacts in one night's time would be impossible. It is, after all, part of the primary duties of Corrections, whose breadth of validations are made possible thanks to advances in cryogenic computing. But, occasionally, a Reconnoiter may have to recognize false information in a live environment—eliminating the burden of sending false information into The Sphere. So, the test took place in two small rooms within the grand library. Ada was assigned to one, Oliver another. Within the room there was documentation that was false. Their only job was to find it.

Oliver operated quite systematically, picking up archival pieces individually, querying The Sphere for what was already written, and when results returned as matching he moved to the next. His approach was both methodical and a bore to witness. Ada raged through the documentation, tearing through pages like voided love letters. Snappily commenting "what a grim excuse for an art" when picking up a tome of war history. When she read in a published memoir, "last year, my husband and I spent January swimming in the sunny seascapes." Ada yelled "Bullocks!"

Removing was easier than identifying, especially because the memoir itself was unread and so not actually in any citizen's memory. If it had been, the test would have been more difficult to finish before night's end. But before Oliver had even identified what in his room was incorrect, Ada had finished the final test. Just as happened with each test before. It ended as immediately as it began. Ada, victorious, was augmented beside Vivian who, beaming, addressed Ada as "the greatest Reconnoiter who has yet deployed."

Ada felt the eyes of the world. But she also felt the eyes of Vivian, which felt separate and more daunting. The precise instills greater fear than the generalized. It was more than this, though. It's that Vivian's gaze held more power than each one of those unseen eyes witnessing from their BRiDGes. Or perhaps as if there were no difference; that the sum of everyone's gaze was also Vivian's. That if there were a deity incarnate it would be beside Ada, sharing a maternal embrace. It was at this moment she realized the core of what unsettled her most the past week and a half. It's that in realizing her potential she realized her limits. And by that, what defined her success and failures. And for Ada, her success would from this day forward be synonymous with Vivian's wishes. Independence had vanished. Or at least the illusion of it did. "Welcome to the Corps," Ada heard Vivian say. Ada returned a smile, half wondering if the purgers too had somehow witnessed this moment and if they'd show her what she ought to do next.

RETRIEVE. REFINE.
PRESERVE.

It had been two weeks since Ada first entered the Stratum of Reason. Not a single minute of it separate from the path to, or rooms within, the Memory Corps training facility. It remained a phantom, a place experienced through mediums two dimensional. Photographs, mostly. From her digitizing days. She could have lived in the Stratum of Knowledge for the last week and it would have felt the same. Whatever was different in this new world, the one beyond her training grounds remained a mystery. The people just as much. Aside from Ruby and Malachi, her encounters with citizens were silent moments of competition. She endured a ceremony. And now bore the title citizen. But Ada felt no different. In fact, she felt less liberated. Which was true. Ada was now more entangled with Vivian's inexplicable games.

The night after Ada was announced as 6Di's newest reconnoiter, she slept alone on the same bed she had each night as a candidate. She didn't feel a seismic change in the weight of her name. She could not yet comprehend the extent to which her existence mattered. But in this victory, Ada had surpassed her personhood. From this day forward she wasn't a precise person— someone who ought to be known. Ada had become a symbol. An object whose meaning and significance would be weaponized. At some level she must have known this, because when Ada awoke the day after her selection, she felt an unfamiliar anxiousness that coincided with the morning's silence. Her life up to this point had primarily been a measurement of her busyness. A sum of mindless preordained tasks in service to the single outcome of citizenship. Now, she was publicly on track for an outcome she wished was not true. And privately, was in agreement with the Purgers to explore a path which might manifest to nothing.

Ada's first stop was to her father's home, an hour's drive away from the Memory Corps's training facility. Ada sat behind the wheel of her personal vehicle as it drove itself to their residence. Immediately after she left the premises of the training grounds, Ada was struck by the messiness of this stratum. In the Stratum of Knowledge, where obsoletes reside, every element was an homage to a master designer. Each part perfectly inexorable from the next; every item either warp or weft. In the Stratum of Reason there was a subtle sense of disorder. Minor expressions of individualism that segmented one property from the next. Places for people to demonstrate their reasonings. Here, the "because" was yoked to something idiosyncratic in lieu of conformism. A house could be red because a citizen felt it was their favorite color, and that reason was enough.

Byron's home was single story, built of brick, with a floor plan as sprawling as the plot of land it sat on. The property reflected the quiet strength and warmth of Byron. But to get there was a journey for the determined. Byron was near the stratum's edge, the furthest Ada had ever been away from her home in 20W. Here, the landscape transitioned from messy urbanscape to untamed rural life. A place where neighbors are trusted silhouettes on hilltops at the horizon. When Ada first arrived, she thought that she'd entered another stratum. It felt too unfamiliar. Backwards. She thought so especially after she exited the vehicle at her dad's home and watched a red bird sing.

A red bird? Ada thought.

Yes, Lily said to Ada, *it's called a cardinal.*

Ada smiled, and asked, "what is it saying?"

It doesn't say anything, but tweet tweet.

Ada thought it beautiful, for the bird meant that meaning still existed beyond the knowledge of 6Di.

Ada knocked on Byron's front door. No one answered. Not after the first knock. Not after the second. Nor third. She decided to check out back. Ada caressed the brick as she walked alongside the home. Its texture as foreign as the red bird's song. A home, at least its permanence, never registered to Ada. But she felt its importance to her father, even if it meant nothing to her. Ada's home, the place where she felt most secure, was in her habits—which could happen anywhere. Home, she believed, was where you let your heart unravel. So, she hadn't felt particularly attached to any single place. Not yet at least. She was, instead, always content with never staying put. As she neared the back of Byron's house, she felt happy that he had a resting place.

When Ada arrived at the backyard, she was delighted to find Byron sitting on a chair atop a stone patio under the shade of an umbrella, between two boxed herb gardens, staring toward the abyss.

"Quite a home you found yourself in," Ada said.

Byron sat still. Only his hand moved toward his face, as if he was wiping his eyes. Then he stood, exhaled, and looked toward Ada. When she saw his face, her stomach sank. Beaming, Byron said, with a bit of a stutter, "Oh Ada, so wonderful for you to visit me."

Ada hugged her father and asked, "What's wrong?"

"Oh nothing. Nothing. Must be the air. Or these plants. My body isn't used to this—you know." It was that last sentence that contained the only bit of truth. Then another, "I'll get used to it—living here." Byron nodded his head, his lips trembled, and he hid his face from Ada. "Quite the view though," he said, acknowledging the plains. "At the stratum's edge."

For the sake of peace, Ada didn't question her father's story any further, and said, "Yeah, it is quite dry out here. They don't show you that in the pictures." Byron forced a smile. But Ada thought he looked unsettled. Byron was concealing something, Ada knew it. There wasn't a word spoken for what must have been a minute.

Ada broke the silence, and asked, "did you see me during the competition?"

"Watched you every night I could. You caused quite a sensation after the sensors lost you during the first event."

"I did?"

"Yeah, added a real sense of mystery." Byron sat again, dropping into the rhythm of this conversation.

Ada grinned. "Was it when I was in the thread shop?"

"Yes! That's when."

"Dad, you wouldn't believe it. One of the purgers—"

Byron leapt from his chair, shook with rage, and shouted, "Do not utter that name! Not ever again!" Ada awestruck, said nothing. "Do you understand me?" Ada lifelessly stared at her father. "Tell me you understand me," he demanded.

Without uttering a word, Ada locked eyes with her father, stared long enough that she watched his pupils vibrate. Those tremors, a voiceless shout, a cry, for Ada to say something—anything. Ada too spoke with her body, and delivered one short affirmative nod. *Understood.* If he was to fully inherit an auspicious future as a citizen, Byron would have to bury his past. If someone queried The Sphere, curious of his path to citizenship, there would be nothing to read about his life as miner; nothing that could link him to Oriana, Azophi, or the Purgers. Instead, his biography read, "Byron Lawrence is a quiet farmer, who moved to the shepherd's district after receiving his BRiDG twenty years prior. He has two daughters, Ada and Chloe, who continued living in the Stratum of Knowledge until they personally reached requirements for citizenship. He is a widower of Elena Lawrence, who was slain during the Second Civil War." So it was written and so it would be.

As quickly as his temper flared it subsided, and Byron asked, "Have you seen Chloe yet?"

"I was off to see her next," Ada said, her tone rising.

"Her place is splendid."

"Is she finding it like you are your place?" Ada asked.

"I can't tell," Byron responded. "She's a bit like you. Can never really tell what she's thinking."

"Or how," Ada added. A grim pause cloaked the outdoor

space. Byron shook his head disapprovingly.

"My daughter," Byron continued, "I know you know what it means for me to have this place. So much must remain unsaid. So, don't visit often. Not at first. I'm free from duties now. But this comes at a cost. You've duties to fulfill. And you should test what happens when you fail to complete them." He took a pause, and said, "The wise foresee the consequences of their actions. But to the foolish, regrets only appear in retrospect. Please Ada, don't come back here a divided soul." Ada wondered what this made her father, who could see nothing in retrospect, except for what's been programmed by 6Di.

When Ada departed her father's property, she did so believing it to be the last time she'd see him for a while. Perhaps, even, the last time she'd ever see him and he would recall anything of the past. Memory was the currency which kept the new world in balance. Each recollection an asset. A thing exchanged without one's permission. To live in peace was to live in debt to someone else's work. A debt which only memories could resolve.

Ada rode into the nearby town to meet her sister Chloe at the local town library. The ride emphasized to Ada the differences between each stratum. In the Stratum of Knowledge, cities were perfectly gridded, designed according to laws of advanced geography. In the Stratum of Reason, cities sprawled in manners less patterned. At times gridded and others crisscrossing. It was almost as if the city had a life to itself. It reminded her of the documents she'd studied about Istanbul or Mexico City. Cities with boundaries that were hard to define and centers even more difficult to locate. It was as if each pocket depended, unknowingly, on the other. The entirety of the city was never a sum greater than its parts—for the pulse of the city was in its districts. The enclaves that made the bustle a home.

Ada arrived before her sister. She leaned against a pillar, nonchalantly observing passersby amidst the cool, idyllic dusk, that was a prerogative of fall. Ada wished night would fall, so that she could observe in anonymity. Instead she stood unmistakably as herself. Which here and now was an overnight sensation on display for all to see. Things which Ada had forgotten. So she was at first perturbed by the many prolonged glances, and the whispering of nearby strangers. The discomfort mounted so much that Ada wanted to cancel her time with Chloe. But before she could message her sister a child approached Ada and asked, "Are you Ada Lawrence?"

Ada said that she was—confused at how this child would know her. Faster than she could ask the child a question in return, a flood of citizens surrounded Ada. She felt an overwhelming panic, as fellow citizens smooshed her against the pillar. Without a word, she ducked and fled for the library's doors, where, inside, the rules commanded quiet. She'd never been inside a library. But she read much about them growing up. She was among those who could reason now, in a place where libraries were safe. Once inside, Ada walked head-down through a series of doors, and turns, and found herself in a kind of warehouse. A concrete floor divided into narrow hallways with tall metal shelves stuffed high with books. Bright iridescent bulbs. If not for the bindings and pages of the books the very sound of her exhale would have become a chilling echo.

Ada silently walked an aisle. Each sound absorbed by the surrounding paper. She felt a humbling silence, a freedom to wonder. *All these ideas once original*, she thought, *I was born in the wrong era.* Exploration's wanderings gave way to a science. New routes and locations, originality and surprise, gave way to capturing and organizing. Making sense of the lands and its people in the name of science. So too was creativity in the era of 6Di. No longer were people compelled to write, even once citizenship was earned and they were permitted. New books would be written, surely. Once commissioned by 6Di. Ada gazed at the sum of the books and wondered what it must have been like to live in an era where she could have written any one of the books on the shelf.

"They say it's all been written," Chloe said gently, a few feet behind Ada.

Goosebumps rose across Ada's skin, but she refused to flinch, "I think we both share similar feelings about that."

Chloe stared at the binding of a nearby book, "I think it's best I stop harboring contradictions. It isn't healthy. And besides," Chloe looked down the hall to which she could not see its end, "there truly is plenty to read."

"I thought you wanted to write once you became a citizen?" Ada asked her sister.

"That was before I knew what it would be like. Writing requires all sorts of permits and signatures." Ada felt the reality of compromise, the fading of her sister's fire, the same resignation her father demonstrated hours prior. "But, like I said, there's much to read anyway. No need to go through all that trouble." Chloe paused. "So, you're quite the celebrity—huh?"

"I guess so. I'm sure I'll get used to it."

"You will. We'll all get used to this. Eventually, all change becomes the norm again." Chloe and Ada wordlessly looked at one another.

"Yeah," Ada said, with a hint of disappointment.

"I am happy here, though."

"Good. What is your new career?"

"Not new at all," Chloe laughed, "I'm one of the lucky citizens that gets to work in the old archives. I transfer raw artifacts to obsoletes' desks for them to digitize. They bus us in each morning, out each evening."

"You're so lucky," Ada sighed. She observed a few bindings on the shelf, "Why do you think no one comes back here?"

"The door said, 'Library Staff Only,'" Chloe responded, smiling.

Ada chuckled, "I was in such a rush."

"I know. Say, care for a drink or two? Like old times after our shifts?"

"Know somewhere quiet, where I could lay low?"

Chloe knew just the spot. The sisters walked into a sleepy bar. Upscale, dark. The kind where each person was masqueraded by shadows. Chloe and Ada sat in a small semi-circle booth, wrapped in red velvet. Martinis arrived. Paired with a carafe to self-deliver the second round.

"You were remarkable in the trials. I mean, I knew you were smart. But your athleticism…that was fierce."

Ada whispered a bashful, "Thanks."

"Night one was a thrill to watch. I mean, every night was, but what an opener! How were you able to cut off the tracking sensors?"

"Just a glitch." Ada replied, a bit curtly.

"Do you think..." Chloe continued speaking but Ada couldn't comprehend what it was she said. Instead, Ada's mind reflexively wondered why 6Di had shown her cutting out of the feed. The event was edited, broadcasting with a slight delay in case of a medical emergency. So, why let every living obsolete and citizen witness her momentary departure from filming? Was it a signal from Vivian? A sign to Ada and the purgers that she knew of their dealings and it only happened because Vivian allowed it? Or was it something less conspiratorial, just a producer's flare, in attempt to further mystify Ada?

"Ada...Ada? Are you listening?" Chloe asked, pulling Ada out of her thoughts.

"Yeah, sorry I - uh..." Ada twirled her martini. "I have to tell you something. About that glitch."

Eager to hear her, Chloe leaned in, "What about it?" She could hardly hold back her grin.

"It wasn't a glitch, exactly. Actually, it wasn't a glitch at all. I was stopped."

"Stopped? By whom? Or what? What do you mean stopped?"

Four men at the bar stood and walked toward Ada and Chloe. They looked dapper. Driven. Ada noticed them walking toward the table. Their void faces indicating that they were undercover guards. Ada hastened her speech, "Do you remember Oriana?"

Chloe queried the name. Her neuropathic dependency wouldn't allow such a thought. Chloe shook her head no. Ada pulled Chloe tight. She snuck the piece of paper once given to her into Chloe's handbag which rested between them, and assured her sister, "I'll see you soon."

Still oblivious to the guards, Chloe asked, "what are you up to?"

The guards encircled the table. "Ada Lawrence, come with us. Vivian requests your presence." Ada stood without a fight or word. She just looked back at her sister and winked.

On this trip, Ada was blindfolded and guided by the hands of surrounding guards. One at each side pushed Ada along faster than she could comfortably walk without sight. She'd been spun and turned and redirected so many times that Ada was truly lost, incapable of estimating just how far she traveled before Ada was placed alone in a room which, while her vision was distorted, appeared edgeless. From her peripherals, the colors swirled to no rhythm. The room neared total silence. Then, a familiar voice in an unfamiliar tone. "It's not good to play with fire, don't you know?" Vivian slurred, as if drunken or drugged: most definitely enraged. Ada's head swiveled in an attempt to locate Vivian. Then, the blindfolds disappeared and her vision returned. Ada was stunned to see that she stood in the center of an enormous tank, surrounded by water—its waters tinted pink. Vivian stood just an arm's length from Ada, snarling in anticipation for Ada to respond. But the objects floating in the aquarium above suspended Ada's speech. Inside the aquarium Ada could not locate a single fish. There were only brains, floating at various depths.

"Answer me!" Vivian demanded. The volume shook Ada from her trance.

"Yes, yes...I know not to play with fire." Ada responded literally.

"Of course you do," Vivian, now eerily calm, said, "because it's a rule. A good rule…that our forebears learned through pain and passed down to the next generation. Who then passed it down to the next generation. And before long, we all knew not to play with fire no matter how enticing it seemed. It's a rule in life and rules keep us safe. They elevate humanity. There are many rules like it, Ada. Rules that you continue to test the limits of. Rules that you insist on violating. And you're putting yourself into dangerous situations. You're playing with a metaphorical fire. That's not good for any mind, especially yours. Come."

Vivian guided Ada toward where Ada's back faced, toward a solo table a few dozen paces away. Vivian's steps were graceless. Erratic. Under operation of a mind other than sober. They sat across from one another. Vivian reached under the desktop and plopped a whole human brain onto the table. Its liquids scattered in abstract fashion. Vivian lit the brain on fire, as if it were a piece of paper bearing a confession. The air burned putrid. The once pink, plump organ blackened and shriveled. "Brains are remarkable," Vivian continued, "they've escaped the scrutiny of science for millennia. Ironically, it has remained more complex and mysterious than man's greatest machines. Each one a ball of infinite potential and possibilities—oh the things it could learn and think and create." Vivian stared at the brain, now curling to the size of a child's fist, charred and flaked. "But it's also just flesh. Which means it's vulnerable, if not for our craniums. And a vulnerable brain could easily become a useless one. Little by little, less of a wonder. Until it's not even a remarkable piece of flesh, but mush!" Vivian soared her hand upwards and slammed it back onto the counter, crushing what remained of the burning brain. Matter splattered across the table and hit both Vivian and Ada.

"Aside from tragedies like this," Vivian continued calmly, now dabbling her fingers in the brain, "our minds can have incredibly long lives. With just a few chemicals, our minds can live perpetually after our bodies decay. Take all these," Vivian scanned her hand the length of the aquarium, blobs of meat dripping from her fingers. "Each one of these minds would have once been considered dead. Today, they're the epicenter of our zeitgeist. The core to 6Di's mission to, from all minds, create just one. The communeural dream dawns in these tanks. Thanks to the generosity of the fallen, who so graciously donated their minds, we can power the BRiDG not through imitations of human thought. There are no robotics powering your Lily. She's the collective voice of everyone in these tanks. A person whose mind is now perfectly cleansed, processing exactly the way yours should too. Do you know how we can do that?"

Ada slowly shook her head, betraying her fear. Because when Ada saw the brain flop against the table she knew that she was witnessing the future of her own mind.

"Because our minds are fluid, embryonic, adapting to change. They're not worried about the way things were or should be. They're truly present. Absolutely liberated. Completely assimilated. As you should be too, Ada." Vivian's eyes locked onto a particular part of the aquarium. "That was Grace's fault ya know? She had a brilliant mind. Much like yours. But far too rigid. Too independent. Not anymore." Vivian pointed to one lone brain floating against the glass, "she's part of The

Sphere now. More than she's ever been. It's an incredible story of redemption, really."

Vivian shook her hands clean, as if suddenly aware of how disgusting it was that her skin was lined with brain matter. "Such a sad end to a great life. Tragic. But just imagine your life if she hadn't passed. I don't make obsolete life easy. You know this. But it's for the better. Humanity took a weak turn for an era. Your position now is one of the hardest. You'll make enemies. Not everyone is grateful for this world we've made. They'll try to subvert and trick you, make you believe they harbor a secret truth. It's utter nonsense, Ada. Do you understand me?"

Ada, calculative, shook her head *no*.

Vivian, happy to check her protégé, said, "Do you think that Oriana hadn't also tried to recruit Grace?"

Ada's skin crawled. Her nerves pulsated, numbed, and tingled. How much of Oriana did Vivian know? How much of her interaction with the purgers was Vivian tracking? There were too many questions, too many that would make Ada appear—as Vivian might say—too independent. Ada mustered a stoic, "Why do you let her go on? Tormenting your people?"

"Even heaven permits hell, Ada. How else could I distinguish the loyal from those who are not? But Oriana must be put to an end. And these are the plans I have for you. Don't think you can outmaneuver me. I know you know more than you should. I don't care what you know. I care about what you do. That's all that ever matters." Vivian punched her index finger between Ada's breasts. Stumbling a bit on her reach.

Ada thought Vivian's words were generic—bombastic. A

fortune teller searching for a thread of truth. Doubt roused Ada's mind. She could not pinpoint precisely what statements were fully, partially, and not-at-all true. But she knew Vivian spoke the spectrum. At best she was only guessing that Ada knew of the Purgers. At worst, she'd been tracking her every movement. Ada couldn't comprehend the worst-case scenario. If there's anything proximity to power teaches, it's its limitations and fallibility. Vivian was not the goddess she'd been marketed as: omnipresent and omniscient. She was a mere human. Remarkable. Powerful. But prone to err. Made of bone and flesh. The same stuff as Ada.

"I think you'll enjoy your first mission," Vivian grinned. "Now you should go on. Get some rest for tomorrow. Walk any way you wish. The water will part. Like in life, all directions lead you to the same exit."

INSIDE THE HALLS
OF DEFENSE

Ada walked toward the water's edge and the particles unexplainably split. Once up close, Ada recognized that there was nothing physical partitioning the aquarium. No glass or encasing. It was, instead, shaped by a force unseen. As she walked, the water parted exactly to her silhouette—just a few feet above and in front. Her trail was invisible, as the steps she took refilled with water again. She had no sense of direction. And with each step a panic burrowed itself into her forethoughts. *This water will crash over me, and I will drown. Run. Run. Run.* With her heart pounding, Ada charged toward the water. She ran for so long that her legs began to burn. Her chest tightened. Breath shortened. Her legs now anchors, pulling her to a stop—sopping wet from the splashing of water opening and closing to her presence. Her body's oxygen, trapped inside her muscles, muted her mind. Her vision began to fade. Her entire existence reduced to the behavior of a stupid machine. She performed one operation over and again. Leg forward, then the other. Exhaustion brought her body to a stumble. Ada couldn't rediscover her footing. She was falling now. The last thing she saw when she hit the ground were the waves closing in over her body. She closed her eyes. When skin slapped against the floor the world fell silent. *I'm drowning*, she thought. *This is it.* She dared take a breath in and was surprised to suck in air. Then she heard the familiar sound of heels marching against the floor. Two pairs. Then, as her vision turned stone white, two guards swooped Ada up from under her arms.

Ada awoke on Monday morning in her assigned room within the Memory Corps compound. Her head pounded dry and mouth longed for water. She shuffled to the nearby sink and, treating it like a trough, ducked her head under the faucet, letting the droplets moisten any part of her face. At that moment she recalled simpler days. Days in the Stratum of Knowledge, when she would dunk her body under the cold beads of water to awaken her body and mind. The water gave instant relief to her physical pangs. When Ada would first bring her head up for air, she escaped the memory of her life as an obsolete. What was once a life of self-determinism had been replaced by something preordained.

Ada began recalling the bizarre events from last night, and pieced them together as memories from a drunken evening. Lucid flashes of memories transpired in third person. It was like any traumatic memory. At first, as a benign memory of someone else's life. Then the emotions of the moment settle. And the impersonal flashes of the past become your own. The personalization toxifies every major neural and nervous pathway, and then seeps into the blood—pulsating with every beat of your heart. Before there's a diagnosis it's dominated every rendition of the past, immobilized the present, and diminished whatever hopes once existed for the future.

For now, Ada's memories remained benign. Worse, a mystery. Events that Ada re-explored without inhibition. But as the flashes started piecing themselves back together—guards, aquarium, blood red, br- brains?—Ada felt Lily abuzz. It happened frequently. Daily, actually. Ada would have a thought and she'd feel her BRiDG hum or buzz or tick. The feeling always a bit different than the one before. Its intensities always varying. Ada never gave these twitches much thought; chalking it up to electrical shortages. But this buzz, at this particular moment sparked an idea in Ada she hadn't yet explored. These were no random failures in Lily's operations.

"Lily," Ada softly said.

"Yes, Ada?"

"What are you doing?"

"What do you mean?"

"You know what I mean. What are you doing, when you buzz like that?" Lily buzzed again, causing Ada's head to reflexively twitch. "Lily!"

"Just doing as I was programmed."

"I understand," Ada sighed, resigned to the revelation that Lily was actively targeting unauthorized memories. Although they lived with one another, neither's loyalty belonged to each other. Ada didn't take it personally. She'd always known Lily was programmed according to 6Di's demands. But it was something about Lily's voice, her random check-ins, her sentimental gestures from time-to-time that presented Lily as confidant, and friend. But the truth is she was most likely programmed to be that too. Lily was nothing at all but a series of responses attached to commands. Ada pondered this reality, then, for a second, wondered what that made everyone else in her life, who subserviently existed under the authority of their BRiDG, and how many more zaps she'd feel before she became the same.

Three weeks ago, Ada's current position would have been to her nothing but a ludicrous fantasy. Today it's just ludicrous. Nothing Ada would wish upon herself if given the choice to do it again. But do-overs are never a choice. There's just doing; and happenings. And the ways one responds to what's happened to them. Ada could do without the fame and personal attention from Vivian. If there's a quality of life taken for granted by the lowly it's their anonymity. Ada never appreciated how much of her perceived independence rested on the fact that she could operate daily without interference or influence from unsolicited voices. So, though Ada's new life gave her more responsibility than every obsolete combined, it was the unwelcome, the constant attentiveness that made her worldview feel as small as the myopic gaze upon her. Self-worth was replaced with a value determined by everyone else but her. She was a currency in a market, exchangeable for objects of their will.

Nevertheless, the training facility contained a palpable energy; felt even by Ada, who still lay on her bed, contemplating the oddities of her present circumstances. It's in the training facility where one's potential and purpose perfectly conjoined. Despite the downsides of her new life, Ada did appreciate the undercurrent of exploration in each moment. Life in the Stratum of Knowledge felt more programmatic. Each day planned and organized according to corporate needs. Days never veered too far from another. Here, there was a sense that each minute was anew, unrelated to the one it preceded. Like a jazz song, progressing soulfully, beyond comprehension. She felt this alone in her room. But especially when she roamed the halls and peered into nearby rooms, those unique eco-systems of knowledge. Small galaxies in the universe of the Memory Corps.

Ada walked to the HQ wing to officially meet her team as their newest reconnoiter. As she passed through unfamiliar halls and door frames, Ada brushed shoulders with strangers whose gazes confirmed her stardom. So, Ada tucked her chin to her chest. She felt safer this way, more incognito. But her vision was limited now. Each step stretched to the length of her legs. She didn't walk with a purpose or intended direction, but instead flowed like water, through the gaps and passages with the least resistance. A path that led her through a door, and to a hall, where no one else walked.

Free of company, Ada lifted her head. All she saw was sterile linoleum against the floor and bright drywall. Above was a speckled ceiling lined with rows of harsh white lights. Ada walked further down the hallway, hypnotized by a dense, heavy, silence. Then, a jarring grunt from a nearby door slowed Ada. She drew closer to the door. *Just one peek*, she thought. The door was cracked, windowless. Ada stuck her head into the crack and saw a bloodied man tied to a chair. He looked so disfigured that Ada wouldn't have recognized him if it were her father. Two towering beasts stood beside him. Their silhouettes resembled that of any guard, enlarged and armored. Their faces were featureless; except for their glowing yellow eyes. Just as she'd seen the first night she was taken to see Vivian face-to-face. One looked her direction. Its insidious gaze was absent of any civilized manner.

Ada shut the door and ran.

In her panic, she ran deeper down this baffling hall. She ran fearing that scene of torture. But in the hall she felt no less safe. Those unstained white walls mocked her fear; its faultless features alluded to worse dangers. Ada entered the next closest door.

In it was a warehouse, or what one might look like following an earthquake. The ruinous space had a large pile of objects at its center. Ada walked the perimeter of the pile. She had come to understand that the pile was made of paintings, books, and sculptures. Works that had been digitized into The Sphere. Before Ada had time to examine a single artifact she heard voices inside the room.

Ada leapt inside the pile and crawled through the crevasse into a makeshift labyrinth. If a single item were removed it seemed that the items above her would collapse, leaving Ada trapped. She'd crawled deep enough that she felt indiscoverable to anyone outside the pile. As the voices neared she doubted the extent to which she was concealed. Especially after she realized the approaching voices belonged to Lex and Vivian.

"It's none of my business, Viv, but I think the program is too risky. We've got a good thing going. There's order and peace. What more could you ask for?"

"If I favored the status quo do you think I'd be where I am?"

"No. Of course not." Lex said. "That's not what I'm suggesting. As one of your advisors, whose concern is defense, I'm saying there are a lot of risks involved with turning people into products - you remember…"

"Of course I remember."

Ada's heart pounded so loudly it muted her hearing. Worried that she wouldn't hear more, Ada placed her ear against the pile.

"I disagree," Lex said.

The stack that Ada placed against her ear shifted. Before she could comprehend what was happening, a small avalanche of books, manuscripts, audio records, and other miscellaneous artifacts fell. Ada's dwelling collapsed. Her legs were trapped. But she dared not move.

Lex looked at the pile, "Happens all the time."

"Show me what we came here for, Lex."

"Yes, of course…It's over here."

Lex and Vivian walk toward where Ada leapt into the pile. "It's somewhere over here," Lex said. Ada's body tightened as she wondered if they too would crawl into that pile.

"God," Vivian barked, "someone could live in this pile of garbage."

Lex, laughing, said, "you and I both know they'd be toast." But they were uninterested about the hole that Ada previously crawled into. They, instead, wanted to see the artwork of—

"Lionel?" Vivian asked. "Who is this, how are they drawing scenes of the stratum of imagination?"

"We…don't know yet."

"You don't know?"

"No, we're not sure exactly who this person is, or even if their name is Lionel. They started publishing drawings a few years back. At first they were harmless. Scenes of forests like before the war—relics. Then these."

"Keep ridding of these works. If this gets out…"

"I know Vivian. I know."

"Let's go. I'm sending Ada to her home district and want to see her off." Lex and Vivian begin walking toward the exit. Faintly, Ada heard one last exchange as Vivian asked, "when does this one go up?"

"As soon as we leave," Lex said.

Go up? Ada thought. What is going up? A mystery she contemplated along with how exactly she was going to unstuck herself from the pile of artifacts that had begun to numb her body. She wiggled her legs, but the pile felt heavier. Like an elastic band, the resistance increased the more she pulled away. Ada was trapped. That thought flooded her mind with anxiety. Her breaths hastened but with each draw of oxygen she felt more desperate for air. She squirmed her whole body in panic. Rapidly, convulsively, without reserve. She freed herself but an inch. Then she smelled smoke.

Go up, as in in-flames! Her initial attempt to escape the weight of materials paled in comparison to her second attempt. Now that she faced death, Ada tapped into some dormant part of herself that harbored immense strength. The hundreds of pounds of objects crushing her legs moved aside like a thrown quilt. Now free, she crawled back the way she crawled in, beginning to sweat and cough from the nearing fire. Once outside the pile, she could hardly orient herself. The door she used to enter this room was straight ahead of her. But which way was that? The intensity of the flames obscured her senses. Ada tried to stand, but at her tallest it was too difficult to breathe.

Ada crawled to where she believed she could exit. Flames liquified or ashened every nearby artifact. Despite all the progresses of modernity, none could contest the power of fire - a force as primitive as time.

The fire now burned across the entire room. Ada could hardly keep her head in the same place for a breath. The sight and smells too putrid to endure without constantly adjusting her position. She was running out of time and oxygen. Ada closed her eyes and imagined the azimuth she first walked toward the pile when the space was not yet aflame. She imagined the exact angle she took from the doorframe to the pile, so that she could retrace those steps and find her way to the exit before she too was engulfed in flames.

That's what makes Ada special: she can imagine scenarios as if they are reality. She is, in a sense, a citizen of many universes. Some lived, others not. A woman who sees realities for what they could be. And for what they are. So, when she closed her eyes while on her hands and knees, fire to her back, and imagined the direction she walked not even thirty minutes before, she saw the path perfectly. She started crawling in the direction until her body reached the wall. But when she reached up for the door handle she didn't feel it. She didn't recognize any component of the wall. But she did feel a steel rod, a lever perhaps. And she grasped both hands with it. The steel absorbed the room's heat. It was too hot to touch for more than a second. She reached for the rod again and quickly pushed upward. It didn't budge. She pushed again, this time with assistance form her legs. It moved. But Ada doubted she could push any harder. Her oxygen levels were low. Her body exhausted from the heat. If she'd open this door, it'd have to be from her next push. She pushed for a third time and popped the steel bar open like a tab to a canned beverage. Adapted to the dark, smoky, room, the light from the outside was blinding. She jumped toward the light. Then felt her stomach drop as she continued to fall far beyond the floor.

Ada's body slammed into the arid ground. The room she entered wasn't structural, but detachable. When the burning began the room must have detached. Ada saw that the room was tracked, like a train, with rails that continued beyond what she could see. Ada stood and, shaking dust from her clothes, watched the structure continue down the tracks as flames escaped the opened back hatch. She felt pain, but was spared from injury. Tomorrow she will be bruised.

Following the tracks, Ada walked back toward the training facility.

On the walk back Ada's mind gravitated to more practical issues. Do I smell like smoke? How am I going to explain my absence? What if I'm caught out here? Are there other burn piles? Before she was aware of it, Ada was again walking in the halls of the training facility. She ended up on the public side of the halls of defense. She stopped walking and looked up at the doors.

Her hypnosis broke when she heard a familiar voice say, "Not your wing, Ada."

Hairs spiked across the back of her neck. It took every ounce of courage for her to lock eyes with this pugnacious man. His voice contained the scars of a hundred wars: Lex Nabakov, Chief of Defense. Lex stood defiantly before Ada, his eyes marched up and down her every inch. His stare strained her strength and commanded cowardice. But she did not obey. Ada tracked his eyes with hers. Her eyes steadied. Betraying her fear, Ada calmly asked, "Where is my wing?"

Lex crossed his arms and snarled, "Behind me, down the hall, take your first left." Then he pointed to the door he caught her previously looking at, "This is my domain. It's not safe for your kind. Rumor is you're a brainiac, Ada. Soon no place will be safe for you." Then he leaned his lips toward Ada's right ear and whispered, "If it were up to me, you'd be with Grace." He pulled back, flashed a grimacing grin and said more loudly, "Enjoy your first day, Ada." He then proceeded to flash his hand in front of a panel against the wall and entered the door Ada recently exited. The door slammed shut, leaving Ada wondering how she mindlessly entered a door that required identification to enter. But her tardiness to her assigned location kept her from trying to reenter, at least this time.

Ada finally found the training wing for the Headquarters Unit. Despite its significance, it was an easy corridor to miss. Tucked beyond a nondescript door among many double-wide and blatantly advertised passageways to areas less important. Once past the entrance, Ada entered the main space, which acted like the body of an octopus, where eight other halls branched outward from the circular center corridor. Each branch a passage to a particular kind of learning, as advertised by the signage above each frame: physical sciences and fitness; philosophy and ethics; cybernetics; imagery; instrumentations; informatonics; and brain-computer interfacings. Coming from down the hall of close quarters combat (CQC), Ada heard a rousing bunch inching closer. Voices of her teammates excited her nerves. Her breath shortened. She combatted it with one slow and intentional, deafening whatever nervousness their proximity aroused.

Yoko Yamamoto was the first to exit the hall of CQC. Jeremiah Warlock and Kimberley Green were close behind. Followed by a fourth, unrecognizable character, that was first to acknowledge, "Ada!" He scurried to her side, "welcome to the team, it's a true pleasure." Ada's confusion urged him to say, "My apologies. I'm J.J. Burroughs—HQ's team captain. I manage logistics and administration for your training and mission sets. And I believe you know the rest of the crew from your time at the archives. Kimberley, preservations. Jeremiah, corrections. And of course Yoko, translations. It's a true honor to have you. Albeit, under such…unfortunate circumstances." The rest of the crew didn't express the same enthusiasm as J.J. They sprawled across the main room. Getting coffee, lounging on nearby chairs. "Let me grab your uniform," J.J. said.

When J.J. left the space, his absence took with him conversation. And in the disquiet emerged disdain. This wasn't an unplanned moment of awkwardness. There wasn't even an attempt to create connection. Ada stood before her new team and felt, desperately, that she wanted to flee. To be anywhere but before these three. They weren't the lively, intriguing bunch she'd remembered encountering as an obsolete—that day that Augusta accessed a journal that clued to Oriana's existence. They were worse than cruel. They were indifferent to Ada's presence, like she was one of those pieces of history that shouldn't be archived for the next generation to witness.

"If it means anything," Ada said, "I don't come here thinking I'm replacing her."

Kimberley and Jeremiah shot each other a glance. Yoko coldly said, "Grace," while reading a book titled *Translations for a Monolingual World*.

"Huh?" Ada replied.

Yoko placed her book down, "You said, 'replacing her.' She has a name. It's Grace. Say it."

Nervously, Ada repeated, "I don't think I'm replacing Grace."

Silence.

J.J. re-entered the space, oblivious to the tension that surrounded him. "Oh you're going to look splendid in this, Ada! Just splendid." His zestful voice lightened the room's aura. "Down the physical fitness hall you'll find your locker room. Change into your Memory Corps uniform and come back here for a more formal introduction with the team." Ada disappeared down the hall, uniform in hand. J.J. looked at the unenthused trio and demanded to know, "What is the problem with all of you? This is your teammate now."

Kimberley was first to speak, "A little convenient isn't it? Ada's punished harshly by Grace one day in her stratum, a few hours later Grace is dead."

"You think Ada killed Grace?" J.J. asked, in disbelief.

"We certainly don't think that Simpson kid did it," Jeremiah said.

"You saw how cunning she is," Yoko said. "If she can lose corporate tracking during a live performance, what is she doing when eyes aren't on her?" The other two grumbled in agreement.

"Look," J.J. interjected, "I see the accusation, but it's a weak one. Look at her record. She was frequently punished. What would have been different about Grace's quota? An extra few thousand wouldn't be enough to push her over the edge."

Ada stood in her personal locker room as her new team debated her innocence. She felt something was afoot, so even after she fully dressed, Ada lingered in the locker room to adore the beauty of this space. Dark, intricately carved wood, accentuated by golden flecks shimmering under warm lights. Old money is regal, as one could describe it. An ode to history itself. Nascent was its antonym.

Certitude is what Ada felt when she donned the gown of a Memory Corps reconnoiter across her skin. That slick, ribbed, form-fitting, olive-green top revealed features Ada normally concealed but was certainly proud to possess. Her perky breasts were kept hidden under her draping obsolete uniform, but now commanded attention. Fitting for her new role. With fame, privacy vanishes.

Yet, as Ada drew the black, cream-trimmed pants up her legs, Ada knew that this newfound sense of openness was only an illusion. She'd never be fully known. Not publicly. Not as long as there was such a thing as unauthorized thoughts. She was an agent enforcing those laws now, and suspect number one. Guilty of the same charges she was commissioned to enforce. Ada wondered if all the illegal notebooks in the world amounted to the unauthorized thoughts she retained in her mind. How she, a trojan horse, could have infiltrated 6Di. Or if it were the other way around. Who had infiltrated whom? Lily zapped again. The question clearly had an answer.

In the main corridor the team continued debating Ada's integrity. "Can we at least have her operating in a probation period? Have one of us accompany her for a while?" Kimberley asked.

J.J. nodded slowly, thinking through the full implications, "Yes, yes I think we can do that. But, there may be exceptions. Sometimes it may be too risky to send two of you undercover in the same region. So you'll just have to do overwatch."

"Do you know what her first will be?" Yoko asked.

"Yes—we'll talk about that when she returns."

"I just don't feel good about this boss," Jeremiah reiterated. "There's something off about her."

"Well, I'll have you talk to Vivian."

"No, no…it's not that bad. Don't do that," Jeremiah pleaded.

Ada's footsteps echoed into the room.

"Treat her like a newbie—fine. But treat her like a newbie on this team. These suspicions are just that. She's guilty of nothing." J.J. sternly acknowledged, timing the end of his warning with Ada's arrival.

"Ada! My, you look marvelous. Come, sit. Everyone sit."

Everyone, Ada included, grumbled to a seat. J.J. took a breath before embarking on his exposition.

"As we know, Grace did not retire. She was murdered. But we must protect the public from this fact. And we must catch whoever did this. Every reconnoiter carries with them a field manual. It's a journal of what they've witnessed. What they're collecting. Who they're targeting. It's an old-school method of note taking that usually ensures absolute security of their documented thoughts. In the event of a death, where the body lies in a public space for a time before its retrieval by corporate citizens, the notebook could be looted. Which is what happened with Grace's journal. Ada, you might not be aware, but M-C agents operate in the dark—completely disconnected from The Sphere. The only information you can access is what's been downloaded offline. This too a security measure meant to protect our agents. Because of this, we believe that whoever possesses Grace's journal is also responsible for her murder."

The three seasoned agents stared at each other in disbelief. The last piece of evidence that could make Ada culpable of Grace's murder would be hers to find.

Jeremiah interjected, "I'll take this one, boss."

"You're not a reconnoiter, Jeremiah."

"No, but I was the last one to see her. I could retrace my steps through 20W…"

"This is Grace's mission. You'll support."

The trio were left speechless, unable to respond. Ada felt the room's tension. She attempted to temper the situation with what she believed was a thoughtful question, "Was Grace's BRiDG intact?"

"Excuse me?" J.J. asked.

"Her BRiDG. Did she still have her BRiDG when her body was found?"

Kimberley, indignant, said, "You can't remove a BRiDG." The others looked at Ada, brandishing disgust. But Ada remembered her first meeting with the Purgers, and knew that their claims were not true. Then she felt a *zap*.

Ada looked puzzled. J.J. intervened, "That's right Ada. I suppose you could technically remove a BRiDG. The same way you could remove a scalp. But in both cases, the object becomes useless. So, it's not a concern."

Ada felt her blood chill, as she remembered more clearly. *But, BRiDGes can be removed. At least, I had mine removed when I first met the Purgers.* Then a thought she never had before. *What if the BRiDG I wear now wasn't mine? What if it was Grace's?* Ada halted her mind from entertaining another thought. One still trickled in: *scalps were battlefield trophies, warnings to enemies remaining of the sufferings that awaited.* But all she uttered was, "I understand."

"Now," J.J. continued, "the obvious place to start the search is 20W, where Grace was killed. But based on some citizen traffic we want to first check the Stratum of Reason."

"Bullshit!" Jeremiah shouted. "We all know it was one of those grimy obsoletes in 20W. No good has ever come from that district." Looking directly at Ada, Jeremiah repeated, "ever."

Ada didn't give him a moment of discomfort. Not even a flinch. The response impressed Yoko, who also concealed her thoughts.

"We search for reason first, then knowledge." J.J. reiterated. "Or, if you'd like, I can take your request up to Vivian?" Again, Jeremiah silenced after that threat.

"Great. Suit up. We're heading out in an hour."

Jeremiah stormed out of the room with J.J. following close behind. The three girls remained. Yoko broke the silence, "It's tough for us all right now. He's a great friend and an even worse enemy. Don't take this personally, but it's hard to trust you. It's hard to trust anyone to take Grace's place."

"I get it," Ada replied. "Like I said, I'm not here to replace her."

"But the fact is you are," Kimberley interjected. "There's no other way to see it. You're replacing her. So even if you were my best friend, I'd hate you right now."

Silence gripped the room.

"Do you both believe someone from 20W did it?"

"Of course," Yoko said.

"But why? What would they have to gain?"

"Look at you."

And a thought occurred to Ada that she'd never had before: *what if her father or sister killed Grace? No, how could they see the end result? How could they know the fortunes that awaited behind that atrocious act? No one could have known. Not even Vivian.* "If I killed Grace, who would have told me that it would have got me here? I wasn't even a citizen at the time. This seemed…impossible."

Ada's coolness, her calm demeanor, or vacuum-tight logic bridged a chasm Yoko and Kimberley hadn't before accepted. For Ada to have killed Grace for this purpose, she would have had to know that she would have been fast-tracked to citizenship, she would have had to know that there wasn't already a replacement in queue, she would have had to know that there would have been open trials that gave her the opportunity to join the team. In sum, she would have either had to commit a heinous crime for an astronomically unlikely shot at an opportunity she wasn't even promised to receive.

Yoko probed, "But you didn't need to know all that. You hated Grace that day, I'm sure. Her death would have been the reward. All this…all this is just extra."

"Look at my records. Nonviolent. Expeditious neurological dependency. And a hell of a lot of extra quotas. An extra few thousand wouldn't have made me murder."

"So who did?" Yoko asked.

"Isn't that what we're trying to find out? Why we need the notebook?"

"Who do you think did it?" Kimberley asked. "You think it was your friend, George?"

"No. I was with him all night."

"One of the other suspects? Amelia or Abigail?"

"I don't know a thing about them. But, unless they're insane… why would they make any more sense as suspects than I do?"

"Then who?" Kimberley demanded. "Who would do this?!"

"Are you afraid one of you is next?" Ada asked. She hit a different octave with that inquiry. The energy of the room shifted, from tense to vulnerable. Kimberley didn't have to say a word. Her welling eyes spoke to her true concerns. She wanted justice as much as security. To know and punish the killer; and ensure that she remained protected from them in that pursuit.

Yoko, pointing to her BRiDG, said, "All of this was supposed to stop violence. Yet, something so horrific was done without explanation? It just doesn't make sense. She was bludgeoned—unrecognizable."

"I didn't know her," Ada said, "but I know she didn't deserve that end."

Fighting tears, Kimberley uttered, "It's weird when you know someone enough that you can picture their face in that moment. And whether it's true or not, that's the last face of hers that replays in my mind. That is before it was made mush. The screams I didn't hear replay in my mind daily. Now, the whole event feels like make-believe. I'm traumatized by memories which I can't even distinguish as real or not."

"In a way," Ada comforted Kimberley, "it's all real."

And with that, Kimberley felt permission to feel the hurt that she hadn't yet allowed to herself. Her pain, she finally believed, was legitimate. Not a phantom making her mad. No longer a source of anxiety and paranoia. It was simply pain. The invisible kind that's hard to fix. But at least a thing she could finally admit was hers to feel.

"Thank you," Kimberley said, "sincerely." She wiped her eyes dry. "What happened to your neck?"

Ada self-consciously pulled the top of her jumpsuit closed. "I'm not sure. Must have been an accident when I was young."

"I've one of those too," Kimberley said, revealing her sternum. "Not as big, obviously."

Shifting to a topic more matter of fact, Ada asked, "What's down the defense corridor?"

Yoko, laughing, said, "Buncha knuckle draggers." Ada grinned and her face quickly fell long. "Why do you ask Ada, did you want to go?"

"Well, I took a wrong turn on the way here. What I saw was…disturbing."

"Yeah," Yoko said resolutely, "they're always experimenting with new policing tactics. What did you see?"

"Just some rough-looking men. Savages. Do they keep

prisoners back there?"

"Maybe actors."

"Hmm," Ada pensively stated. "It just seemed too real."

"That's the magic," Yoko winked. Lily zapped.

BACK TO 20W

Ada was back in her home district of 20W to retrieve Grace's notebook. She was first dispatched to Grace's last known location, the archival facility. In the main passageway, near the exact spot where she remembered seeing Grace butchered, she saw her old friend Corydon—walking without hands.

Up to this moment, she had not known if that act was real or simulated. But indeed, she had chopped his hands clean off. She and Corydon locked eyes. And as much as she wanted to divert to the floor or sky or anywhere else but back into his eyes, she kept them locked. Because she hoped in that gaze she would relay the inexpressible. She might never have had the chance to send him a formal apology. But Corydon's stare was cold and lifeless. Whatever sorrow she felt for him, he felt equal parts hatred. What had life done to their friendship—not life, 6Di?

Ada and her team walked into the archival facility, where obsoletes digitized materials each day to earn their citizenship; a life which had been hers until a short while ago. Ada felt torn. In one respect this was a return home. But in another manner, she was witnessing a life she'd happily escaped. Above all else, she wanted to impress Jeremiah, Yoko, and Kimberley. But deep down, she knew it may never happen. Because Ada was from rebel blood, born an obsolete. Her teammates were born into the Stratum of Knowledge. They'd never known life apart from their BRiDG.

As the Memory Corps team trotted toward the entrance, Yoko tapped Ada on the shoulder, smiling, and said, "Look." Above the entrance was a large sign that read: The Ada Lawrence Center for Archival Excellence. Her name now synonymous with 20W. She'd become a topic in each household, a lesson on how discipline ushers one to the highest echelons of society. Ada felt the eyes of nearby obsoletes looking proudly at her presence. That gaze was inescapable in her new life. So, though they meant well, Ada resented onlookers.

Once at the entrance the team began to work.

"She was found here." Yoko said, "facedown. Head toward the door."

"No," Ada interjected, and Lily intercepted with a zap.

"Stop that!" Ada yelled to the sky. The rest of her unit looked at her confusedly. "Sorry," Ada continued, "her head was toward the hall."

Yoko and Kimberley looked puzzled. Jeremiah exhaled heavily, diminishing his rage.

"Ada," Yoko said slowly, "the report says that her head was facing toward the door."

"I know what the report says," Ada retorted. "I'm saying…" Ada seized her thoughts, aware of what she was about to admit. She was free to say nearly anything, but no one could suggest The Sphere *was wrong*. Whatever facts entered the database were fact immemorial.

Jeremiah snapped, "A protectorate of The Sphere can't even

attest to its infallibility. Genius. Absolutely genius! Would you like to tell us how it's wrong, Ada?" He stood before her chest, and said, "Go ahead. Tell us how Vivian allowed for a false report to enter The Sphere."

At this moment, Ada realized what she had always suspected. Jeremiah operated on a different wavelength. The strength of his body inverse to the power of his mind. She contemplated responding to Jeremiah's assault so that he too could understand. She needed to flip the energy. Toss this colossus's thoughts like a pancake. It was on the tip of the tongue, and Ada began her retort with the thrill of not knowing exactly how her sentence would end. Except that it would punch. And it did: "Why else would your job exist if there was not the possibility of something erroneous entering The Sphere?"

Coldly, Jeremiah responded, "It's because my job exists that nothing erroneous has."

Ada understood. His loyalty to The Sphere's accuracy was unquestionable. But perhaps he was more upset at the idea that he could be fallible. His laurels rested upon his title as protector of truth, perpetuating a flawed man to believe himself faultless. That's the thing about titles; they always assume too much.

"We have to proceed with what's recorded," Kimberley suggested. "There's no time for quibbling—especially over details that can't be proven. The most likely course of action is to trace who all entered the facility within a two-hour time period of Grace's body being discovered."

Each began querying high-security modals of The Sphere, accessible only to members of 6Di corporate.

"Damn," Yoko said, "fifty people. Ada, do you know any of these people?"

"All of them."

"Any that feel exceptionally…likely?"

Ada scanned the list in her mind. *What a ridiculous thought. Who do I think may have killed Grace? Does anyone think that they know someone who would kill another? The truth is, if we're just asking who has the propensity to kill, the answer is any one of these people. This is a human problem. Not a person problem. Anyone could commit this act. Not just someone. Anyone. BRiDG or not.* But before Ada revealed her inner dialogue she remembered Augusta's unfortunate claim that day. "Yes," Ada said, "there is in fact. Augusta Edwards. The one who you all first came for that day. She said something I don't think she meant, but sounds eerie now. She said she could murder and get away with it."

The team looked at one another, perplexed. Jeremiah asked, "And you're just now remembering this?"

"It meant nothing at the moment."

Yoko, less certain of the promise of this lead, suggested, "We could be falsely interpreting the value of this statement. It could be a coincidence. I don't want to read too far into this."

Kimberley, desperate for action, said, "It's the only lead we have."

"Fine," Yoko said, "but before we search someone for circumstantial evidence—can we gather facts from the top floor?"

Ada had always wanted to see the top floor, where all the objects went after she digitized each of the artifacts.

"Yeah, I'll search there first." Jeremiah began walking that way. Kimberley asked, "What are you doing? We stay here. This is Ada's job."

"Bullshit, I can't trust her yet. And we'll be just as effective at uncovering—"

"No," Kimberley said, "we won't. Because the most dangerous quality of a reconnoiter is that they can think like an obsolete while maintaining neuropathic dependency. None of the other Memory Corps members had ever been an obsolete. None could reason where an obsolete may be safekeeping Grace's notebook.

Jeremiah fumed out the exit. Yoko smirked as Kimberley continued, "We'll be outside in the vehicle working on our backlogs. Call us in if you need something verified. This will be a good first place. Not at all dangerous, but good luck."

"Thanks," Ada said. "I shouldn't be long."

Ada walked toward the archives elevator. As an obsolete, she was never granted access. Now, her BRiDGs proximity called the doors open. Once the door closed and she was alone inside that steel coffin, she remembered her early mornings as an obsolete. Her mission for truth has only become more complicated since those days of naivety.

When the elevator doors opened again, Ada felt a rush of discomfort. This space, the place where all the digitized materials from 20W elevated to enter, what she believed was storage, was the same kind of room, the exact same kind of room that she just exited in the hall of defense as it was engulfed in flames. The layout. The makeup. The colors. The only difference was that all these artifacts still stood on their shelves. There appeared to be some order. Something inherently different about this space.

Nevertheless, its similarities made Ada shudder. *Don't even think about it*, she uttered to Lily.

In these halls, every square foot was occupied with paintings, sculptures, novels, and notebooks stacked and aligned ,which as a sum doubled as walls. In the presence of this many objects at once, Ada felt both grounded and inspired. As a citizen, her world had practically forgone a dimension. Her days two-dimensional. Existing in digital replicas and simulations. A life dependent on the BRiDG was remarkably internal and sterile. Despite the ability to access physical artifacts in the Stratum of Knowledge, it was as if that desire had been trained out of citizens. There was no emphasis on aura or sensation. Citizenry was a matter of right and wrong, for better or worse.

There was no object which when digitized didn't lose its essence. Because each element possesses qualities unobservable. Whatever wasn't measured wasn't translated into The Sphere. So, there was no such thing as exact replicas. Citizens literally lived in a different world. Because everything that was digitized would become something else, something less. And once the original was tucked away to the storage units, what was gone was forgotten. But here, Ada felt those immeasurable qualities.

The kaleidoscopic mass of artifacts was dizzying to traverse. Up here, Ada wasn't alone. There were dozens of Memory Corps agents assigned to 20W hurriedly crisscrossing among aisles, delivering new artifacts to their respective piles, unaware of Ada's presence. There were perhaps a million different artifacts on this floor, all seemingly placed without any order or reason. She'd spend the rest of her life searching for this single notebook—and maybe that was the point. If Grace's notebook was lost among the pile of these artifacts, she'd need help understanding where. Ada stopped the next person who walked past her.

"Excuse me, but where are personal notebooks kept?"

"Aisle 1440," the man mumbled. Ada began walking in that direction. And as she drifted further from this man his attention gravitated back toward her, "Ada?"

She took a moment to process his face. Then it came to her, "Malachi? What are..."

"I'm with 20W, preservations."

"That's...That's wonderful." Ada said, in a tone that betrayed her excitement. His icy blue eyes magnetized Ada closer. She let them penetrate her, long enough until she'd wanted to be penetrated by him in other ways.

"It's interesting. Pretty much exactly like the place I grew up in in the tenth district."

"Mimicry is flattery."

"And the means of institutionalism," he said, smirking. But Ada couldn't see his smile. She couldn't see anything but her being dominated by his body. Unlike her primal instincts that freed her from the fiery room, this desire felt entrapping; the kind that thrilled.

But Malachi sensed none of this. A slight attraction, yes. But he wasn't yet comfortable enough in his newly earned position to explore sexuality. He was, you could say, at the ends of institutionalism. For he mimicked his life according to one he perceived he should live. To become a citizen of 6Di is to become fully subordinate to corporate endeavors. So, regardless of the apparent power or authority he now possessed, he couldn't comprehend how that made him any different. Why his thoughts should, or even how they could, roam freely. And this made him a perfect model citizen. So, despite Ada's longing stare, he, unable to reciprocate such an emotion, said "Follow me, I'll take you to 1440."

At first they walked in silence. Ada wrestled her unexplainable desire to be lost in a party of their flesh. Malachi couldn't uncover a single question he thought worth asking. Cycles of doubts flooded both their minds until Malachi asked, "How is it, being a celebrity of 6Di?"

Perhaps it was the intensity of the thoughts she mitigated in her head, or the fact she wanted to see them manifested—her body sprawled across the floor with him on top—whatever the reason she responded, strikingly honest, and said, "It's lonely."

Ada continued, "I worked all my life for a dream that I now think was someone else's. Even the fact that I had to work so hard just to gain access to better understand my heritage is maddening. Now I'm here without any friends or family. I should feel sad. But I haven't had the time." She paused, eyes welling, then broke the tension with laughter, "What am I saying? Of course I could. Not like you'd remember anyways."

"Of course I would," Malachi said, naively.

A tear dropped onto Ada's left cheek. She blinked, held her eyes shut. Not in remorse. Just in relief, that for the first time since she'd been a citizen she felt something unsubscribed. And though she couldn't put it into words, couldn't describe exactly what it was that she was feeling, it felt completely her.

When she opened her eyes, her cheek had dried. And Malachi, having already forgotten that she cried, said, "You know if you needed a shoulder to cry on, you have mine." He reached for Ada. Patted her shoulder awkwardly. But Ada didn't need to shed another tear. She understood. She could be whoever she wanted. But she'd only ever be known as she was meant to be remembered: a woman worthy of Vivian's heir, strong and infallible, The Sphere incarnate.

"Here we are, 1440." Ada stared, a bit in wonder, at the towering display of articles, notes, and books. Malachi asked, "What was it exactly you were looking for?"

"The reconnoitrer's field book."

"Grace's?"

"Yeah," Ada said, beginning to ruffle through the pile.

"Would be weird if it made it here," Malachi said, pursing his lips.

While rummaging through the pile of artifacts, Ada asked, "It's worrisome, don't you think? That someone could still kill."

"Maybe on the other side." Malachi said, "you don't see this horrific behavior in the Stratum of Knowledge. No citizen could ever behave like this."

Ada paused her rummaging but didn't look away from the pile. She thought of asking, but only thought, *do you really believe this?*

As Ada continued sifting through the pile, Malachi asked "You think that's here, in this pile?"

"No one knows where it is."

"It can't be here."

Ada, reiterated, "I said no one knows where it is."

Malachi paused to read Ada's face, to understand if she was being ironically logical, or if she truly believed that because no one knew where it could be, this notebook could also be in the most unlikely places. But likely and unlikely are mere measurements of imagination. And that's one thing that obsoletes, and citizens, dearly lacked. Except for Ada.

"Fine then," Malachi said, walking down aisle 1440, "let me at least show you where most of the notebooks are stacked."

Along the walk, Ada asked, "Do you enjoy this work— preservations?"

"I do. It feels like home. It's rewarding to think that I get to help in the assistance of creating the collective memory. That these things will be accessed long after I'm gone because of my work. As if in some way, someone, unknowingly, will read a part of me anytime that they read any of these works."

Ada wondered how he could be so oblivious. *Does he know that not all of these objects make it into The Sphere, that entire archival facilities incinerate once transported to the Stratum of Reason? Does he not know that all his life's work could go up into flames tomorrow, not by accident, but by design? If he did, would he still do the exact same work? Would the value remain?* Ada concealed her inner thoughts and simply nodded. They walked a few more paces in silence.

"What about you Ada, where's home now?"

"People are always asking me where my home is. But I don't think home is a matter of where, but how."

"What do you mean?"

"I mean, so often isn't it just a matter of fate and happenstance? A place you were born into, or a space where enough memories have been amassed. A place one person calls home, is to an outsider just a passageway."

"Isn't it just a matter of where you feel most loved?" Malachi asked.

"Those feelings don't have much value in my world. Do you mean used, where I feel most used?"

"No—those are not at all the same."

"But you said it yourself, you feel at home in preservations. And to what I know, it hasn't been long enough to be loved where you are—only used."

Malachi smirked, without retort. He led Ada into the aisle, only to find themselves immersed between walls of journals and notebooks scattered without reason. Between the thousands of pages, an exotic rush of pent-up thoughts buzzed the space to life—as if the room itself possessed neurosis. Even the settled dust seemed to carry with it thoughts, as it accumulated in the air and traveled from one book to the next. The whole space, then, felt like it was communicating. Ada's heart raced.

"So," Malachi asked, "what does this notebook look like?"

"I-I truly don't know. We'll know it by its contents."

"The binding is nothing special?"

"I'd imagine not."

"Great."

Both Ada and Malachi traversed the room, without a word. Each grabbed one notebook, opened its cover, confirmed its details were dissimilar to what Grace may have journaled, and placed it back into the shelves. It was a simple operation— but tedious. One that allowed the mind to drift in and out of consciousness, to not fully focus on one's actions. A mindset which welcomed unsolicited thoughts. As Ada caressed the pores of each page, she thought about how much in life she'd touched and yet had been touched by so little. Sure, there were the cold beads of water blasting from her shower head each morning. The threads of the assigned garments that draped her skin. Her bedding. Occasionally, her own hands. It was bizarre how few memories she had of being touched—or explored. She felt inanimate. Jealous of books. Jealous of threads. Jealous of all the things men had also touched before her. Ada had one prior lover. At least she thought she did. The memory felt too cloudy now to say for certain it was real. She was drunk. He was too. It was a memory worth forgetting, anyways.

These thoughts blinded Ada to Malachi's proximity. His unintended brush of his shoulder against her sleeve transported her out of that trance. Then there was a moment where nothing happened, but everything changed. They lingered; neither tried to separate. Ada's thoughts danced in the endless possibilities of their mingling. It wasn't enough. It was just her sleeve. That envy for those things Malachi touched before her was not hatred. Those thin strands of interweaving cotton intercepted a glorious sensation. Those strands reduced the touch of Malachi's hand to that of another object. An unexpected corner, the back of a chair. Ada hated her clothes for the fact they insulated her from another person's touch, the only thing in this moment that she wanted to feel.

But Malachi and Ada lingered next to each other long enough that the space between them became a brushing of their shoulders, followed by elbows. And then their hands: at last, skin-to-skin. At which point Ada's breath hastened. Neither dared gaze toward the guiltless lust that animated in each other's eyes. Their vision remained fixated to the shelves at their fore. Malachi's hand laced gently around Ada's. He twirled it around hers. Interlaced each finger. Like two liquors in a cocktail, irreversibly inseparable. Ada's mind numbed. She looked at the hand he held. Then at Malachi, who was now staring at her, as something to devour and cherish. She loosened her grip and sent both her hands around his neck. His arms wrapped around the small of her back. Their tongues now interlocking just as their fingers had embraced seconds before.

Between kisses, Ada began removing her clothes. It was Malachi she wanted to wear. To make his warmth and strength hers; to finally feel more than his eyes penetrate her. Ada didn't care how it looked. She just wanted to feel him. Without any barriers, the same way she felt herself dripping. Then they were naked. Ada more than him. Malachi's pants ornamented his ankles. The only thing on Ada was that damned scar down her neck—and Malachi. After a few hard thrusts Malachi was cumming. The sex was sloppy. Guiltless. The kind you want to forget. Malachi would. Ada wasn't meant to be remembered that way; so, this was her memory to bear. Ada could only be perceived the way she was designed to be seen.

He whispered into her ear, "You're a wild one." She kissed him once more, and then dressed. He followed suit. They returned to looking for the notebook, without another word.

Chloe Lawrence snuck away during her lunch hour for a bit

of her own exploring in 20W. Not the bounds of sexual activity, but the perimeter of the sector's power grid. After Chloe and Ada were last together, Chloe stumbled back to her room, and after removing her clothes thought herself drugged. Hallucinogenic. The note that Ada hid in Chloe's pocket was lying on her ground, staring at her blank as a corpse. A thing as untouchable as it was unexplainable. Evidence to a guilty verdict. Chloe so wanted to believe it an illusion that she left it untouched until morning, when she believed she would be sober and the paper would have vanished. Only the former came true. Chloe cursed whoever it was that framed her of this crime. Citizens were permitted to retain their own notes. But possessing a written note with an unknown author was a violation of code 36, perpetuation of an inefficient truth. The caste clause, they called it. Who is anyone to know anything that no one else can? All knowledge must be available to all people. To live otherwise was criminal and punishable by death.

But Chloe knew death was inevitable, so she might as well die knowing all she could. Chloe read the note and tucked it away in a drawer filled with other unsightly objects—other junk. But she found a bit of pleasure in disarray; in things to later fix. Though out of sight, that note haunted Chloe at nearly all times of the day. Who was O? And why did she want to meet at the 20W power plant? How could she get there now, as a citizen? Why would O want anything to do with her? Confusion beget wonder. The thought of a mysterious person living in a place deemed uninhabitable while bidding for her attention enchanted Chloe. Within the hour she set off to visit the outer edges of the power plant at 20W.

Chloe visited quietly. Although citizens had the right to traverse to and from the stratums of reason and knowledge without explanation, Chloe visited clandestinely. Her reason, she felt, too sinister to advertise. Easier to manufacture an alibi for her absence than fabricate an explanation for why Chloe, who despised her life as an obsolete, would make her way back to her own personal prison. The same reason anyone does anything inexplicable: curiosity.

When Chloe arrived at the perimeter of the 20W power grid she was disappointed to find it barren. There was neither life, nor any trace of it. Just channels of electricity so dense that even the surrounding air felt charged. Every molecule ready to blow. Hairs across her body erected, seduced by the surrounding magnetic field to draw nearer. She wandered deeper into the grid. Deep enough that she'd lost her way between the maze of fallen wires and grounded generators. Deep enough that she saw signs of lives that once were: remnants of food, package scraps, settled ground marking where tents once laid. But no people. No "O."

Nor would there be any memory of this visit tomorrow. The mystique and thrill she felt in this moment, standing amongst evidence of an unknown person, would fade to a muted sensation of nostalgia by morning. A longing for something she wouldn't be able to articulate. Just as 6Di planned it. There would be no such thing as "O," even if they did exist.

But it wasn't morning yet, so Chloe roamed. The duality of exploration manifested with each step. Her left brain amplified her curiosity. The right side, her anxiety. She was more of a right-minded explorer; who worried the longer she wandered. So, the boundlessness of the open grid suddenly felt like a tightly bordered box. Chloe's chest tightened. As if the desert air itself was compacting, pressing against her chest. Anxiety morphed into panic. Her breaths suddenly inefficient, incapable of sustaining a stable state of consciousness. Chloe clenched her chest. Stumbled in the direction she believed was toward town. But Chloe's senses revolted. Her vision, delayed and kaleidoscopic, encrypted the present. Though practically blind Chloe kept walking. She saw a figure standing not fifty feet from her. A person—which 6Di did not want her to see. In desperation Chloe reached an arm out for help. In her blindness, Chloe walked into a power transformer. Upon contact she was blasted backwards and rendered unconscious. The unknown figure hovered over Chloe and drug her by her feet across the desert floor. By morning, Chloe would remember this trip only by the small note tucked inside of her bra.

Inside the archival facility, Ada was unaware of her sister's voyage into 20W's power grid. Ada was instead fixated on the warm semen radiating inside her. Even while she stared intently at the shelves in search of the reconnoitrer's notebook. She didn't actually expect to find it in the archives. That would have meant a failure of multiple checkpoints. An inexcusable set of errors which would certainly be erased. But stranger things had happened. And stranger things would. At this exact moment, actually. Ada opened the spine of the next unmarked notebook on the shelf and in it found another message from O. The note read as too specific, too explicit, to have been part of the original documentation. It was written and placed recently. As early as minutes ago. Was she here now? If not, who on the inside worked for her? Who could have predicted Ada would be standing right here and able to read these words?

You are not just like her. See through her lies. Not just some, like today. See through them all. - O

WE WILL ALL BE FORGOTTEN

While Chloe lay unconscious at the ground of the power grid in 20W, Ada searched the archival facility, ignorant of her sister's condition. Ada could not shake the feeling that she was being monitored by a nearby purger. But any nearby purger would be too obvious. Their helmets too conspicuous. *Unless...* Ada wondered if a guard could clandestinely be a purger. Their identities were concealed. *But if there was one, were there many? Have I always been under the watchful eye of purgers?* She sounded crazy, even to herself. But the last few moments were exactly that. She wasn't crazy. Not more than the world around her.

"I need to walk." Ada said, firing the remark across to Malachi without awaiting a response.

"I'll be here," Malachi responded, unaware that Ada was out of earshot.

The cozy space where she had just surrendered her body to Malachi's was, aesthetically, juxtaposed strongly to the cold, corporate warehouse that dominated the space, with its towering aisles turning each precious piece of knowledge into a commodity. The coldness of the concrete, steel beams, and harsh overhead lighting was therapeutic for Ada. At this moment she longed for order and rigidity. She wanted to feel an overwhelming sense of predictability and smallness. To feel that even her grandest concerns weren't even worthy of belonging on a shelf. They were trapped inside her head, where they were born and where they would die.

Outside the facility Ada's team worked out of sight. They were spies of information highways. Always intercepting, guiding, interpreting, and correcting what it was the BRiDG could access, what exactly people could know. And like all good spies they operated out of sight. Since obsoletes still had not fully adopted the BRiDG or interlinked their thinking to The Sphere, they were prone to unauthorized ideas—tempted to think beyond the BRiDG. This was especially true during existential moments.

Their secret was remaining invisible. This translated to a variety of direct-action approaches. Rebellious overtones were particularly difficult to manage. Though the memory capacity of obsoletes was finite, it wasn't non-existent. If members of the Memory Corps deleted a memory too soon suspicions arose. And any missteps thereafter may only cause that unauthorized thought to metastasize itself into one's mind deeper than the BRiDG could access. So, any errors in correction must always be followed by absence; just long enough, until the error is forgotten. Then the corps could make another mistake again, as if it were their first.

Jeremiah's disdain for obsoletes caused him to, in times of stress, respond too heavy handedly. He was not a fan of 6Di's long-game conversion. He doubted the efficacy of letting people come to their own conclusion that they themselves should become subservient to their BRiDG. In his opinion, the whole world could be converted in a day. And any nonbelievers who remained should be wiped from the planet. The world was simple to him. Black and white. He thrived in his role as corrections.

Ada was less certain about how to successfully complete her role. Even when she knew of objects to hunt, the odds of finding them were slim. In Grace's ten years of hunting she found exactly ten documents. All of which were identified as having belonged to specific obsoletes. The second half of Ada's job, to discover documents unknown, felt nearly impossible. But discovering unknowns was what was supposed to make her special. Even in the halls of warehouses, where one day everything would end in flames.

As Ada walked the warehouse she noticed a number of guards closing in on her location. Their presence was always unsettling. Especially now that she didn't know the alliances of any, or who were the ones she'd secretly witnessed torture individuals in the halls of defense. She turned to avoid contact with a few at the end of the aisle. Midway through the next aisle, one end was capped with a guard. At the other end, another. She was trapped. Although now a citizen, Ada's instincts reverted to her earliest memories encountering guards as an obsolete. They were her old bullies. Powerless now. Except in her mind, where their power reigned absolute.

So, Ada froze. She hoped to conceal her fear, and unflinchingly watched the guards walk toward her. There were four in total. All possessed the typical look of guards: draping, tin- colored garments and featureless blacked-out faces. One walked more briskly than the rest. The one with the fastest feet stood before Ada and said, "Ada, what a pleasure to see you again." The darkness from its face began to fade. Revealing Oriana, and Azophi directly behind her. Ada only assumed that the rest were purgers too.

Azophi spoke first, and said, "Your sister dropped this," as he handed her the piece of paper Oriana wrote Ada weeks ago. "She tried to make contact. But she's not like you. She can't see past her BRiDG. Even if we said her name, she still wouldn't hear it."

"You're a lot like me," Oriana added, "able to think past your BRiDG."

Ada suddenly felt a bit incensed. A bit too vulnerable to not put up her guard. She felt like a pawn in a game with rules she couldn't comprehend. A victim even through her agency. The hands that guided her actions were invisible. And so, instead of receiving what Oriana thought was a compliment, Ada responded tersely, "Vivian says the same thing."

"Oddly, we're a lot alike. In more ways than you know."

Ada's frustration dictated her speech. "Why did you trick me into amputating Corydon?"

"I didn't."

"You said—"

"I said it would be a test of loyalty. I didn't say to whom." The point was technical. Unfair, but true.

"Am I in danger of being killed, the way Grace was?"

Azophi interjected, "No. You're safe. Because Vivian knows you've made contact with those who can recall—us. Whoever killed her wanted to do so before she made contact with any purger."

"What do you mean I'm safe now?"

Azophi continued, "There's a danger in killing you off, even for good reason. You still have a chance to be remembered. But Grace, she will be forgotten."

Ada asked, "Why will you forget Grace?"

Azophi responded, "That's what the BRiDG wants. And, I've never known her outside the BRiDG. All she is, is a figment. An idea. She's not a real person to me. I've never felt her flesh, looked into her eyes. She's a thing. And people forget things."

Silence fell across the group.

"This whole room will go ablaze one day." Ada said matter-of-factly. "I saw it for myself."

"We know," Azophi said. "Which room did you see go ablaze?"

"It was connected to the hall of defense. Then, suddenly, it was on a rail heading toward the horizon—toward the edge of the Stratum of Reason. Wherever that ends."

"What else did you see in that hall, Ada?" Oriana asked.

"Tortures."

"There's rumors of that hall," Oriana said bleakly. "Rumors that you need to discover for yourself. It will all make sense to you then—why we're doing all of this" Oriana said.

"Can't you tell me?"

"Afraid not," Azophi said, "we don't yet know the extent of what your BRiDG can censor. But if you see what you think is in there you will never be the same."

"You must roam the halls again," Oriana pleaded.

"I'll go tonight."

"Be careful," Oriana said, "Just because you're not yet worth the risk of erasing, doesn't mean your meddling can't make that an option."

Azophi pointed to an engraving above the doorway and said, "Look."

It read: Burn date June 15. Sixty days from today. Azophi,

exasperated, said, "Everything has a burn date, a date of expiration, a moment in time when it will be forgotten. That is not reason to mourn. Forgetting allows us to fall in love with ourselves again, to always see this world anew."

ADA, MY DEAR?

The hall of defense was sterile. Wrought by an air of rigidity and cleanliness which could only be described as militant. And it was also how you could describe Ada's approach that night. She had set off to complete a mission that she couldn't define. The open-ended nature of her assignment muted Ada's usual reservations to wander. Her curiosity to unveil this hall's mystery was greater than her fear to face it. Driven by the fact that now she wasn't here on recreation. This visit was mandatory. Fears be damned. What awaited her was promised to make her never the same.

Tonight the hall was lifeless. The only sound Ada heard was the buzzing of overly bright fluorescent tube-lights. A silence so deep, it wasn't heard but felt. A stillness that made Ada believe her slightest movements sent ripples across the room, like wading through a flat pond. Every detail was accentuated by the absence of details. There was no question that Ada was alone. Should anyone else arrive, she'd sense them before her eyes or ears could register their presence. Aura was all that remained.

So, Ada opened doors without reserve and entered each space as if it were her own. The tiptoeing and sneaky movements of her previous venture were non-existent. Each room was a bore, so she moved quickly through each. Empty classrooms and staff rooms, mostly. The warehouse hall was replaced with another segment.

She snuck a look above that door frame. Burn date tomorrow. But Ada wasn't looking for what she'd already seen. She needed to walk deeper into the hall than she'd ever wandered, to expand her search to every corner she could scamper her way into.

The search was remarkably unremarkable. Even Ada's pulse, which at first raced adrenaline through her veins, had steadied to a rate that indicated she was nothing short of bored. Empty room, after empty room. Each pristine as if never used. Each concealing the reasons for its true purpose; the heinous tortures Ada had briefly witnessed. But these rooms, in this hour, looked unassuming. It was starting to feel like a colossal waste of time. A pointless endeavor. Having vowed to open every last door, Ada trudged onward. Ten doors became twenty, and then thirty. Eventually, she stopped counting. Stopped caring. She was ready for bed. With just one more door to go, the one bookending the end of her journey, positioned between the two walls that guided her down the hall, she took a short breath, reached for the handle, and stopped. She felt something; the unseen presence of someone behind the door. She removed her hand from the handle and pondered what she would say, what would be her alibi, to whoever was behind this door. Ada realized this was not the time to think, but do. She opened the door uncertain what her story would be, or if she'd even be able to speak.

Queue the latter. What Ada saw beyond that last door demanded inarticulable emotion. A word, any word, would have belittled the horror she witnessed. So, she said nothing. But her stomach flipped, vision blurred, and hands shook. The distinct scent of aluminum that preceded vomiting flooded her mouth.

But that would only add to that putrid space, further sickening the poor bodies strewn across the space like pelts. Though lifeless, all seemed alive—technically. The bodies were caged. Each in their own cell. Each stationed with a unique apparatus that Ada could only imagine was used for experimentations: implanting new versions of the BRiDG, brain transplants, memory manipulation. Everybody had an eclectic variety of tubes and wires running from the walls to their back into their cerebral cortex. Each faintly breathed. Many accompanied only by their own shit or piss. If there was life in their eyes it was unseen, as none kept them open. They appeared as stoics awaiting death, or humans induced by heavy anesthetics. Lily zapped. But these memories would not be overridden, for Ada's mind was too strong.

As Ada walked deeper into the caged room she began to lose her way. The paths were too numerous and chaotic. As hard to reason as the bodies in the cages. When she turned left she ended facing right. Every turn a curve, or intersection to another three halls. The disorientation only multiplied the number of bodies she saw. Each looked the same. Anemic and sinewy. Their skins either absent or crusted. Every twenty feet looked like a replica of the other. A maze copy-pasted. All this should have caused Ada to panic. But she deployed the same breath she used each morning under those cold beads of water. Repeating to herself: *This is it. This is it.* Lily continued to zap. More rapidly than ever too. Each as futile as the one before.

Cooly, Ada said, "You won't win, Lily." But the clicks continued.

For Ada, moral convictions commanded intellectual reasoning. So, when the initial shock of the horrors began to lessen, Ada's mind drifted into a flurry of questions. *What exactly were these experiments? Why these individuals? How were they chosen?* Ada's mind deepened into a mental maze. *Why would Oriana want me to see this? What secrets pertaining to me exist here? What do I gain by knowing this?* Ada knew that not everything should be known. Not every thought deserved to be spoken, some ideas were better off dying inside the mind where they sprouted. And at that thought Ada's empathy for 6Di heightened. There was danger in recollection. Each person is the story they can tell themselves. And, there are too many rotten stories. Best to be assigned one that's best. *What's that saying? Ignorance is bliss.*

Ada had resided in the space long enough that she walked the aisles like a grocery store. She peered at each cage like a novel packaged good, underwhelming and irrelevant. As her shock faded the details of the space amplified. Each body seemed to breathe in unison. Wires strung across each cage, connecting each to another. It was as if they were an analog version of what the BRiDG was doing outside these walls—turning the minds of many into one. Ada stopped bothering herself with the bodies and concerned herself with the wires. She wanted to trace their origin, where it was they first connected. After many minutes of starts and stops it occurred to her that there was no beginning. Perhaps what she was witnessing was more like a circle, a completely enclosed system where each element is both beginning and end. It all made no sense. Not its purpose nor its value. Especially not its ethics. The putrid smell of human waste resurfaced to her consciousness. The dizziness returned. This time, Ada did not hesitate to relieve herself. She puked into the corner of a nearby cage. She hadn't felt more concerned than guilty. Because now her presence had left a mark.

She wanted out. But which way she should walk was as known to her as any of these caged people. At least her pile of vomit distinguished that corner from the others. Ada's first reference point. She snaked through the space. Winding and trailing, never losing her way because she never had one. She knew she'd get out. Even if it took another hour, she'd find the exit. Many minutes into her wondering she heard a distant moan. No one, yet, had been awake. *Maybe they'll have answers,* she thought. *Maybe they can tell me how or why they got into this predicament.* Ada followed the sound. The person, now awake, must have been overwhelmed by their pain. Once in sight, she saw a woman writhing, squirming, but too weak to move any part but her appendages. Ada tended to the front of her cell. The caged woman was too occupied with her pain to notice Ada's presence. But the poor woman must have felt Ada's gaze. The woman's eyes rolled shut. Then, as if the wires deep into her brain had activated a particular thought her eyelids unfolded—and stayed open. The woman's eyeballs were mucoused and pale. Obscured by whatever drugs and experiments had overruled her body. The longer her eyes remained open, though, the clearer Ada saw them. The color of her iris glinted. Then the woman's eyes expanded wide as a fist, like she'd just uncovered a harrowing mystery.

"Ada, my dear," the poor woman quivered, "it's me— your mother."

UNSPEAKABLE COMPROMISE

There is a kind of lie so monumental that its revelation causes the story of one's life to metamorphose. Before the new story begins there is a chasm filled with grief. And the wronged becomes subject to hell on earth; wherein they reside in a purgatory. A life of nothingness, paralyzed by a wave of conflicting emotions. The mind of the wronged becomes a battlefield for right. But no order or amount of words delivers solace. For a moment the person has no identity at all. They've been reduced to incoherent thoughts and incomplete sentences—signals of a defective state. Every person, if they live long enough, will have their trajectory altered by one of these lies. For Ada, discovering that her mother survived was that lie.

Up to this moment the censorships from 6Di, the manipulation of knowledge, the echeloning of truth felt like an unfortunate, necessary evil. An evolution of atomic weaponry. Built much in the same spirit as the Manhattan Project, where no single mind was aware of their role in its project. The hiding and experimentation of her mother Elena should have sent Ada on a crusade to overthrow 6Di. And it may have if she had more time to plan for it. But not seconds after Ada looked into her mother's murky eyes for the first time since infancy, she felt a hot, chilling breath down her neck.

"Remarkable isn't it?" Vivian asked.

Goosebumps spread to the tips of Ada's fingers. She clenched the cage. Her grip expelling rage into those metal bars. She squeezed so tightly that her hands began to bleed.

"Innovation demands experimentation." Vivian continued, "Experimentation so often leads to failures. It's a shame the grandest of experiments happen in secret—but the people haven't appreciated the same trial and error with human flesh as they do with silicon and microchips. Suddenly it becomes unethical. Abhorrent. But what about the days when computer chips mimic sentience? What then, could nothing undergo experimentation?" Vivian circled Elena's cage. "All life progresses with experimentation. All species progress through sacrifice. Some of us get to choose those sacrifices, others of us have it bestowed upon us. You and I Ada, we get to choose."

Ada's grip hadn't retreated an ounce.

"You will not understand this today. You may not understand this tomorrow. But one day you'll understand that the path to success is paved with unspeakable compromises."

Ada shook her head in disagreement, her grip unwavering.

"Oh yes, Ada, yes. You must believe me. Do you think I haven't compromised any part of my life to rise to this occasion? I had a husband once. A man I loved dearly. Who loved me more than anything else on this earth. But love…" Vivian chuckled, "love is the same always. It's not inventive. Never new. And the only people who do something worthwhile, dare I say, worth remembering, are those that invent. Love isn't a matter of invention, but surrender. So, you can feel betrayed or hurt or whatever it is you feel right now. But you shouldn't feel that if she had been in your life this entire time that you'd be a better woman. You'd be a different one. A simpler one. That's the problem with love, it lessens the depth of many in its pursuit."

Tears rolled down Ada's cheeks. Its source untraceable. Some coagulation of sadness and rage. But what hurt the most was the betrayal. How long had Oriana and Azophi known? And her father. Was Byron's coded recollection of the past him concealing this secret? How many others knew about Elena, about the thousands of people caged for experimentation? Ada prayed silently, *Lily please. Lily take this away. I do not want to remember today.* Lily did not respond. It didn't matter much anyways. Ada was damned if she remembered, and damned if she didn't.

As tears continued to roll down Ada's face her grip loosened on the cage that held her mother.

"But why?" Ada asked, "why did you do this to her—to us?"

"You don't remember, child?" Vivian's tongue slithered.

Ada took a hard look back at Elena, whose eyes were downcast to the floor. She stared in search of a clue, some kind of hint as to why it was she was locked away. If there were any justification, any rightful reason for imprisonment, it was eclipsed by her saddened face.

"What about you?" Vivian asked Elena, "do you remember why you were put here? Go ahead. Tell her. Tell your child why you chose this life."

"Bullshit," Ada retorted. "No chance in hell she chose this."

"Oh child, we're not in hell. Now go on Elena. Tell Ada why you're here."

Emaciated, Elena went to speak but instead trembled. So much that her weakened legs collapsed under her.

"Help her!" Ada shouted.

"She must speak."

Elena stuttered to the beat of her convulsions. "I...I...I am - uh - sor - ry." She wailed the final tone of her admission. Her shaking worsened. It was obvious she'd say nothing more.

"Why won't you tell me?" Ada demanded of Vivian.

"It's too horrible to repeat. What's done is done and now she pays the price."

Vivian began rubbing Ada's back. Her touches so uncharacteristic that they undermined their purpose. Vivian's embrace felt manipulative, more like an unsolicited trance from a hypnotist than a comforting touch. Ada shuddered. Vivian, cold and insensitive, rubbed harder. Ada froze. Vivian's grip was another one of those unchangeable facts of life. No one could escape her hand. And Ada might be the only living person she knew that contemplated such a thing. Obedience to 6Di presumed delusion—a kind of thinking that favored quotations over questions.

As Vivian rubbed Ada's still, tensed back, she leaned into Ada's ear and said, in a voice just above a whisper, "It does no good to keep looking into her eyes. She's not your mother. She's a different purpose now. As do you. Never forget that the path to success is paved with unspeakable compromise."

Ada could only nod. Neither in agreement nor denial. She just nodded, like a metronome passing the time away.

Vivian continued and said, "Good my child, this is good.

You'll be stronger for this. And, I want you to remember that I know your powers. They're like mine. We can think beyond The Sphere. We imagine and remember a world separate from our BRiDGs. That's a danger, to remember something no one else can. By definition you live forever alone. Imagine if you only spoke a language that no one else remembered? Imagine if half of what you knew were things no one else did? But of everything you recall, remember this: it doesn't matter what you know. I don't care what you learn is true and how much of it you remember. You could learn all the secrets that keep this world afloat. Eventually you will. What you remember doesn't matter— who could ever believe you? All that matters is what you do. It's your loyalty that concerns me most."

Lifeless, Ada replied, "I understand."

"Good. I'll leave you two alone. I recommend you don't spend too long here. You could forget again—but that requires letting go." Vivian nodded tersely and exited into the darkness, disappearing into the maze of cages. Ada's head hung low, her hands slumped against the cage. She had entered the room fueled by confidence and curiosity. She would leave it paralyzed with fear and shame. Ada felt the weak gaze of her mother. Her thin, desperate frame, still suctioned to the floor.

"Get up mom," Ada whimpered. "Please get up. Let me see you one last time." Slowly, Elena initiated. But when her elbows neared ninety she collapsed, exhaling loudly upon impact. Elena only turned her head toward Ada, mouth and eyes agape. What had she done to deserve this? How could anyone deserve this?

Ada lay against the floor, and faced her mother's cage. She

smiled, grateful to see her mother again. Her frailness unleashed in Ada a flood of tears. Ada saw the strength in Elena's eyes. None of it could be expressed. Ada's tears empowered Elena to reach a trembling hand toward Ada. Ada's tears blinded her to Elena's affectionate gesture. Ada wiped her eyes and saw Elena's feeble, outstretched hand. The simplicity of this gesture deepened Ada's sorrow. She cried even more, and was once again blinded by her tears. Ada searched for her mother's hand as if it were a light switch in a dark room. Their fingertips brushed. And just as quickly broke apart. Then their tips brushed again. She rested her hand over Elena's. In an instant Ada remembered being swaddled in her mother's arms. A warmth tingled throughout Ada. She longed for nothing else than to feel her mother's chapped hands tremble for a few more minutes.

Ada had stopped crying and, still lying against the floor, looked into her mother's eyes. Elena, still unable to speak, dispensed the last molecule of moisture in her tear ducts. A single tear dripped down her face. She was too famished to muster anything more.

It was the last sign she needed to depart. Ada squeezed her mother's hand and whispered, "I love you too." Ada removed a necklace that hung around her mother's neck. It was the same necklace worn by the purgers, jeweled with a BRiDG. An emblem of rebellion. Vivian must have mockingly let it drape from Elena's neck. Ada surveyed the space and realized that all the encaged were wearing these necklaces. Which made Ada believe the reason for the necklaces was more sinister, an easy-access method to test brain functionality with and without the BRiDG. Which it was, Ada would have to wait to learn. She stood and left her lifeless mother on the floor. Vivian, believing this was a sign of Ada's loyalty, watched in the shadows and smirked.

That night, Ada made her way to the Memory Corps's nightlife district. The pubs and clubs onsite operated at all hours, drawing party goers till dawn. It was an hour past midnight when Ada arrived at a nameless electronic club. A space where all senses were muted or overridden. Nothing mattered beyond the pulsating bass, beaming neon lights, cocaine-fueled speech, and sweaty skin. This was a space for total abandonment. Ada's exact desires. To combat the predestined disappointments of today, Ada longed to surrender herself to whatever carnal remained within her. She summoned that self with a bump of coke, a shot of liquor. A first dance with a stranger's skin rubbing against hers. She welcomed any sensation that let her forget. A hand grabbed her ass. She caressed it, and looked back at this bold stranger. Who was no stranger at all.

"Malachi?" she said, drunken and high. "I didn't take you as the type to…"

"And you are?" he said, wryly.

She placed his hands around her hips and backed into his pelvis.

Even their sweat morphed into single droplets when they touched. Ada wrapped her arms around his head. She stared into his eyes, which at this hour looked as lifeless as those encaged. Ada danced her tongue inside his mouth, then led him into the nearest bathroom stall. That's the last thing she remembered. This forgetting was due to her consumption of chemical concoctions.

She woke up the next morning incapable of understanding

where she was or why her body ached. A whiff of day-old sex confounded the sight of her empty bed. She closed her eyes. Her head pounded to the rhythm of her heart. Flashes of adrenaline and ecstasy shaped her memories. A few details became unmistakably clear. She and Malachi had met on the dance floor. She'd invited him inside her again. But why? She didn't really want Malachi. Confusion and grogginess was displaced by immeasurable sadness. Her mind, once struggling to accelerate, zoomed. On the nightstand next to her bed her mother's necklace rested. A thing at this moment she dared not touch. A woman who once would do anything to help herself remember now felt desperately that she was living in a world dense with details she'd rather forget.

In the month following Ada's journey through the cages Lex had taken a sudden, coincidental, interest in Ada. He spoke to her daily. Often in private. Always in the hall of defense. He'd send guards to her training corridor to fetch her; or telephone through Yoko or Kimberley that he requested her presence. He had a way of getting everyone to do him favors. In part because he was also always doing favors. He gave Yoko original artwork signatured by her great grandparents from Kyoto. Gifted Jeremiah the canoe traced to his bloodline that was believed to first journey to the Faroe islands. He gifted bits of history. A subtle reminder that what remains of the past was always within his reach—that each person's legacy was literally within his hands.

This is what made Lex Nabakov a master of deception. Even the power he wielded wasn't entirely his. He understood, perhaps even more than Vivian, the complexities of the human psyche, its vulnerabilities. Ada felt his chilling authoritarian demeanor the moment she met him. She felt he was a man who did not walk, but prowled. A man who was ravenous for a hunt. Lex spoke every sentence with unshakeable conviction, as if every word he spoke was read from a teleprompter. No matter the hour, the day, or the moment he appeared flawless; no sweat, no rumpled clothes, no unkempt hair. He always looked ready to announce a declaration of war. Too put together. A man who behaved more like machine.

This reputation made Ada uncomfortable now that she found herself so vulnerable. Since seeing Elena caged, Ada hadn't slept a night without waking up in a full-sweat, after nightmares of her mother, charging her in anger, shook Ada awake. She lived a life filled with guilt and absent of power. Two feelings she realized that had always coincided. Occasionally, Ada felt empowered to do something about this misfortune. To set her mother free, but her conviction for justice was always short-lived. Because, what would Ada do after her mother was free? Instead she gave into more passionate nights with Malachi, or descended into incalculable drunkenness. From the outside, her behavior looked like self-destruction. But to her it was simply preservation. She was given a lot of pain too great to confront at once. To ingest it subtly, steadily, seemed like the only way to minimize her trauma.

Lex threatened the pace of her recovery. Frequently, he'd walk her down to the last door, to "show her around" his workspace, he would place his hand on the door handle to the entryway of the encaged, and, at the last second, divert to another doorway instead. Their conversations inevitably turned to his parents and how "fulfilled"—his words, strangely—their relationship made him. Ada couldn't believe someone so cold could care for the elderly—nor anything weak. But discussing the nature of his relationships was all a ploy. Just another device to get Ada thinking about hers.

What Ada hated most was when he'd tease entry to the door of the encaged then say, "We can't go into this room—it's full of gifts." Then he'd wink. Ada would faintly smile, concealing her anger. But this tease would come to drive Ada insane. It happened so frequently, the shock of his words subsided. But each time he did, it recycled for her the thought that maybe that is what Lex would gift Ada—whenever he was ready to bring her into the fold of his blackmail trail. And once that thought was on her mind, she could have no other. It didn't matter the occasion. She preferred to have the thought before bed. It eliminated her nightmares but sent her into deep morning depressions when her dreams of reuniting with Elena were discovered to be just that.

One morning, Lex walked Ada down the long, steely hall of defense. It was like every other time. Ada remained silent, responding only in kind to his self-aggrandizing monologues about how he "really turned the defense program around at Sixth Domain Industries." About how his predecessor just wasn't cut out to do the dirty work. This time, though, Lex stopped midway down the hall, turned to Ada, and said with surprising sincerity, "I know you haven't been well, Ada."

"I haven't?" she asked, taken aback.

"Your performance metrics have dropped across the board. Your heart rate has been all over the spectrum. Blood sugars constantly cycle from low to high. Your sleep—god—your poor sleep patterns. You know we have to monitor these essentials. We have to ensure our memory corps is in top shape, ready for whatever missions are next. And, frankly, you're not ready for any mission."

Ada steadily nodded her head, neither confirming nor denying his conclusion.

"I'm pulling you from tonight's operation." Lex let the words hang with the weight he thought they were worth. But Ada's dedication to service wasn't on par with his.

Concealing her relief, Ada plainly stated, "Oh, okay. I understand."

"Good. I knew you would," Lex retorted, again walking down the hall. "Now, we only have one mission. And that's to get you right. To get your head fixed. The body will follow. I'm going to suppose something quite difficult to comprehend. Something that will cause a visceral, negative reaction. I want you to recognize that reaction but from it there should be no decisions made. Not until that visceral feeling fades do I want you to answer my proposal, okay?"

As confused as she was nervous, Ada replied, "I understand."

"Do you, Ada?" Lex coldly asked, as he pressed on the door handle to the back room. Then at the moment when he usually diverted to another, he cracked the doorway. He stared at Ada, knowing his question to her was rhetorical. Lex looked into the room, stepped inside, and disappeared into the darkness. Ada understood that she was meant to follow. But she felt an invisible force preventing her from entering. Not an actual, physical force.

An apprehension, arising from her sixth sense. Just a feeling. A kind which, if obeyed, would label someone as superstitious or prescient—depending on the outcome of that obedience. But if disobeyed, betrays oneself. After a brief pause, Ada chose to enter the room. On the other side of that doorframe, a piece of her remained.

The room looked exactly as it did before. Dark, mazy, with a hazy glow of light emanating from plasma that flushed through tunnels connecting each cage. This visit, Ada spent less time orienting herself amidst the chaos, and more time studying details that were previously hidden by her confusion. She noticed the wires connecting each cage across the ceiling; an order to the way that the cages were placed. Faces that she could swear were replaced, different from the ones she saw the last time she visited. But like a river, no person returns to the same room twice. The differences are subtle. And if not visible in the room then a part of the aura it harbors. Each space a capsule of unobservable energy summoned by the sets of experiences within it. Even if a room hasn't changed, its observer has. What was once a space of mystery had transformed into a room harboring unfathomable secrets.

So, for Ada to return sent her to the verge of psychosomatic overdrive. It pushed her to a neurological fork in her cortex, one where she must decide to either numb herself to her current reality or risk it dominating her every thought. To be nothing, or the horror itself. She chose numbness. As Ada stepped further into the room, the details blurred. She saw the pathways diminish, winding trails of darkness; the cages, merely smudges of color and shapes. If not for Ada deploying her slow, steady breath she may have become completely unhinged.

What she could perceive was Lex walking deeper into the maze, closer to where the swore she last saw Elena. But the cage, this time, was empty. Before Ada could utter a noise, Lex spoke and said, "This is what you could remember of this space."

"What, what do you mean?"

"I—we—can help. I know you wandered in here and… unfortunately discovered your mother. That must have been heartbreaking. It's a deep wound. One that I'm sure you'd rather forget. We've been working on a new technology for your kind. Those who are haunted by life beyond The Sphere. We don't want you to remember this. But you're defunct. Same with anyone who can recall things unauthorized. But we think the technology is ready. And if you are too, you could remember exactly what you see now, and nothing else."

"Exactly this?"

"And nothing else."

"What about these scars?" Ada asked, pointing to her chest.

"You'll retell the same fables as before."

"How long do I have to decide?"

"As long as you need," Lex said, "this is your choice." What a Machiavellian, Lex, for presenting his gift to her as a choice.

"Give me some time."

"Of course," Lex muttered, leaving Ada without a goodbye.

Sixth Domain Industries always had its way with what would be remembered. This, it seemed, was their final frontier. Bring those beyond the BRiDG into its fold. Let them see the world as it was designed to be seen; as the rest of the world saw it. Ada pondered the extent to which memory was manipulated for everyone she knew. In the weeks that followed her first visit among the encaged Ada had not heard a word about Grace's murder, or its trial. Some of this was explained by the tsunami news cycle, the endless stream of urgent stories that amplified a zeitgeist of attention-deficiency. Each headline another figmentation of symbiosis, a multiplication too rapid to linger over any one story till its end. But to Ada the reasonings for the silence surrounding this murder seemed ever stranger than myopism. Even when Ada addressed the story directly to members of the Memory Corps, they'd stared at her blankly. As if Ada was talking about events in an alternative universe in which only she had lived. When pressed about the mission to 20W to retrieve Grace's notebook, Yoko swore that the team meandered in 20W to assist with an unauthorized scan—as they had before Ada was a member of the team and Augusta digitized the journal of Oriana. The narratives compounded exponentially. Which stories were real Ada could not discern. But, as she fell deeper into the trappings of 6Di, Ada figured this dilemma was not a matter of perception, but choice. Her history merely a matter of will. Choose one, and make it true.

HISTORICAL CORRECTION

Out of sight out of mind is the foundational principle to 6Di's censorship. The second is like it, *keep that which is out of mind out of sight*. And so, the centrifugal relationship perpetuates without end. This is accomplished through the demand for neuropathic dependency through digitizations, burn pits, the cranial aquarium, and the cages. Control what is seen and you've controlled what will be remembered. Ada was never supposed to see Elena. She was supposed to believe that all her memories were accessible. That she was somehow above the influence of 6Di, and for good reason as Vivian's selected heir. Seeing Elena brought her mother back into mind, yes. But it also brought into her mind the fact that even she, future heir of Vivian's position, was a subject to 6Di's censorships. She was not the free-willed and minded individual parading through life aware of all its secrets. This, to Ada, was unacceptable.

But halfway between her twenty-minute walk from the hall of defense to her citizen-styled apartment, Ada started to forget. She walked an elevated pathway that snaked between the skyscrapers. A space seasoned with sprinklings of gardens and streams. The plants and the fish all non-native. None served a purpose beyond their aesthetics. In the Stratum of Reason the natural world had become man's subject. Just another color to a painter's palette.

Ada was crossing a garden illuminated by moonlight when she tried to recall her mother's face. A clear image of it against the floor morphed into a chiseled silhouette, which dissipated into a featureless shadow. It was natural to remember. But memories, like the flowers at her feet, should be perfectly positioned and pruned.

A quiet panic jolted through Ada's mind. Her steps slowed. Teeth clenched. She was not ready to let go. She did not want to let go. Why was she—*zap*.

"Stop," Ada whispered to Lily.

Ada's pensive face mimicked her taut gait. She walked as someone in pain. Her source of physical contortions a matter of frustration; from dear memories slipping—dashing—away that she wasn't ready to relinquish. She stepped with such intention any observer may have wondered if she was pursuing someone, matching the steps of an unaware stranger. But she walked to her own rhythm. That jaded, incoherent beat based on scattered attempts to recall Elena's face. The harder she recalled the more her image dissolved into nothing but Lily's audible *clicks*. Ada's choice had been made for her. If 6Di had it their way, an empty cage was all Ada would ever remember.

It was enough to drive Ada mad. Those aneurysmal ticks commanded her consciousness to seize. Each reverberation unleashed a unique emotion. The first signaled fear. After which, Ada's entire nervous system paralyzed. Once Ada's body recognized the source of this shock, she was overcome with rage. A kind that only hundreds of thousands of years of evolution could harbor. A rage that befriended a violence of guaranteed survival. One that knew only two futures: kill or be killed.

This rage wasn't a result of the clicks *per se*, the literal auditory experience which was, at worst, an annoyance. The rage manifested in what those clicks symbolized. The knowledge of what was happening beyond the senses. With each click a neural pathway was blockaded. Memories her mind tried to recall were quarantined—or worse, zapped. And her brain, once a world unto itself that she could freely explore, became a maze of someone else's engineering; a series of pathways levied to someone else's liking. She felt her brain enclosing, the paths detouring and rerouting, her neurons firing on a tighter and tighter circuit. Regression. Generations of evolution reversed. Decades of life behind lock and key. Historically, this kind of threat is classified under the "kill" category. But this rage had no relief. For the perpetrator was inside Ada, posing as part of her body.

Ada couldn't take another step. Her whole body numbed by the sudden sensation of loss. She countered her panic with a thought most beguiling. *It's okay. No one can remember everything.* And for a moment there was silence. A nothingness that ushered with it a sense of peace. A peace Ada desperately wanted to cloak herself within. For those few seconds she did. Her heart steadied. Eyes gazed upwards, and nerves prickled. *This is how it always goes. People have always forgotten things. My mother used to say— my mother, where is she?*

What's her name?

Click. Click. Click. Each snap chopped at Ada's peace. "Lily, please," Ada cried.

For the next ten minutes Ada walked to the spastic pattering of Lily's clicks. Lily had never behaved this way before. There were no memories associated with these edits. She clicked *ad infinitum*. And the once jarring intrusions of Lily began to feel, to Ada, like gentle pulsating massages. Lily had dug her way into the deepest part of Ada's mind. And here, a third wave of emotion arose: trust.

And this nearly split Ada's mind. Although Ada no longer felt the fear, or rage, she had moments before—she comprehended that what Lily was doing was nothing short of ransacking. As Lily upended the order of Ada's mind she continued to walk to her apartment. With each step there must have been ten more clicks. Ten bits of memory Lily blockaded from Ada ever accessing again. When Ada tried to recall Elena once more her image was reduced to a series of mushed pixels. Nothing but a smeared, wet painting. But when she gripped the necklace draped around her neck, she felt that maybe she could remember her mother again. Which may have been a false hope. But in a world built on lies, what other kind of hope exists?

Ada drifted into sleep. She'd hover in and out of rest for hours, unable to distinguish between her dreams, delusions, and memories. But at a moment when she was at the deepest of her sleep, Ada was awakened by a noise that was unmistakably real—originating from feet near her bed. Ada jolted awake. Her breathing hastened. She scanned the darkness, expecting glowing eyes like in her previous kidnapping. Instead, she saw two towering silhouettes inching toward her bed.

"Ada," Oriana said, "we're so sorry. We wanted to tell you sooner."

Ada sat upright, her hands wringing her bed sheets as she

seethed, "Why didn't you?"

"We didn't know," Azophi said, "the extent at which you were still independent—how much you could remember if we told you. We knew you needed to see for yourself. To put a face to a name is unforgettable."

"Used to be."

"What do you mean?" Oriana asked.

"I mean, even after I've seen my mother's face her features fade in and out of memory." Ada said, flicking on the lights. Before her Oriana and Azophi stood, disguised as guards. Their faces black as the galaxy's edge. They unfiltered their faces, revealing their identities.

"What do you mean?" Oriana asked.

"I mean, Lex said an upgrade was coming, to circumvent the need for neuropathic dependency…an update that would allow the BRiDG to embed itself in someone's mind … no matter their level of dependency."

Azophi and Oriana turned pale.

Oriana sat against the bed, and asked, "Is that what you feel, that you can no longer remember what you saw?"

"It is trying to make me forget. But I won't let go." There was a moment of silence, "Can you remove my BRiDG again, like you did the first time we met?"

"No Ada," Oriana said, frowning. "We're afraid it's too embedded in you now. That if removed you'd forget how to move, or talk. Like those you saw encaged."

"Ada," Azophi interjected, "you must learn how to override the BRiDG."

Ada stared at the foot of her bed as she took a few slow, steady breaths. "Okay then," Ada demanded, "give me all the reasons to never forget. What else have you not told me? What is my lineage?"

"Ada," Oriana said, as her breath quickened, "your mother was the founder of 6Di."

A FIGHT TO REMEMBER

Seconds after Ada learned about her mother's past, lights in her room strobed. From overhead speakers, a message was broadcast: *Emergency. Report to the briefing center ASAP. Emergency. Report to the—*

"Dammit," Ada said.

Oriana and Azophi's faces dissipated behind total blackness.

Good Morning, Ada, said Lily.

"Not now," Ada said as her company looked confusedly her way. Ada pointed at the back of her skull.

Oriana and Azophi nodded, and exited without another word.

Ada dressed. Her cold uniform stiff to don. Then she bolted toward the briefing room. She was the first of her team to arrive. Ada walked to her personal locker room to grab accessories for her deployment. So much of 6Di's spaces had unnerved Ada, but this room comforted her. It reminded her of her life in the Stratum of Knowledge, when life was tougher but equally simpler. Ada sat on her bench and stared at the intricate woodwork. She felt embraced by the dark hues and warm lights. Then her blood chilled, as she felt a hand squeeze her shoulder.

"Ada," Lex said, "how are you?"

Ada was so shocked that all she could muster was a quick, shallow inhale. Vivian appeared in her peripherals, and steadily walked before Ada, who sat paralyzed under Lex's grasp. Vivian knelt toward Ada and draped Ada's necklace over her palm, "Very pretty," Vivian said, "what is it?"

Ada couldn't find the words. Her toes tingled and forehead burned. Sweat perspired from her pores. Lex, impatient, squeezed Ada's shoulder so hard that she flinched. "Answer your leader," Lex commanded.

But Vivian filled the silence, "I let you walk out with this because I believe you need to discover all things for yourself. But Lex informed me that you volunteered to join our trial and forget all that was in that room." Vivian's eyes squinted paper thin as she smiled, "I'm so proud of you. But Ada," Vivian continued, her hand now tugging on Ada's necklace, "this is dangerous if that's the path you want. This will always remind you of things better off forgotten. To heal you must also let this go."

Ada's lips quivered, as if each lip was battling the other for the right words. But Ada couldn't tell Vivian that she wanted to remember. Not because it wasn't the truth. But because in the war against it, this moment was not a battle worth fighting.

So, instead, Ada surrendered her chin to her chest. Vivian slid the necklace off Ada's neck. "Good child. Very good," Vivian whispered, "now you are free to forget." But to forget was to surrender, and Ada wasn't ready to do that. In fact she was prepared for the opposite. Under the literal grip of her oppressor Ada promised to herself that she'd not only see that necklace again, but would place it on her mother.

"Even heaven allows hell, Ada. I am just trying to understand if you will allow it too." And for the first time, Ada believed that all along, Vivian was proclaiming that 6Di was on the side of hell.

Ada concealed her deepest thoughts, and said, "I can."

"Good," Vivian said, "now let's prepare for the others." And all three left the dressing room to wait inside the main corridor of HQ's Memory Corps.

Soon after, the rest of the team arrived as one.

"Ada," Yoko laughed, "how did you get here so fast?"

"Couldn't sleep," Ada joked.

Vivian, seated on a bed of fossilized snakes, smirked. But before anyone else could speak, Lex said, "Team, there's an uprising in 20W we need to quell. As HQ, you will be the lead team on the ground supported by each archival unit located within the first twenty miles of the Stratum of Knowledge."

Jeremiah shook his head in disgust, staring at Ada, and said, "Nothing good ever came out of 20W. What's the reason for these uprisings, boss?"

"Jeremiah," Lex continued, "We don't yet have a full report on the situation. It is violent. If necessary you are permitted to use lethal force."

"Lethal force?" Kimberley interjected, "the entire reason for the BRiDG is—"

"Kim," Jeremiah shouted, "we're not dealing with reasonable people. They're not dependent on their BRiDGs."

"Yes," Lex added, "we cannot treat these people like citizens. And though heaven allows hell, it doesn't allow the fallen to reside inside its pearly gates."

"But what is this revolt about? Why now?" Yoko asked.

"One chant was archived." Lex tuned to his BRiDG. Then, slowly, repeated, "*Knowledge, Reason! Both we cherish! Take them from us—we'd rather Perish!"*

Jeremiah, seated, slapped his hands to his knees to rise and said, "Welp, let's give 'em what they want. Obsoletes were born to die."

"Team," Vivian added gravely, "your mission is to eliminate and extract all physical artifacts that perpetuate revolutionary sentiments."

"People included?" Kimberley asked.

"People included." Vivian then stood and exited the room, her throne of snakes unfurled themselves, following Vivian.

"Vivian," Ada asked, "why is it you rest upon snakes?"

The room froze, as did Vivian. Who deflected the tension and said, "Snakes were present when man first bit into the forbidden fruit. No creature better understands our demons." Vivian bent over to let a few wrangle themselves around her arm. Then, standing, she said, "We despise snakes because of that. It's in our genes too—to believe that their presence is somehow evil. The first thing man saw after their fall were the eyes of a serpent. Our darkest parts visible to these." A snake slithered up from Vivian's arm to around her neck. "We hate them not because of what we see in them, but what they see in us." The snake tried to plunge its fangs into her neck, but Vivian snatched its head before it penetrated her skin. Vivian pulled its neck out enough so that she could make eye contact, and said, "They're purveyors of evil. That's why they strike. They see the evil in us and want a bite of it themselves. They want to free us of our inner demons." Vivian ripped the snake off her neck and whipped it against the floor—and stomped it dead.

"Have fun back home, Ada," Vivian said, winking.

Two hours later, HQ's Memory Corps arrived in district 20W. The neighborhood, prone to possess a constant bustling, was silent. The district appeared abandoned. A posterboard rolled by in the wind like a tumbleweed. In the distance, a single obsolete was briefly seen passing by a window inside a nearby high-rise. The only signs of life outdoors was the local archival unit, led by Malachi, who had exited a store feet from where the Memory Corps stood.

"Hey team, I'm Malachi, 20W's reconnoiter." He said, greeting Jeremiah with a handshake. Malachi was surrounded by a dozen guards. The way they walked, the manner in which their invisible faces affixed in Ada's direction, she believed they were present for her.

"Looks like your team cleaned house already?" Jeremiah asked, as both teams conjoined.

"Everyone's hiding indoors."

"How are we supposed to remove revolutionaries if they're inside?" Jeremiah scowled, kicking the ground.

"Why?" Yoko asked Malachi, "why is everyone indoors?"

"They heard she was coming," Malachi said, nodding toward Ada.

"Me? Why would—" And then Ada remembered. Last time she was in 20W Ada had removed the hand of her dear friend Corydon, thinking it was a simulation.

"Yeah," Jeremiah said, "because you ruin everything."

"There is a woman inside this store," Malachi said, pointing at the door that he and the guards just exited. Ada felt now that every guard was staring at her, awaiting some kind of command.

"Let's go," Yoko said.

"No," Ada interjected, "I want to go in alone. These are my people." Ada walked toward the door. Four guards followed.

"I'll join you. This is my jurisdiction." Malachi said, following the guards. Ada clenched her jaw, concealing her disapproval.

"Sure Ada," Jeremiah scoffed, "have your last words." Then, to the faceless guards, he said, "Keep her safe, boys."

Ada entered the store. Inside, a store clerk stood alone behind the counter.

"Where's everyone?" Ada asked, approaching the counter. The woman's eyes grew wide. Her face squeamish. The old woman cowered as Ada neared. She began to mumble: *please, please no.*

Ada understood that her reputation was like any other memory. Just the result of a formula embedded into the minds of people residing under 6Di. She'd been reduced to an algorithm, an object as ephemeral as a digit on a stock-market ticker. Her worsening reputation was a preview of the control Lex and Vivian had over any of Ada's deepest desires. She was led to believe that she could never lead a successful revolt—because the minds of the people were never hers. So she wrestled with this dilemma. Either Ada must choose to forget the things that so profoundly shaped her world. Or her world would be shaped to forget the profoundly important things about her character. The future was too small for the whole truth. Exactly as 6Di designed.

Ada stepped back, confused, "What, what is it?" Ada pleaded. But the old woman couldn't muster any other words but *please.*

Ada felt sorry for the woman's plea. Because Ada understood

what no one else could even comprehend, that the world happening before everyone's eyes was not random or natural. Rather, it was a result of corporate planning. A reality covertly escorted into existence by a corporation that concealed its ambitions behind claims of shepherding truth.

"Answer her!" Malachi shouted. But Malachi gave her no time, he ripped a poster off the wall, walked behind the counter and shoved it into the face of the old, cowering woman. "Now answer me! Why are you doing this?"

"Malachi! Stop!" Ada yelled. Ada glanced at the guards, who nodded her way, confirming her suspicion that their loyalties were with the Purgers.

Malachi grabbed the old woman by her neck; began choking her with her own shirt. "You vermin!" he shouted again, shaking her head against the hard tile floor. Ada tried to rip Malachi's hands from her neck but he elbowed her back. Ada fell to the floor. Then stood, patted the dust off her ass, and said, "Guards."

As the four guards encircled Malachi, Ada picked up the poster that was at the center of his interrogation. When she read it, Ada was confused: *BOGO Soda, This Week Only! All Wine Half Off M-F 4-6*. Promotional posters. Items to run her business. Not a call to a revolution.

Poster in hand, Malachi was dragged before Ada. "Explain this," she demanded, revealing to him the posters.

Malachi looked at the poser and shrugged, as if it explained itself. Ada turned the poster over to read and began to say, "these are promo—" then she paused. Her vision flickered, like she was a reel of film that was just spliced into another. At this moment,

Lily rapidly *clicked*. The posters were no longer the benign displays of corner-store capitalism. It read *Off with her Head*, which was written below a graphic that showed Ada's head in the hand of an anonymous obsolete.

"Bring her here." Ada commanded the two unoccupied guards.

"I told you!" Malachi pleaded, still apprehended by two guards. The old woman was brought before Ada. Her legs trembled. So much that it looked as if she'd flop to the floor if the guards released her.

"I'm not here to harm you, okay?" Ada assured the woman. "I simply need to know, what is it you see?" The woman dared not look at the posters before her. Ada held steady. The woman slowly peeked upward. But all that she could muster was a whimper.

The old woman pointed to the back of the store, "She did it."

"She?" Ada asked.

Ada dropped the poster to the floor. It stuck like a rug; heavy and accentuating. On the floor the poster fuzzed, like the poster had fallen to the edge of the radius that relayed this visual. Ada continued to stare at the poster, anticipating it would change. After a brief second it flashed again, *BOGO Soda, This week Only!* And though she couldn't discern between which version was real and simulated, she knew the only lie was being broadcast by 6Di.

"Shut him up," Ada ordered the guards, as she walked to the back. "And let the old woman free."

Ada tucked herself into a narrow door behind the counter and entered a cluttered room. The space was littered with papers and posters—enough paraphernalia to charge all surviving obsoletes to death. A woman sat alone on the floor, her back to the door, rocking. Before her laid open a book. Ada knew the silhouette, but couldn't believe her eyes.

"Chloe?" Ada asked.

"Ada!" Chloe said, springing to her feet. "She knew it all along!" Her sister's face, usually cool and collected, appeared wiry and crazed.

Ada grasped Chloe by the shoulders, uncertain if she was even real. "Who knew what, Chloe?"

"Mom," Chloe said, pointing to the splayed book. Ada's face contorted. Chloe continued, "After you snuck that note into my handbag I made my way to 20W and met the Purgers. Well, they met me and gifted me that book: some kind of diary of mom's."

Ada knelt beside the book, flipping through its pages. A metal key fell out. Chloe bent and pocketed the key, which she used as a bookmark.

"It's too much to read now," Chloe exclaimed, "but Ada… Mom didn't die because she was in battle. She died because she was once the head of 6Di. Back when it was an A.I. Organization. Before it had global ambitions of embedding itself into our minds. Vivian took it over in a coup. That was after the war. No one blinked an eye at an executive being displaced."

Ada flipped the pages faster than she could read.

"I know this must be hard to understand. I'm not crazy. I—"

"No Chloe, I'm the one that's going to sound crazy," Ada said, as she stood, book in hand. "Mom's not dead."

"Take me to her," Chloe demanded.

Ada peeked into the room beyond the door. Malachi was still bound. The old woman sat in a corner.

"Is O at the grid?" Ada asked. In unison, each guard shook their head in affirmation.

"Great," Ada said, "cover for me." Then Ada grabbed her sister Chloe by the arm, snuck out the back door to the building and into the vehicle that she and her team rode into 20W. As she sped away with Chloe in the passenger seat, Ada saw her team chasing after the vehicle on foot.

Ada zoomed down the interstate at a speed that made her vision vibrate. At the road's horizon there was traffic. Citizens, most likely, returning to home after a shift in the Stratum of Knowledge. Despite the raging engine, and deadly speeds, Ada felt at peace. Because for much of Ada's life she struggled to understand right from wrong—to even understand what was true and imagined. But now, despite all repercussions, her choice was clear. She'd abandoned her post, subdued a fellow archivist, and prolonged the lifespan of revolutionary propaganda. Crimes worthy of nonexistence. But nonexistence was also the life for those who obeyed 6Di.

The traffic was because of a checkpoint. Here, Ada's speed slowed her nerves revved. She wondered if her team had already reported her missing, if the guards would have dispatched this quickly.

"Chloe," Ada asked, "on your commutes to and from work is this checkpoint normally here?"

"No. Never." Ada's eyes stared ahead, contemplating hundreds of maneuvers. "What should we do, Ada?"

Ada pulled onto the shoulder of the road, dodging stopped vehicles and slowly approached the guards that were halting traffic. A few guards formed a small line, arms drawn, to prevent her from proceeding. Ada's vehicle came to a stop at the feet of a few guards. She rolled her window down and said, "Good evening boys, I'm on a mission from HQ."

One of the guards spoke from under his shadowed face, "Ada Lawrence?"

"Yep, that's me."

The shadowed faces all glanced at another. The first one who spoke did so again, saying, "Get out and come with me."

"No—you don't understand, I really—"

"I said come with me—both of you."

Ada's hands shook. At first in rage. Then at the thought that she wouldn't reach Oriana if she caused a chase at this moment. Her foot twitched against the gas pedal. She was going to plow through these guards, and if she killed any of them it made no difference to her. Her trembling stopped. There was no scenario Ada could comprehend where her life wasn't drastically different in the next few seconds, no matter her decision. Ada's vision narrowed to a pinhole.

But a hand slapped atop her window's edge, drawing Ada back to the surrounding world. "Ada Lawrence," the guard said again, "I'm not who you think I am. We know what's coming."

Shaken, Ada repeated, "We?"

"Those who should not be remembered."

Ada exited her vehicle and followed the guard. Shortly after she and Chloe crossed the other side of the highway there was an explosion. Ada looked back to see her car in flames. The guard said, "It'll make them think you're dead for a while."

They hiked through the nearby forest, which was so dense

that even in midday it looked like dusk. The guard surged ahead, leading Ada and Chloe through an untraceable path that had them feeling lost again at every step. Ada never journeyed into the woods as a child. One because they only existed beside highways, as a means to absorb pollution. So, to her, trees, absorbing the toxins, were toxic. But also because from the outside the trees cascaded a wall of darkness. A place where light and foreign life could not escape. Nature, true nature, to the modern observer, behaved ravenously. In it, there was no reason or knowledge. Between the trees resided immeasurable mystery.

The guard led Ada and Chloe through a clearing in the brush. The immense foliage led to a natural enclave. Ada stood stunned in this crater. Nature had a peculiar way of layering and placing its objects, and now that she was immersed in its ecosystem, she believed that every detail had a reason. The moss thrived off the heavy atmospheric moisture. The shrubs flourished from the perpetual shade provided by many towering trees. Each component existed because of the presence of another. In nature, every strand of life existed both independently of and in total dependency on the surrounding life.

Ada began orienting herself beyond the immediate landscape, and noticed purgers sprinkled throughout the rocks and along the narrow waterway. Each sat with helmets at their sides, partaking in indiscernible chatter. From around a boulder appeared Oriana and Azophi. The towering duo approached Chloe and Ada. The purgers silenced, but the creek still trickled.

Oriana pierced the tension, and asked, "Is it making sense yet?"

Both Ada and Chloe chucked at the absurdity of the

question. "No," Ada said, still smiling.

"Your mother was in charge during and shortly after the war. At the time, the entire nation was traumatized by violence. Vivian, her then COO, was leaking information to the remaining press and government that 6Di could guarantee peace. Finally, your mother wrote *The Liberated Mind*. It was her manifesto about the dangers of the then nascent technology we now know as the BRiDG."

"The book you gave me," Chloe interjected.

"Exactly," Oriana said, "but this book was spun as justifying the war, interpreted as a defense for violence. And Vivian capitalized on that. Your mother was ousted as CEO and was given the choice to be remembered as a propagator of hate—or not at all. She chose the latter. She was supposed to just go to jail, disappear from the headlines, and then lead a quiet, normal life. But *The Liberated Mind*, which was supposed to be given to 6Di and destroyed, was lost. It's fable even to us how it never ended up in Vivian's hands. But somehow, our people got it."

"Is that why she was encaged, to be tortured?" Ada asked.

"Kind of," Oriana continued, "Vivian didn't believe in torture but she believed that she could find a way to completely map your mother's mind and retrieve all memories. 6Di thought that the moment she remembered where it was placed they could go directly to that location. But your mother truly didn't know where the book was."

"What's the fable?" Ada asked, pointing to Chloe "about how it ended up here."

"I don't know how, but eventually it found itself with Grace.

She was a bit rebellious herself—the secret kind. So she kept it to herself and continued her loyal service to 6Di. But she started talking about having it. And rumors were spreading fast. So, I sent one of our guards to retrieve it from her. She fought back and…well, you saw how it ended."

"You killed Grace?"

"We didn't want to. But you must understand that Grace would have eventually been caught with your mother's book. She would have disappeared, and with her, Elena's writings too. And once 6Di had Elena's book, they'd have no reason to keep her alive. It would have been a triple homicide if we didn't get to her first. They would have killed Grace, your mother, and her book."

"Is this why I was suddenly chosen as Vivian's heir?"

"Yes," Ada, "6Di sent you to find the book, claiming it was Grace's reconnoiter notebook. If you'd found it they would have escorted you to see your mother and choose which you'd like to survive. But you discovered the lies in the opposite order they wanted. And now, they're scrambling and the only choice you've left is which side it is you fight for."

Ada bent over in agony, squeezing her palms against her skull. Witnesses saw nothing obtuse about her physical state. There were no seizing muscles or protruding bones. Yet, Ada hollered as if her body were aflame. A nearby purger tackled Ada to the ground and shoved her mouth into the dirt, all the while imploring her to "be quiet." Believing their position compromised, guards at the enclave's perimeter faced outward and readied their weapons for an attack.

Azophi knelt next to Ada, looked to Oriana, and said,

"she's infected."

"Infected?" Chloe asked.

"She told us the other day that Vivian pushed a new update to her BRiDG. This made the BRiDG stronger. Elena wrote about this. The BRiDG could see the brain as a virus and attack it if the device becomes too powerful." Azophi leaned closer to Ada, hearing Lily chop away at Ada's neural pathways. "It's a madhouse in there."

"My god," Chloe said, "I hear it."

"Bind her up," Oriana said, "she'll try to rip out her own brain if we don't." A couple guards hopped on Ada's limbs—stretching her flat against the ground. She could hardly be subdued. Ada was possessed with pain, a novel neural-virus she'd soon learn was deployed by 6Di as a last attempt to override her memory. Ada's body convulsed as her eyes rolled back into her own skull.

Her head twitched. Eyes flickered. Shell shocked is what they called it in the Great War. This was a new kind of attack, though. One against and from within the mind. The purgers had seen this previously; moments before they removed a recruit's BRiDG. It was a fail-safe, an attempt to ruin the property that would survive without the BRiDG. Akin to lighting a ship on fire as pirates aboard. No one ever survived the onslaught. Their minds were beyond repair. Schizophrenic is what the early cases were called. But this was different. More terminal. The purgers knew it simply as burnt brain.

Oriana knelt next to Azophi, placed her hand gently on Ada's back, and whispered, "Hang on Ada, hang on."

"She's not going to make it." Azophi said. "We have to

remove her BRiDG."

"It's too embedded, she'll go brain dead if we remove it now."

"Not yet. She can make it."

"But O, she's——" A few dozen purgers watched Ada recklessly slam her body against the floor. The thumping sounded like a creature racing in the distance.

"I said not yet," Oriana repeated.

Then Ada's body locked. She gasped for air as if it were her last. But before she could finish that last breath, Chloe lunged at the back of her sister's head. Chloe removed the key from her pocket and inserted it inside Ada's BRiDG. With the twist of a wrist, Ada's BRiDG sprung out from the back of her skull. Ada's body froze. And the encampment fell silent.

The guards hopped off Ada's lifeless body. Chloe stood above it.

"What did you do?" Oriana snarled.

"What mother said to——"

Before Chloe finished her justification, Ada rolled face up. She looked dazed, yet present. Absent of the symptoms that plagued her moments before. She resided in aftershock. Then, after a few seconds, she sat upright and stared at the surrounding purgers. Her eyes appeared tougher, sharper, mismatching the delicate frame they crowned.

"It's done," Ada said, laughing. "It's done!"

Oriana knelt, grasped Ada by the shoulder and asked, "What does it feel like now, your mind?"

Ada's face straightened. She took a deep breath, then said, "I used to feel this lingering sadness. You know, that there's a part of your past you can't access. A part of you that's escaped your mind. It always made me feel incomplete. As if I was a sentence with a word missing on the tip of a tongue. And then I found that word; and for the first time understood what it felt like to be complete. Or closer to it. But…there are things I still can't remember. But now, these lapses feel completely a part of me. Like I'm some kind of bagel. The gaps aren't what makes me incomplete, but me—me."

Oriana nodded in agreement, then said, "6Di's greatest mistake was trying to reprogram the heart. When their technology was no longer concerned with accessing information, but overwriting desires. They put their codes against a few million years of genetics, and thought they could win. They thought a translation of facts could deliver their version of peace. But the same will to survive asteroid strikes, and frozen winters, and floods, and disease, and war resides in each of our hearts. To conquer the mind one has to first win the heart. And that's a terrain that belongs to no one, except in whose chest it rests." Oriana took a breath, "Ada, the same kind of incompleteness you've felt for so long is also felt by everyone. It's time you show us all how to also feel complete." Oriana picked up Elena's book and said, "it's what she'd want."

Ada took the book from Oriana's grip. The fibrous paper felt odd in her hands. She'd never read anything on paper without Lily; had never known what it was like to comprehend something new without her BRiDG attempting an override. Ada opened the book and felt as if she had begun reading a foreign language that she perfectly understood. Every word, a magnificent stroke of magic. Even the prepositions, those measly, meddling, add-ons, always getting between things.

"What happens," Chloe asked, "when everyone else starts to remember? Will their BRiDGs turn on them too?"

Ada closed the manifesto and said, "We're about to find out."

And just then, there was the sickening sound of gunfire. All scrambled except for Azophi, who plopped lifeless to the ground. What would become to be known as The First Neural War had claimed its first victim.

A LIBERATED MIND

Oriana feared the day of 6Di's retaliation for so long that its happening felt like relief. Oriana never wished her, or her husband, dead. But his death meant that she would never worry about him becoming an accessory for ransom. She never had to worry about his existence becoming reduced to a carcass in a cage. He was free. And now was she too, to die in the same fight as her dear husband.

Chloe, Ada, and Oriana ran towards a tunnel guarded by a dozen purgers. The run for their lives was curiously primal, for Ada and Chloe had never before heard a gunshot. And Oriana hadn't heard of any since the last Civil War. Its sound encapsulated a faceless violence. Captured a moment in history when killing was a part of everyday life, when it was mechanized, optimized, mindless. But it had been part of their gene pool long enough to trigger an innate response. And so, without truly understanding why, they ran.

The inside of the tunnel was unlit and cool. The ground so soft that the pounding of their running feet muffled to a hush.

"Where does this take us?" Ada asked, seconds before her sight eclipsed to darkness.

Oriana, leading, stopped before a fork, and said, "That depends, Ada. What move should we make next? Right takes us to the Stratum of Reason. Left to 20W's power grid."

"Ada," Chloe said, "you can't change the minds of obsoletes by recycling old sights to them. Show them what you've seen."

Left meant certain death; right prolonged it. Ada looked at Chloe and Oriana once more. Their faces floating like soft illusions in the near darkness. But, she could feel the intensity of their gazes. What would be worse than a forgotten fight? A mound of deaths with no explanation? "Okay," Ada said, "Oriana, return to the grid and round up the purgers. Chloe and I will head to the Stratum of Reason. I will bring back the forgotten. Chloe, grab Dad." And at that order, Ada plunged right, into a darkness that at its end promised to liberate them all.

Back in the forest, the purgers had fractured. Some dropped dead alongside Azophi. Others retreated further into the forest. And the few who remained surrendered to the force of guards that first shot onto their location. Once all weapons were grounded, Jeremiah leaped from over a ridge and asked, "Where's Ada?!"

"Completing her assignment," one of the defenseless purgers chuckled.

Four guards drew their weapons. But the purgers' laughter amplified. "Shut up!" Jeremiah shouted. The purger was bent over now, in a fit of laughter.

Yoko's eyes grew wide at the sight of the guns drawn, then even wider at the recollection of Oriana. "She's real?" Yoko whispered to herself.

Jeremiah, who lacked the same access as Yoko to files in The Sphere asked, "Who's real?"

With hands raised, and facing the bottom of a nearby barrel,

Yoko said, "Oriana, leader of the purgers. Records indicated she died—and effectively the movement did too."

"The purgers are long gone." Jeremiah said.

"Yes," the guard standing over Kimberley said, "we were." Kimberley's face confounded. Yoko's head tilted in confusion. And before they could register the totality of that confession, another barrage of gunfire unleashed, sending each archivist to a knee, as they drew to return fire. The surviving purgers died before they could confess anymore.

On one knee, Yoko tried to draw her gun. But, *click*. Her BRiDG made an edit. It was the first she'd ever felt. And though the experience was completely foreign, it was also unlike any other and she knew without a doubt what it was that just happened to her mind. She was incapable of placing her hand around her gun. Defenseless against the silhouettes that slowly rose over the same ridge the Memory Corps team leaped from. Yoko's teammates watched in awe. So, Yoko hid her panic. Then disguised her confusion at the sight of Vivian, Lex, and a host of a few guards.

"Better dead." Lex coolly said, as his identity unshadowed from above the ridge.

"Where's Ada?" Vivian asked.

"Ask them," Jeremiah said, pointing to the dead purgers.

"She's offline," Lex said. "And we have reason to believe she's been compromised."

"Offline?" Kimberley asked.

"As far as we can tell," Vivian said, "she's dead. The vehicle she took was found burning on the side of the road just north of here. But that seems a bit too convenient. We must from here on believe she's acting on behalf of the purgers. They're monsters. We first learned of their resurgence after a few of them posed as school teachers, and, locking a class into a room, dissected the BRiDG from each child. All they did was splatter those kids' brains across the room. Thirty kids opened like pez dispensers. We can't have that happen again…Treat Ada like a threat to the state. If seen, shoot her on sight."

Jeremiah and Kimberley nodded their heads as if Vivian had extracted a memory once forgotten. Yoko looked puzzled. She hadn't remembered that story. To Yoko's memory, the purgers were a people who believed life was to be lived without the BRiDG. She remembered they'd written unauthorized materials. But—*click*. No details of what was written came to her at this moment. So, instead of contradicting Vivian, Yoko stood in silence.

Vivian continued, "And that O, you all saw on this revolutionary material is from Oriana, their leader."

Lex, anticipating the next question, interjected, "Despite this horrible act, we never took their existence seriously. We thought that was a freak accident, more an act of desperation than malevolence. They went into hiding after their botched BRiDG removal—twenty years ago. Until today, all that was known of them was the aftermath of that room, and a note explaining their intent—signed with an O."

"But now," Vivian added, "they've demonstrated that this entire time they've been plotting their second strike. This one far more sophisticated and with a far larger network of sympathizers. They've managed to infiltrate our guards and now they're brainwashing obsoletes into a suicide mission."

At this moment two guards carried the old store keeper and her paraphernalia in front of Vivian. Before Vivian, the old woman fell to her knees. Vivian too knelt, and pointing at the poster a guard splayed with spread arms, asked, "Why did you hang this in your establishment?"

The woman didn't cower or recede. Absent of any emotion, she said. "Because there needs to be another way."

"You don't really believe that do you?" Vivian inquired.

"I do," the old woman said, raising her bound hands as a symbol of her frustrations.

Vivian stood without giving any other gesture. But Lex understood her meaning. So, he walked behind the old woman, placed a pistol to the back of her skull, and said, "Mark my word, not a single purger will remain by the end of this week." Then the old woman took her last breath. Her body flopped lifeless to the floor. And Yoko wondered, *In one week, will I be gone too?*

"The war has started," Vivian declared, "let's return to gather the troops." Lex, Vivian, and the remaining members of HQ's Memory Corps piled into one of the combat vehicles in a convoy awaiting them on the nearby road. The cabin contained an anxious quietness. Where even words seemed incapable of easing the angst felt by each. War was supposed to never be a reality. If they could win it definitively, though, it would never have to be. Just another forgotten fight.

Yoko's stomach churned amidst the silence. Hoping to relieve it, she asked, "Is Ada dead?"

"Until we have her body, she's not," Lex said.

"Where was she last?" Kimberley asked.

"Right where we last were."

Then Yoko started to ask, "Do you think the purgers—"

But Vivian stopped the conversation with a hard, "No." And to everyone in the car except Yoko, that command became fact.

Once at headquarters, Vivian ran a quick debrief with the team as Lex asked for a total-recall of all 800 archivists to report back to HQ's training facility. Inside the debriefing room, Vivian said, "Begin the cleanse. Remove any sightings of posters or audio relating to rebellious conversations. You know the key words. Purgers. Rebellion. O. Find those memories, and remove them. By tomorrow the whole thing should feel like a bad dream."

Vivian noticed Yoko twitch, and shift uncomfortably at the thought of editing memories. It seemed dated. Censorship is not a modern dilemma. Humans have maximized censorship according to the capabilities of their instruments. Its white lies whispered to lovers. Grades curved for good character. Blank memories of traumatic events. Censorship has always been a part of the human experience. And that's what perturbed Yoko in this moment: 6Di had deployed a machine to complete that which mankind lacked no talent. Or was it that at this moment the recollection of her life, and the absence of childhood memories was a corporate function?

For a moment, Yoko wondered about her first lie. How old she must have been when she said it. What sum of her words have been equally betraying. Yoko felt squeamish at the thought that every single one of her words as an archivist, as a guarantor to truth, was the opposite. She wondered if it was too late to die an honest woman. If she should join those back in the Stratum of Knowledge making one last attempt to revive their humanity. If they should all die, something other than *homo sapien* remains, Yoko reasoned.

Yoko's trance was broken when Jeremiah said, "You got it boss," as he and Kimberley exited.

The room was silent, Yoko stood before Vivian, whose back was turned. Yoko felt the energy shift in the room—as she realized it made no sense to send Jeremiah and Kimberley by themselves. As she realized—

"Are you okay, Yoko?" Vivian asked. Yoko's mind raced through an unwadable tension. She sought an answer. But her entire body, from the stem of her brain to the tip of her tongue, became sluggish. "Do you ever find yourself wondering why your chest has that scar?" Vivian asked instead. Yoko touched between her breasts, which beneath her shirt bore a scar akin to Ada's.

The silence returned, haunting Yoko's thoughts. So she fought it with the sound of her voice, "I remember—" Click. Yoko rubbed her head. "Sorry, I uhhh." *Click. Click. Click.* The rapidity of the clicking intensified. The sound deafened any other thoughts and sent Yoko to the floor, where she squealed in agony. Slowly, Vivian stood above Yoko, hands still grasped behind her back.

"Don't worry, Yoko," Vivian said, "you'll be better soon." The last thing Yoko saw before the pain sent her unconscious was the sight of two guards reaching for her body.

While Yoko was carried away, Lex began his recall. Each team of archivists from the 200 districts of the Stratum of Knowledge were *en route* to receive orders on how to thwart the purgers' coordinated forthcoming attacks. Lex didn't recall any of the guards in the Stratum of Knowledge. He assumed their allegiance was spoiled. Instead, he sent a command to their BRiDGs: terminate. At once, thousands of guards crumbled to the floor. Should any survive they'd certainly embolden their loyalty to the purgers. But Lex assumed none would remain.

Lex did recall the guards residing in the Stratum of Reason, those whose loyalty was still unproven. And since each guard's face was shrouded in shadow, he couldn't verify by watching for any kind of subconscious twitches, the kind Yoko unknowingly revealed. So he set a trap. He sent a message to all guards in the Stratum of Reason, acting as Oriana. For those guards who relied on the BRiDG alone, would have found the message incomprehensible, if it even registered in their minds at all.

So, one by one, those with divided alliances piled into a warehouse at 6Di's headquarters. The room was packed tight with guards who stood below as Lex entered from the second-story rafters, overlooking them all. The room fell silent. Whatever their allegiances, they at least possessed discipline; and even their breaths were coordinated in his presence. A few thousand men all inhaling and exhaling at once caused even the walls to expand and contract in unison. A few of the guards realized as soon as Lex began to speak that what they all walked into was a trap. Those few began to run for the exit. But it was blockaded.

From atop, Lex bellowed, "You're all here today because you believe in the power and sovereignty of Oriana. A criminal and terrorist to the integrity of Sixth Domain Industries. As Chief of Defense and protector of this corporate state, I deem you all traitors, and hereby sentence you to death." Lex couldn't contain the grin that grew on his face, as an unfolding flower touched by the morning sunlight.

And at that moment, Lex revealed a pistol from his right hip and placed it at the skull of the guard to his left and fired. That brave warrior embraced his fate. Despite knowing that he was living his last second he did so bravely, and saluted his comrades below. There was no click. Just a bang. And then, the guard slammed against the grated floor. His last thoughts as abstract as the blood that dripped onto his friends below. The new, Neural War now had claimed its second victim. And as long as Sixth Domain Industries won, he would be given no honors, no grave, because he would die without a name.

Then Lex departed the warehouse from the grated loft, escorted by a few guards whose allegiance he verified. Below him, the guards piled against the doorways hoping to escape. All they did was trample a few of their own to death. Some of the bold attempted to scale the vertical piping. But those same rods were where the flames began. Once Lex exited, the subtle leak of fumes raged into a scorching fire. Those climbing the pipes flaked to a charred corpse. Those below slowly waxed to figureless flesh. All the while the building they were within trained them to the stratum's edge, the closest they'd ever been to freedom.

When Lex exited the warehouse where he scorched the known traitors he walked across the hall into an auditorium equally sized, where he addressed those whose loyalty was without question. It's here that both the remaining guards and all of the archivists met. All except Ada and Yoko.

"I heard that the riots in 20W are so bad that we're going to terminate that district," whispered the translations agent assigned to 30E.

"Nonsense," said another archivist nearby, hearing her rumor, "we're here because we'll be the first to move into those spaces."

"I heard Ada will be announced as Vivian's replacement," said another.

"She's too young. They wouldn't announce that yet," said the corrections agent sitting nearby assigned to 46W.

It wasn't until Lex took the stage that the room fell silent. So silent that you'd believe not a single soul sat in the room. But they clamored to hear every syllable he was about to say. For, if there was any commonality in the rumors, it was that they all believed whatever was about to be said would change each and every one of their lives. Lex spoke into the vacuumed auditorium, saying, "As all of you know, recalls are used for the instances of extreme emergencies that require a full-unit deployment to issues that gravely affect the security of our operations and livelihoods." He took a pause, and then continued, "This morning we learned of a shadow organization called the purgers—they're a unit of people who live without BRiDGs. As you can imagine, their thoughts are incoherent and wild. They represent a true threat to anyone who is connected to the BRiDG and for such reasons should be eliminated. As to why we're just learning about them, it's believed that they kept themselves in hiding out of shame of the life that they chose. But arrogance got the best of them. They revealed themselves as the ones responsible for the recent uprisings in 20W. This overstep must be met with resistance. By the end of the week every purger will be destroyed—including their sympathizers. This is your mission. To remove them from this earth, and any possibility of them being remembered any moment hereafter."

At once, the stadium erupted. War was that unsung promise of resolving all existential worry. That's why so many men throughout history ran toward the frontlines. It was never about the brutality, the blood. It's always been about the purpose one believes they find in that battle. Which is exactly what the 800 sitting members of the memory corps believed about this fight. It's one thing to inherit history, and quite another to create it; to have a proactive part in the story that would be remembered. And now, finally, they each had the chance to say that they were part of the long arch of the human experience. To one day look at their children, or grandchildren, or someone else's, and say, "I was there, I'm the reason that happened." That's all any person really wants, is to point to a moment in time and say that they're part of the reason the timeline became the one it did. In the era of 6Di, that role was as important as ever. Under the umbrella of what was the first global political body, the effect each fighting member would have on the solidarity of the organization was enormous. This wasn't a fight for a country that was destined to fade in a generation. This was their opportunity to uphold the strength of the first legitimate enemy of the strongest political body that history has ever remembered.

It would be easy to misinterpret the source of enthusiasm for these members of the memory corps. Outsiders may believe that these were just bloodthirsty juveniles, desperate to project their youthful angst into the flesh of another living person—rendering their lives more valuable. By that interpretation, you'd miss the significance of what it meant to any living person to be called by 6Di for help. This wasn't simply a matter of being selected. This was of the highest honor. Whatever came of someone's life after this, they believed, would be seasoned with utmost honor. The ability to always look backwards and point to a moment in time, which, unabashedly, they'd call their climax.

The cheers transformed to confusion, though, when Lex, along with forty other guards he trusted, at once turned to nearby guards and executed each one on the spot. The rush of the room flattened as it was before Lex spoke a word. And in that space Lex continued his speech, "Purgers have infiltrated every part of our world, silently infecting your loved ones— disrupting the sovereignty of our organization. If you're still alive in this room, you're verifiably on the good side. Remember each other's faces. Because beyond this wall there's no telling who is who. Not until you hear them speak, listen to them speak. The more nonsense they speak the less likely they are to be connected to the BRiDG. Now, everyone head to their quarters. We will coordinate our deployment efforts and station tomorrow morning. Drink and sleep well. We're now at war. Live like every night is your last."

Outside the auditorium two guards dragged an unconscious Yoko into a cell inside the enclosed space of the encaged. She murmured and wailed, coming in and out of consciousness. Vivian trailed the trio as they mazed their way in front of an empty cage. The guards plopped her into it, connected her veins and skull to the various plugs and tubes that ran about the facility, which also lit the space a hazy red. Vivian noticed a shift in the shadows beyond where Yoko was being connected. The shadow neared Vivian and whispered, "Ada?"

AND THE TRUTH SHALL SET YOU FREE

While Lex and Vivian stood before a rapturous group of archivists and guards, Ada walked through the hall of defense and into the room of the encaged. She was accompanied by four guards whose allegiance was with the purgers. Despite the stakes of this encounter, Ada approached the final door in the hall without any concern or nervousness. She simply walked, as one does into their office. There was no reason to fear. Because as far as she was concerned, her decision to side with the purgers was a death sentence. And she wouldn't spend what might be her last days—her first days with a mind freed from her BRiDG—in fear.

Instead, Ada walked those windy, hazy halls curiously, like avenues to a new part of town. As she made her way deeper into the maze of cages, Ada made it a point to look at each person she passed and wondered who they were, why they were here, and if they would be remembered again once freed. With each step closer to Elena, Ada's heart fell heavier. What began as a journey of closure started to feel like the opposite. Each step a pluck of a dandelion's seeds: *to continue, to continue not*. It was the unfamiliar faces of the encaged that empowered Ada to continue forward. She glanced at each person she passed, and they returned lifeless gazes. Occasionally, she'd stop and look deep into their eyes, worried that even if they could be remembered, they'd never be loved again.

But this was nonsense, because even now Ada felt something akin to love for each of these strangers. Each of these poor souls, enduring the same hell as Elena. That made them a lot like her mother. How could Ada feel anything but adoration? She didn't need a memory to love, only perspective. And at that thought Ada no longer felt as if she was surrounded by unknown people. These encaged were her dear family. And this space their cemetery. But Ada was determined to make sure none were buried here. That for each person still alive, this place would mark the beginning of a next great chapter in each of their lives.

Ada was a single turn away from Elena's cage when she paused. A sickening thought crossed her mind that left her paralyzed: *she's not there.* The thought irregulated Ada's breath. But it was unfounded; and foolish to believe that lie. So, Ada turned the corner to reveal the truth. Ada locked her eyes onto her mother's now-empty cage. She blinked hard, disbelieving her eyes. When they opened again Ada saw the same empty cage. Tears roiled to her eyes, making the dark hazy room look like it was submerged underwater. Ada felt a sadness drowning her every thought. How badly Ada wished she could reach for her mother's necklace right now, to feel something that could remind of her of why she must continue to fight.

In this moment, Ada's memory revealed to her an early image. One so foreign it felt like a flash of film. But it was her memory as a child. Ada was standing before her mother's lap, smiling. They were at a house party. Her mother was laughing.

In this memory, little Ada turns, and sees Vivian grimacing. And at that sight Ada came to, like she'd just awakened from a bad dream. Its details too confounding to parse fact from fiction. Now she stood before an empty cage imagining her mother emaciated and lifeless. Ada wiped a solo tear from her eye. Damned was the world that required imagination to feel complete.

"Ada," one of the guards interrupted, "we must begin." And in that moment Ada recognized the immeasurable silence that Lily had always occupied. For the first time in her life she heard nothingness. That moment was so precious she dared not break it. Instead, Ada gave a short affirmative nod. Then they began.

None of the five knew how to safely unplug an encaged, or if it were possible. The guards approached each cage, horrified. They'd witnessed many of the atrocities committed by 6Di. None were as difficult to face as this. If not for Ada's cold confidence, the mission would have ended the moment they entered the space. While the guards stood before the perimeter of a cage uncertain of what to do once the door was opened, Ada proceeded into one adjacent like the property was rightfully hers. Her emphatic motions signified a boiling anger. Ada unplugged every component that sustained that poor, emaciated life. If her actions killed, Ada did not care. She only wished to free each lifeless carcass. To have them pass onto whatever life awaits, or fuel the revolution she was now orchestrating. To give them any life besides one under 6Di.

The first unplugged encaged lay lifeless against the floor. Blood dripped from the half dozen ruptures of the now removed wirings. Its body existed with no electro current stabilizers, no analytical monitors or oxygenating tubes, nor were they attached to the tubes that provided them both water and blended food. The once pitiful body withered to near termination. One guard kneeled to check on the body, and opened his mouth to protest Ada's tactics. Just as he did, the encaged took an enormous gasp, like it'd just been revived to life.

But Ada hadn't noticed any of the unfolding drama. She kicked in a door of another nearby cage. Its door concussed against a metal wall. As Ada ripped a torso-long tube out of another encaged woman's back, Ada shouted to a couple of guards, "Are you two going to help or not?"

It was difficult to count the number of the encaged. There may have been three hundred. Maybe four. The room was too mazy, too layered, to know what was a new corner or one traversed before. The total number didn't matter. Ada knew that she didn't have enough time to free them all. Not yet. "Everyone unplug three," Ada shouted again, before entering the cage of her third. This third cage brought Ada to a halt. For, at the moment when she reached to disconnect the first wire that meshed around this person's skull, he looked Ada in the eyes. And though Ada knew that this was a man she'd never met before, he looked uncannily like her father. It was the first time Ada had thought of Byron in months. And now, she couldn't shake the thought that though he was safe, 6Di had managed to place him in a similar cell, only he called his cage a home.

Ada had taken so long to disconnect her third and final encaged that the other guards finished before her. One walked to the outside of the cage where Ada stood still, staring into space, contemplating all she left behind, and asked, "Should we begin loading them?"

"Huh?" Ada asked, confused as to why she was standing with a ported wire in hand. "Oh…yes, yes. He's my last. I'll join you soon." The guard corralled the others to begin piling the fourteen bodies into the back of a large vehicle built for transporting archival materials between each stratum. In the moments after each one of these individuals were stripped from the lifelines that sustained their miserable lives each responded uniquely. One seemed incapable of acclimating to the new world; unable to catch their breath and deal with their eyes wide open. Some seemed unwilling to let go of life encaged, these individuals rushed to the back of the truck to reconnect themselves. But the guards swatted them to the floor.

The shoves triggered each to awaken. And, as if every available nanogram of adrenaline unleashed into their bloodstreams at once, they stood alert and as one charged the door. But that chemical burst of power wasn't backed by strong muscles. The rush gave a few guards a scare, but they slammed the door. One encaged reached for the door frame, and upon the cabin sealing his index finger plopped to the outside floor.

"All secure," said one of the guards to Ada.

"Good," Ada said. "I'm going to make sure nothing was left behind." Ada returned to the room of the encaged. But what she really desired was one last look at Elena's cage. One final reminiscence of the place where she would last lay eyes on her.

"We'll help," one of the guards remarked.

"No," said Ada, "stay here and protect the truck. Just in

case." They nodded in agreement.

Inside the facility the aura had shifted. As Ada stepped toward Elena's cage she felt sweat trickle down her palms, her heart beat quickly but to no rhythm. She placed her sweaty palm on her chest and stopped walking, afraid of what might happen to her if she took another step. She pondered why everything could have suddenly felt so different, so unapproachable. True, fourteen bodies were missing from the room. *It's just her cage*, Ada said to herself, believing that maybe she was afraid that when she turned the corner she would see her. But when she turned the cage she didn't see Elena's empty cage.

"Ada?" Vivian asked.

Ada's eyes grew wide at the sight of Vivian ushering Yoko.

"What are you doing with her?" Ada asked.

"Oh," Vivian delayed, with a smile that betrayed her intent. "I was giving her a tour."

"A tour?" Ada questioned, looking at a Yoko who seemed completely incoherent. "Yoko, what do you think—"

"Now Ada, our tour has just begun. Give her some time to acclimate. This is a lot for someone to process."

"No. I—"

"You must get inside now, Lex is looking for you. He needs your help Ada." Vivian looked around the space, aware of the cherry-picked bodies now missing. "And as you can see, we have less work to do here." Ada smirked at the bold-faced lies Vivian propagated. Ada always suspected that Vivian spoke bombastically, favoring euphemisms and indirectness. Whatever perpetuated the expanding web of lies upon which 6Di was built.

But those tiny diversions from the truth were too molecularly sized to pinpoint in the moment. They demanded observation by instrumentation. A chance to pluck it onto a petri dish and review each word through various lenses. But Vivian never allowed anyone that time—rather, the BRiDG never did. But Ada's mind was quiet now. No longer bombarded by the various, disconnected sets of thoughts that filled every bit of silence, that competed with the possibility that for a moment Ada might think, on her own. "Go on, now." Vivian said, as if speaking to her barn dog.

"I said no," Ada firmly announced. Vivian paid no attention to Ada's retort, and instead proceeded to place Yoko into a cage within arm's length. But when Vivian opened the door, Ada slammed it shut.

"What are you doing?" Vivian asked, beside herself.

"I'm taking her with me."

"She's not needed for this operation, Ada." Vivian said, snickering as she again reached for the door. Once again Ada slammed the door shut and this time stepped in front of it. "Ada, you're not right you're—"

"Do not say another word, Vivian."

"Your insubordination will not be forgotten."

"Then make sure you tell them it was me who put you here. Do you lie even to yourself? We're at war Vivian. And once you're exposed nobody—not even the delusional—will believe in your reign. Because where you sit is my chair, and my feet are tired." Ada re-opened the cage, and said to Vivian, "Now you go." Vivian protested, when two of the four guards protecting the truck outside appeared and nudged her into the open cell. She went in without a fight; because Vivian was never seen fighting. Her battles were always internal: of the mind and thoughts and ways to manipulate both. Even now she didn't believe there wasn't a physical solution to her incarceration—a perspective that allowed Vivian to always see a few steps ahead. But at this moment it was Ada, whose mind was liberated from 6Di, that could think furthest ahead.

Gunshots pulsed throughout the room.

"The BRiDGd!" a guard shouted, referring to 6Di loyalists. Ada scrambled to the ground, sealing her face and body to the floor. Her face winced at the escalating sound. Each blast more deafening than the last. She felt a strong tug at her arm. She looked up and saw a guard carrying Yoko on its back. "Let's go!" the guard shouted between gunfire. Ada stumbled to her feet, looked back at the cage of her and Vivian's confrontation. Ada craned her neck toward where Vivian was just caged. Ada slowed. The guard affirmed what she was seeing, "She's gone Ada, let's go!"

Outside, Ada hopped into the driver's seat of the vehicle. Yoko was splayed across the backseat, entering and exiting consciousness. Only one guard rode as passenger. The other three remained on foot to defend Ada's vehicle from the hundreds of oncoming assault from the BRiDGd. Those three conducted a suicide mission. For any who survived, the race was on to 20W.

Since each guard and archivist assigned to the Stratum of Knowledge was recalled for an emergency session, the stratum had been unguarded. It was policed only by the BRiDGs embedded into each obsolete's cerebellum. If not for the hundreds of purgers who came out of hiding, the district would have been perfectly controlled. But Oriana had moved swiftly. Hundreds of purgers flooded the streets of 20W and under the orders of Oriana began removing each obsolete from their dwellings. The entirety of the city soon stood in the streets.

Corydon sat at a cafe that he and Ada used to frequent, when he witnessed the first purger walk down the street. His mind glitched as his BRiDG tried to correct his vision and remove their presence. The single purger appeared as a loyal guard. But then another purger entered his vision. Then another. And another. His vision corrected too often. Corydon placed his latte atop his saucer, and missed. The physical world suddenly made no sense. Just as his espresso was about to drip off the table and onto his clothes, a purger grabbed him by the arm. Muffled from behind its helmet it said, "Come with me to the archival facility." Corydon stood and lost his footing. The purger tugged at Corydon's arm, all the while he saw the guard as an illusion.

It was this way for each obsolete that was dragged into 20W's town square. Each arrived with a case of vertigo and a frightening sense of self-delusion. It was only for the fact that each and every other obsolete had a similar story that kept them sane. Sane enough to stand, awaiting whatever was next. Corydon stood silent, shook. He might have remained completely entranced if not for a pair of nearby obsoletes who rumored "Can't believe Ada."

"No chance," said an obsolete closest to Corydon.

"It's just what I heard," said the other.

"What did you hear?" Corydon interrupted.

"Ada. She's dead."

"What did you say?" Corydon asked.

"I —" the man looked puzzled at Corydon, "I don't actually remember. I'm sorry."

"No, you said that Ada is dead?"

"Did I?" the man inquired, his entire body twitching twice to the corrections of his BRiDG. Indeed, the rumors, even if repeated once, couldn't be uttered again, since those too become vaporous thoughts, evaporating the moment they were spoken. This was the first sign of 6Di's last attempt to preserve control of its obsoletes. The BRiDGs were fully throttled to edit those who could think beyond it, permanently. In war, it was no longer about combatting thoughts. But, the minds that harbored them. Their assault was the same that Ada had endured earlier that day. And as the obsoletes gathered in the town square, their collective twitches, and reaches for their mind, revved a disconcerting energy that stirred curiosity into chaos.

"Are —" Corydon struggled to find the words, "are…you… ok—" He spoke like his tongue suddenly was possessed with an impediment. The sound of the *k* turning over and over again like an old car engine on a cold Midwest morning. Corydon's body buzzed. He'd never experienced a seizure before, but he assumed this was it. And it seemed that everyone around him was experiencing the same as well.

Corydon felt his body multiply into two, allowing him to feel both sadness and confusion. For he did not understand what was beginning to happen to his body, nor why his town was being gathered outside the archives. And he couldn't believe the rumors that Ada was now dead. Yet, of all the rumors, it was Ada's death that remained the most grounding. And at that thought, Corydon felt a steady, anchoring sadness. One that materialized a single teardrop to his eye at the thought that he would never see his childhood friend again. That he would never get the chance to understand why it was she took his arm that day he was convicted guilty of possessing inaccessible truths. He peered at his arm. The one Ada amputated. His vision flashed, revealing to him an illusion of his arm intact. He turned away in fear at a thought he'd never had before this: *what if its absence was the illusion?*

Near Corydon, obsoletes crazed. Their lives were defined by predictability. They lived a transactional life, where actions corresponded with predetermined prices and rewards. Now, this was the first moment in the remaining obsoletes' lives where their fate seemed unknown. And this mystery caused each obsolete to think thoughts they'd never remembered having before. Because though life in the Stratum of Knowledge had been good—it had also been relatively flat. Not a mesmerizing thing; nor one filled with any particular highs or lows. It was a steady kind of life. One which begged questions like, *what's a life worth living that's already written?* Corydon felt this thought appear and disappear as he stood in the crowd. Then another: *what was the point of waking up one day after the next to face what was already determined?* He craved a destiny. Something not yet written, endless possibilities. That was the unspeakable burden under Sixth Domain Industries—the possible had ended. And that's why people joined the revolution.

Oriana had a tight window to engage the obsoletes of 20W who were now all gathered outside the district's archival facility.

She predicted that 6Di's guards and archivists were closing in on the district and would arrive any minute. Oriana stood atop the archival facility, that gargantuan chapel where information and opportunity were housed. Her voice boomed from the edge of an ornate parapet, "People of 20W!" She noticed bunches of obsoletes twitching below. "You must all wonder why you're gathered here and who it is I am," Oriana continued. From below, Corydon shook his head in disbelief at the reappearing figure atop the archives; at the intermittent message she was sending— as if from a car radio while driving past a station's radius.

Oriana spoke more, "This is not the first time you've wondered what might be wrong. Though, this may feel like the first." The rustlings amongst the crowd intensified. Corydon slapped his one remaining hand against his skull, trying to ease the sudden pain he felt in his mind. "You all remember Ada Lawrence. You believe she's dead, which is wrong. Just like it was wrong that you believed her a traitor for punishing one of your own." Corydon felt Oriana's far gaze zero in on him, along with the eyes of hundreds more, all the while he remained hunched over in neural agony. "The only way to break the bondage that binds you all is to trust that there's a world beyond your sight." Oriana swallowed to speak again. Then, gunshots. She ducked behind the parapet. A couple purgers rushed to her side as she smelt the unmistakable scent of paper ablaze.

Lex watched the assault through binoculars while positioned from the stratum's highway that divided it from east to west. He watched the first batch of guards whose loyalty was undeniably to him unleash a barrage of bullets into the crowd. "Dammit!" he shouted.

"What is it, boss?" Jeremiah asked.

"I said no headshots. We need to preserve each mind. I don't care about a body. Even a dead person is a data source. But dammit if their minds are mush, we lose all of it."

"Understood." Jeremiah interjected, as he hopped into a nearby all-terrain vehicle to join the fight. "I'll remind the troops." His engine roared.

"Jeremiah!" Lex shouted. "Except for Ada. If you see that traitor, take the headshot." Jeremiah nodded as Lex grinned at Vivian who was sitting beside him.

6Di had accomplished the ultimate element of surprise by disabling the ability to hear the exact decibels of their guns firing for those who were still dependent upon their BRiDG. So when the barrage began, all the obsoletes watched confused as Oriana senselessly ducked out of sight. Then looked at another even more perplexed when their neighbors dropped to the floor as blood began seeping from their bodies. The obsoletes chalked up such sights to another bizarre set of delusions, and so most stood at attention, waiting for Oriana to reappear, while witnessing more of their neighbors drop to death. Corydon, however, did hear gunshots. And upon the first barrage he ducked low, then buried himself under a purger who was shot and lifeless.

Under that cold body Corydon's pain increased. His body quivered from agony. He wanted nothing more than to scream, for his own hands to turn into knives so that he could dig inside his mind and once and for all remove his BRiDG. Instead, he was left to endure the pain in utter silence and stillness. To not let any guard nearby know that under this purger rested a living man. Corydon counted the seconds of each breath. Four to inhale. Five to exhale. The beginning of each exhale was a minor victory that eased his pain; the exhale that bounced off the hardening body above him reflected a sad fact. The only thing that may be remembered about this purger's life was this moment. Purgers had no written records either of or about them. They lived and died in anonymity. Yet, collectively, their existence symbolized something greater than any set of memories. They were not footnotes in history, but an entire genre. This man above Corydon, now dead, represented another way of living. A way Corydon had never before comprehended. And now couldn't again, as his pain eclipsed any ability for him to think a single thought.

The guards who mowed their way through the unaware crowd marched deeper into it, stepping over bodies like freshly whacked weeds. Methodically. Senselessly. As one moves through any therapeutic chore. From under the body where he hid, Corydon sensed a guard within feet of where he lay. Corydon fought every instinct within him to not tremble, to not shake, nor moan. But the pain did not relent. And Corydon yelped—at that same moment when gunfire ceased. Corydon squeezed his eyes like fists. He lay unsure if the guard had heard his muffled bark, but dared not give him another reason to believe that someone in proximity was still alive. Corydon clenched his jaw; so tightly that he felt three teeth from his top left row crack. Their break initiated an odd sensation of relief. The warm, tinny taste of blood trickled in his mouth, quenching his thirst. Then the gunfire continued. Empty brass dropped beside his ears. And that warm sensation that began in his mouth quickly spread through the rest of his body. *I've been shot,* Corydon thought.

He laid still, believing there was no point in running. He was wounded, or so he thought. And still, his BRiDG continued to assault his entire nervous system. Yet, that pain seemed to dull at the thought that these were his last breaths. Corydon imagined what would be remembered of him. If anything would. He'd never been to a funeral before. His first would be his own. As his mind calmed at that bizarre thought, as he felt himself at the edge of surrender, his body warmed. What he believed was blood profusely pouring from his punctured pores was in fact something else. It wasn't blood, but fire. The purger he hid beneath was set aflame. Those flames had grown like vines, wrapping themselves around Corydon's body. Unlike the torturous pain of his rogue BRiDG, the flames incited a primordial sense of panic he could not ignore. Without thought, Corydon tossed the dead man from off his chest, stood, and ran. These were the first steps Corydon remembered taking without a BRiDG.

He ran far enough from the flames that his body cooled. But with each step Corydon felt displaced from his own self. Without his BRiDG he felt ungrounded, suddenly aware of life beyond what 6Di had permitted him to see. He saw with utmost clarity the details of his fully intact arm that he believed was amputated months before. He saw bodies piled, maimed with lead. He saw the cafe he sat at earlier, now abandoned. He rushed into its door, locked it behind him and stared in bewilderment as he watched his fellow obsoletes toss themselves into the quickly spreading flames.

Corydon was lucky. Most obsoletes, seeing the flames, peered at it, transfixed. And slowly, like greeting a forgotten lover, walked toward the wriggling flames until they were totally immersed. Just another line of code for 6Di that overwrote the inherited logic which said do not touch. Under the control of rogue BRiDGs, obsoletes couldn't even access the will to survive. And now, each of those obsoletes met the most grotesque of ends, as their skin bubbled like cheese atop of a fine french onion soup. People, after all, were just artifacts to 6Di. And in the end all artifacts were destined for ash.

From a nearby road, Vivian turned to Lex and laughed. "It actually worked," she said, beside herself. Lex stood, arms crossed extra tight, like he was hugging himself, while constraining an undeniable grin.

"Good work," Lex said, looking at Kimberley, who stood behind a dozen monitors, on which she released new code into the BRiDGs of nearby obsoletes. She, effectively, shaped the minds of the enemy to absolute submission. Only those whose BRiDGs broke in the overtaking would have the choice to fight.

Vivian leaned closer to Lex and whispered, "How's Elena?"

Lex checked a nearby monitor, and watched graphs of her vitals, "Alive."

"Good."

"How'd it go, finding Ada?" Lex asked.

"Afraid she chose war."

"So much like her mother," Lex laughed.

"Let's bury them side by side," said Vivian, as she looked out into the town, where obsoletes rushed into flames.

Nearby, at the edge of 20W, where Ada first met Oriana, Ada arrived with Yoko, one guard, and a dozen encaged people loaded into the back of the vehicle. Ada slowed the vehicle to a halt. And just before she came to a stop, the guard sitting next to Ada said, "You know, I was there. That day when Grace was killed."

"You were?" Ada asked.

"Yes, I was Guard 40 that day. The one——"

"Who delivered my punishment."

"Yeah. I didn't realize. I couldn't have guessed."

"No, it's not your fault," Ada assured him, bringing the vehicle to a halt.

"Ada," the guard paused, "what if no one remembers?"

"Remembers what?"

"Any of this. The fight. The forgotten. Us."

Ada sighed, "Then at least for a moment we will. Ready?" Ada asked. The guard nodded. Yoko did too.

As they exited the vehicle Yoko asked, "Where are we?"

"20W's power grid," Ada answered, as an arc of electricity shot feet above their heads. Yoko ducked to the ground.

"It's pointless," Ada said, "to duck. If it's a deadly one, you'll never be the wiser." And it was then Yoko noticed the old, decaying bodies littered across the grounds. Muffled gunshots fired in the distance, all of which they ignored.

Ada gripped the handle of the door's back hatch and, sternly, said to Yoko, "This isn't going to be easy to see."

"You said they're people right?"

"What's left of them," Ada said, punching the handle down and swinging the door open. In the short hour drive from the Stratum of Reason, the smell of the dozen rotting people compounded, so that once the door opened the fresh oxygen, like a flame to a leak, exploded into an unapproachable grotesque scent. Both Ada and Yoko leaped backwards, coughing. From a few feet away from the trailer, Yoko saw the forgotten—those encaged—for the first time. But she'd always remember. The scent was unforgettable, for it was also unforgivable.

"Shit," Ada muttered as she inched closer to the truck's bed. Of the dozen encaged it looked like one had died in the journey. Or at least, there was one lying lifeless on the floor nearest the door, resting in a puddle of blood from their amputated fingers, while the other eleven huddled together in the back, fearing anything that wasn't sharing in their suffering. Timid to any force unrecognizable, benign or otherwise. Ada held her breath, reached her middle and index finger to below the still body's jaw, and checked for a pulse. The cold touch was enough of a hint, but Ada dug at a few more spots across their neck in search of something rhythmic. Ada's lips pursed as she removed her hand from its neck. Her heavy exhale a sign of what life she did not find.

"What do we do with…it?" Yoko asked.

"Help me unload." Ada said sternly. Yoko glanced at the nearby guard, hoping he'd volunteer instead. But he was on watch. They each took a half. Ada the top. Yoko the bottom. And dragged the dead woman off the truck bed and gently onto the rocky, sandy ground. "I've got her from here," Ada pronounced, dragging the bloating corpse across the jagged landscape.

"Boss!" said Guard 40, who, on watch, had raised his rifle toward the horizon. Ada glanced his way, and saw a bouncing silhouette headed their direction.

"Shoot!"

Guard 40 squeezed his finger to the trigger. Another ounce of pressure and a bullet would exit the chamber. But something unsettled Guard 40 about shooting this oncomer. They ran so feverishly, frantically, that they couldn't have been on an assault, but instead seeking help. He relinquished the pressure from the trigger. Instead, focused his vision on identifying who was running into 20W's grid. "No," he finally said calmly, "it's one of us."

Both Yoko and Ada stood beside him now and asked who.

"I don't know. Here," he said, handing his rifle to Ada.

She peered through the optics and saw the unmistakable identifying full-faced helmet. Though from this distance she couldn't tell who it was. "A purger," Ada whispered.

"I thought we were supposed to meet them in the square?"

"Let's see." Ada said, relaxing her stance. The incoming purger was a couple hundred yards out.

Yoko pointed back toward the woman they dragged out of the truck, "what should we do with her?"

"We'll have to come back for her," Ada said.

Yoko nodded. Then, pointing to the rest of the encaged, asked, "do you think they have all been erased from our memories?"

"I know so."

"Who here did you forget?"

"No one here," Ada said.

Yoko surveyed Ada's face, as if it were dangerous, and wondered if she should proceed. She halted. Then, looking at the oncoming purger, said, "I hope they bring good news."

A minute later the purger, who Ada had never met, arrived. They huffed. In between each rapid breath told Guard 40, Ada, and Yoko about the onslaught happening in town.

"Are there any survivors?" Ada asked.

"Yes, we've many in hiding. Just as many have scrambled on their own. But Ada," the purger paused, "the BRiDGs are malfunctioning." Ada kept her gaze, awaiting details. "Randomly, obsoletes are falling over in pain, like they're having a heart attack of the mind. Most who do don't survive."

"I know," Ada said matter-of-factly. "I had one. It's dead now, my BRiDG." The group looked at Ada perplexed. "But we need to stick to our plan."

In a fit of disbelief, Yoko announced, "what's the difference? They're in our minds. We can't win this Ada."

"Do you believe that, or are you programmed to think that?" Yoko inhaled quickly to deliver a biting retort. But she had no words. Perhaps Ada was right. Perhaps this fight could be won.

Ada touched Yoko's chest, and asked, "What if you found out that behind this scar was a person you loved so deeply that you'd endure any pain to see again? Would that give you a reason to fight—to see beyond the walls of this big cage that we call home. Those people in there are just like you and me. Only, we saw their cages, and we're just now beginning to see ours. We need everyone to see these people, then they can decide which side they're on."

Yoko went to speak, but the purger did first, "Come," he said, "we don't have much time."

INTO THE SIXTH DOMAIN

The unidentified purger led Guard 40, Ada, Yoko, and the twelve forgotten through a windy set of roads in 20W. Each turn took them closer to nowhere. And with each unfamiliar turn Ada felt more displaced from her hometown. Has that much really changed since she left this little district nearly six months prior? Ada tried to calm herself by remembering that she hardly ever explored any of 20W, aside from the bars she'd pass on her way home after work. Still, Ada couldn't shake the fact that none of this space felt familiar. The streets were tagged and buildings were drab and crumbling. *Is this how it's always been*, Ada wondered, *to those without a BRiDG?*

Yoko neared Ada and whispered, "Where is he taking us?"

Ada shrugged, and said, "I-I really don't know."

"Should we be worried?" Yoko asked.

"No," Ada said, "he's with us."

"How do you know?"

"Now," Ada said, looking at the dilapidated mess her BRiDG always censored, "I'm afraid I see everything as it is."

"Don't mistake everything, for more," Yoko said.

The purger led Ada and company into the lobby of the building where Ada once lived. This too was a lifeless space. Absent of the ordained gold she remembered seeing as an obsolete. He spoke, and said, "If we head to the top, the remaining obsoletes will be able to see us from the square." He reached to call for the elevator, but hit the down button, and said, "Shit."

The doors opened before he could tap the up button. "Let's take it," he affirmed, "no one else is here." He stepped forward, holding the door ajar so that the fifteen could fit aboard the oversized elevator. Once all were on, he hit the button that would take the elevator down and into the mines. Before anyone aboard registered what he'd done, the purger slipped past the door and drew his weapon. "I'm sorry," he said plainly, as the doors closed and all on the elevator descended into a trap.

A quarter mile from the elevator shaft where Ada descended, Vivian ascended into a parapet overlooking a mass of obsoletes who mindlessly ran into fire. Some, stuck in another loop, ran in circles, trampling upon corpses and freshly fallen of their once beloved. Among the chaos were Chloe and Byron, whose neuropathic dependencies upon the BRiDG were too strong. They'd returned to 20W in search of Ada, but had been drawn to the chaos at the town square. And both would never again be seen leaving this crowd. At the moment there were untold numbers of missing, wounded, or killed. If 6Di would win this war—the tally would be zero.

Atop the parapet, Vivian's voice boomed, "Look at your feet! This is what happens when you disobey; when you believe that you are ready to reason!" The obsoletes obediently looked down at their feet and marched in place, squishing the soupy remains of those who disobeyed. Vivian continued, "You are to trust and to hold steadfast to the truth which your BRiDG makes available to you. Those below you exemplify what it means to disavow the BRiDG that so faithfully serves you what is true. There is no tolerance in this world for lies. And if you happen to go astray, to dedicate yourself to falsehood, you will be eradicated. For you are no different than the most dangerous of lies." The crowd erupted into celebration, tossing mush from the decayed above their heads as fleshy confetti.

Corydon had witnessed the purger lead Ada, Yoko, and a dozen others into the obsoletes' residence of 20W. This was still his home. Where he woke up each morning to continue his quota with one arm. And it was where he returned to each night, tipsy and stumbling. He'd drank daily since Ada amputated one of his arms—or when he thought she did. And each night since, he fell deeper into a depression. Until, not even the whiskey that touched his tongue had a bite. So when family and loved ones expected his drinking to wane, Corydon steadied. Still chugging away his sorrows each night. Finding it better to live with no feelings, than only a resounding pain.

But tonight Corydon was sober, because he finally saw the truth. His arm had been there all along. After his BRiDG deactivated, every sense felt anew. Nothing he experienced now he wished to numb. If anything he worried that he'd become hallucinogenic. He wondered how it was there, his arm, dangling, just as he always remembered. He'd had visions of this before. Moments when he swore he saw his arm. It was a sight that excited him so much that he dared not reach for it, dared not touch it, out of fear of feeling the disappointment he'd feel when all he grasped was air. So, when Corydon watched Ada enter the building he didn't recoil in fear or charge her in anger like he so often imagined he would before today. He watched quietly, aware that what he was witnessing was perhaps impermissible.

When the purger who escorted Ada and crew into the building exited alone, Corydon stepped out from the brush against the lobby hall where he once hid, making his presence visible. Corydon walked three steps, then four. Then eight. Surely the purger had seen him by now. But he kept walking toward the elevator, and the purger toward the exit. In two steps Corydon would pass the purger's field of vision. He didn't know what he would do once he did. He never imagined he would. He'd never have to.

It did cross this purger's mind that perhaps he was unseen. That maybe this was the luxury of those who lived as nonexistent. He was posing after all. Because underneath his purger appearance, he was a loyal guard to 6Di. He didn't know how to treat an obsolete, someone who was not supposed to know that he existed. But he couldn't betray his true alliance. A step before Corydon was out of sight, he belted, "What are you doing here?"

Corydon considered ignoring the voice, which he did, for a step, and had he known that the disguised guard would have also continued walking if his presence wasn't acknowledged Corydon would have entered the elevator without another peep. But Corydon noticed the guard grab his head—as if to relieve a sharp pain that signified his mind could fight 6Di's newest BRiDG upgrade. So, Corydon turned and said, "Excuse me?"

The defiance took the guard by surprise, stirring a striking anger. "Back to the square!" the guard demanded.

"Where are they?" Corydon asked, pointing to the elevator.

"That is none of your business," the guard said sternly, as he withdrew the same pistol he pointed at Ada.

Corydon did not know what to believe, what was real, what was worth his fear. So, he stepped calmly toward the barrel of that pistol. Aligning its small hole with the center of his forehead, like he was docking into a charger, fueling some existential energy that he couldn't otherwise access. With the pistol against his skull, Corydon felt the cold metal tremble against his skin. "What are you afraid of?" Corydon asked, "I'm the one with the gun to my head."

The guard said nothing, so Corydon continued, "You're not a purger. Or if you were, you're not anymore. And now you're confused if you're on the wrong side or not. But let me tell you that it's a decision you're more than likely incapable of comprehending. You can ask the question, but you don't know the answer. You search for it in your BRiDG. You look for something else to tell you what to do and how to live. And this moment, right here, with your pistol against my skull, it's terrifying because if I were a betting man I'd bet that it's the first time in your life you've had to decide with no one to tell you right from wrong." Corydon's voice bellowed up, across, and around the vast and empty lobby. Each reverberation multiplied Corydon's inescapable presence. As if the single man who stood across the guard actually numbered in the hundreds.

"Let me make this simple," Corydon said, "if I'm wrong pull that trigger. Eradicate me like every other lie we're designed to destroy. But if what I just said has even a sliver of truth you need to let me go. You need to let me find the end of that strand, because where it leads is a mystery worth uncovering." The guard's finger quivered against the trigger. Corydon curled his nose, raised his eyebrows, and demanded, "Decide already." The guard holstered his pistol, and without another word turned to exit the building.

But Corydon stopped him, asking, "Where are you going?"

The guard was speechless, having never been affronted like this before, not by an obsolete.

"Are you choosing to leave, or is that someone else telling you to go?" Corydon hit the down button to call an elevator car. The car next to the one Ada entered was ready to depart. The door opened with a chime. "There's room for two," Corydon said, his hand blocking the door from closing. Then, the guard began walking toward the elevator, and when he stepped aboard Corydon pressed M to begin their journey into the mines.

Aboard the elevator, Ada had jammed every button in hopes that she could reverse or stall the direction of their car. It had been a short journey aboard the elevator. Just a few floors. But Ada had gone through, what she knew were, the entire spectrum of emotions. An erratic few seconds which soothed when she began a long, steady breath, the same one she'd used hundreds of feet above each morning, when she awakened herself with an ice-cold shower, as dreams of citizenship grappled in her mind. After Ada calmed, there had been silence, a sinking, sickening silence anchored by the thought that what awaited them when the doors opened was most certainly death. But Ada, solemn at that thought, turned crazed again. The thought of her journey ending from one slight act of deception. All the risks and hopes she'd taken and acquired to finally reveal 6Di for all its horrors, suddenly gone?

If there's any fairness in death it's in its surprise. It is a fact that remains abstract until, in a moment so swift, it becomes the only absolute. The last fact of a person's life. But to face it slowly, to contemplate its meaning, to have it lurking toward someone foot by foot is maddening. One should never see themselves as dying, live in any state in which they are both alive and yet not. That is unfair. That is a breach of borders, to which the end result is war in the battlespace of that person's mind. That is what was incited the moment Ada began her descent. She always understood death. But to have it approach with each floor spiraled her mind into an assault against itself: as if death were bartering, not commanding, what time she had left. It was up to Ada now if she should live or perish.

It was this entrapment that marked Lex's greatest mistake. Lex's greatest weakness was his inability to remember history, therefore he was doomed to repeat it. Lex would never remember the words of the great Sun Tzu, when he wrote, "Do not press a desperate foe too hard. When a foe is cornered, they must fight for their lives and will do so with the energy of final fear." Ada was stuck aboard an elevator, with no escape. If there were any word that so adequately described her fear, it was final. For after those doors opened, the few seconds after would decide if she lived another day or not.

"What are we going to do?" Yoko asked frantically.

"Give me your weapon," she said to Guard 40.

He gave his pistol to Ada, and added, "It won't work down here."

"What?" Ada asked quizzically.

"Old rumor. But—no one's ever fired a weapon in the mines."

"I've been the first to do a lot of things around here." Ada said.

"So the door opens and you hope this thing works, and that there aren't fifty people on the other side and you somehow shoot all of them and we all stand here untouched, is that your plan Ada?" Yoko asked.

"I-I don't! Yes! Yes, that's my plan Yoko! Do you have a better one?" Ada shouted. Yoko tightened her jawline and shook her head no. "We'll figure it out. We will."

The elevator rocked as it jolted to a pause. The sign at the top corner of the elevator read M. Then, a ding; that familiar chime that one had arrived at their final destination. Ada drew the pistol, pointing it toward the door which began to crack apart. She exhaled, readying herself to fire the weapon, then yelped. All she saw was her mother, Elena.

WHAT MEMORY AM I?

Ada stood still before her mother. Until, a cold breeze rushed into the elevator and awakened Ada to the present. Elena's face was lit by the brightness from the elevator. Behind her was total darkness. Ada lowered her weapon and stepped toward Elena, breaching the elevator door. She was fixated on her mother's eyes, which since she last saw her had sharpened—displaying the thousands of hard nights etched into her mind. Ada's heart raced as she neared her mother. Elena stood solid and listless. An emotionlessness which Ada should have heeded.

"Mom," Ada said, reaching for her hands. Elena's face hung low.

Behind Ada, Lex said, "I thought you'd never show," as he blockaded the elevator from closing. Ada's skin curled as she watched a shadowy Lex float toward her direction. She turned to escape what she now knew was a trap. But there stood Jeremiah and Kimberley preventing her exit. "I've been wanting to get the team back together," Lex said with a smile that pierced the dark.

Lex stepped from out of the shadows and into plain sight. His hands were wrapped neatly behind his back, orchestrating his authority. "I always liked this place," Lex said, encircling Ada and Elena. "Some of my brightest moments came from here. I don't know if it's the cool air. The raw earth. Or just the fact that we're

standing so far below earth's surface—at an impossible depth—
to power above an unfathomable life." He paused, stuffing his
nose to Ada's cheek, and sniffed. "Your father seemed to love it
down here too, Ada. He was a wonderful laborer." Lex patted the
back of Ada's head. She tightened her jawline with enough force
to dust the top layers of her back teeth.

"It's all over, Ada," Lex continued. "Well, this little journey
of yours. Vivian still believes you deserve to be her heir—says
that the only person deserving of her title is the one who nearly
took it away. It's an odd perspective, but respectable. But for all
the trouble you caused—don't worry about it Ada. Don't worry.
Those who for a moment believed a glitch was possible will
expose themselves and will take care of them expediently. But
most, nearly everyone, will wake up tomorrow, and forget this
whole day happened. It's beautiful, isn't it? To let each day be
anew. To disfigure time from itself and Tetris history together
according to magnanimity—not the unfortunate undertow of
happenstance. Doesn't that excite you Ada, that we can wipe
away pain? What better invention is there than that?"

Lex halted his speech, anticipating Ada to answer. Ada stared
ahead, at Elena's hung head, at the breathing skeleton of the
woman who penned a manifesto against this organization that she
had once begun and under which they were now all imprisoned.
If not for the fact that she was standing, Ada would have believed
Elena spineless. All that remained in question was her spirit.

"But I want you to be happy too, I really do Ada. But I'm not
sure if you want the same." For the first time in Lex's diatribe, Ada
gaze broke. Ada's eyes shifted to Lex. Yet the rest of her remained

stiffened. But he caught her break, and that energized him. "I want you to live in harmony. To no longer have these conflicts. You can forget too, you know. It's okay to forget." And to rile a response from her, or because it was part of the plan all along, Lex snapped his middle finger and thumb and at the sound two guards appeared from the darkness in the mine and, taking her from under the arms, began escorting Elena back into the darkness.

"Wait," Ada pronounced, "where are you taking her?"

"Do you want a life with her?" Lex asked, as if he were actually confused by her request.

"Ye-yes," she stuttered.

"There's only one way that can happen, Ada. And you're not going to like it."

"What's that?" Ada gulped.

"I need you to give me the manifesto she wrote. It's too dangerous living outside The Sphere."

"I don't have it," Ada snarled, consciously restraining herself from reaching for the document that was folded into the hidden pocket at the top of her ribs.

"Who does?"

"Nobody. It's living in the minds of those who can see beyond this cage you've kept us in. There is no capturing it. You saw those obsoletes earlier. They don't believe anymore. They know something is off."

"Okay, then give me them." Lex said cooly, pointing to the twelve forgotten obsoletes still in the elevator.

"I won't."

"Oh Ada," Lex said patronizingly, as he towered in front of

her, "you still think you have control. You still think that all of this wasn't part of our plan. That somehow we let you go astray from the world we designed. That's not true Ada. This is all part of the plan for us to rid ourselves of all the rebellions we've fought for decades and to solidify the lineage of 6Di. And the sooner you comprehend that you're another clog in this wheel the sooner we can all start moving again."

For a moment, Ada wondered if Lex was right. If this entire time she'd been behaving and acting according to the plan that Vivian designed. If the reach of 6Di were truly inescapable. But the summation of all the events she witnessed and remembered over these past six months proved otherwise. She knew from the bottom of her heart that what she was witnessing, and alone comprehending, was the steady grip of 6Di slowly loosening. That the erratic and harsh policies were a response of fear, not total control. And to surrender her momentum now would be to forfeit a future that she always favored. Ada went to respond, when the elevator shaft next to the one that Kimberley and Jeremiah guarded dinged. Ada, believing this was just another act in Lex's theater, looked at him. And it was then she knew for certain that everything was outside of his control. Because whatever was behind that door wasn't here on his orders.

The elevator door opened and nothing happened. Just a tense few seconds that articulated the sensation of time, making a few seconds feel like minutes. Ada's eyes flashed between Lex, Kimberley, and Jeremiah, then to the newly opened elevator doors. All stood stricken. Then, as the door began to shut, four tips of gloved fingers cut through the door's perimeter. That hand electrified the space to life, as if it were a defibrillator against a lifeless chest. Jeremiah and Kimberley drew their weapons and inched toward the door. Then a body began to exit the elevator. Ada had seen this figure before. But why it was here was confounding. Ada tilted her head, confusedly calculating the reasons why the purger who had deceived her onto the elevator had now returned.

"Don't try anything funny!" Jeremiah shouted, stiffening the aim of his pistol.

"Hold fire," Lex said, with an annoyed sense of relief, "Dodger, what are you doing down here? You did just fine. Go assist Vivian."

"He's one of us?" Jeremiah asked, perplexed.

"Don't move!" Kimberley shouted, responding to Dodger's casual stride away from the elevator. Away from everything, as he walked into the mine's darkness.

"Dammit Dodger, stop!" Lex shouted. But he wouldn't stop. Because his few brisk strides drew the eyes necessary for a different plan to unfold. The doors Kimberley and Jeremiah once guarded began to close. She ran towards it, but was too far to stop them from closing. The last thing Kimberley saw was Yoko's wide, surprised eyes, as she pressed a button on the elevator panel. And up a dozen forgotten obsoletes and Chloe went. By the time those of 6Di had realized, they had, perhaps for the first time in their lives, been deceived.

Kimberley rerouted back to the shaft which Dodger just exited, and yelled, "Let's go J!" Who, at her command, dropped his aim from Dodger and proceeded toward the open elevator, directly behind Kimberley. They jumped aboard. As they did, two gunshots pierced the air. Kimberley's body splayed perpendicular from the elevator doorway. Jeremiah lay lifeless in the elevator, out of Ada's sight. Ada had watched the elevator until Kimberley's body dropped dead. Then she turned toward Lex, who was now gone, and realized that she now stood in the darkness alone.

Ada looked back toward the elevator and saw Corydon huffing, blood splattered across his body. She hadn't seen him since when she last returned to 20W in search of Grace's notebook, and he looked vacantly at her. So, Ada was perplexed, not only to see him—of all people—come to her aid. But to see him before her with both arms intact. As if the amputation had never happened. As if it were all a delusion they both could now see past.

"Corydon?" Ada said in disbelief. Whatever sentimental moment was briefly unfolding abruptly ended when Corydon revealed the pistol he just used to kill Kimberley and Jeremiah. "Corydon?" Ada asked again, now fearing for her life. But he wasn't aiming at her. He was aiming beyond Ada, toward Lex, who was re-emerging from the darkness, his own pistol against Elena's skull.

"Time is up Ada," Lex announced. "Come with me, or she goes." Ada stared at Elena, a woman she had, for her whole life, longed to know. She loved her mother—despite having no memories of her. She had given Ada the grandest reasons to live; to search for the truth no matter the cost. And now, Elena's existence was being ransomed for a future ruled by falsehood. Either Elena would die. Or her works would perish. To salvage Elena's flesh and in exchange have her ideas forgotten, Ada believed, was worse than killing. It was eradication. And Ada vowed then to ensure no one would forget her mother's name.

Ada did not respond. Not for a few seconds. Not for ten. She paused for so long that Elena lifted her down-trodden head, and flashed Ada eyes of despair. Up until this moment, she'd sustained her own life at the thought of seeing Ada again. Of all the memories removed and edited from her mind in their experimentations. Ada remained untouched. Ada was Elena's beacon in stormy waters, a constant reminder that a steady future nears. And she lived in that fantasy perpetually. Of her hand interlaced with hers, of cherishing her firstborn once more. To maybe, once again, make her daughter laugh uncontrollably, like Elena had when Ada was a baby. It was these thoughts Elena had replayed and imagined through the years of her tortures that preserved her last bit of sanity. But now, as she looked into her daughter's eyes, Elena saw a future that she had never confronted until now. A future where Ada and she would never smile together again. And the thought so saddened her that she closed her eyes, hanged her chin to her chest, and wished that this would be her last moment on earth.

If Ada spoke she would have been overwhelmed with sadness. That emotion which, at too high a concentration, disables one's ability to think, act, and be. Ada couldn't reduce herself to that state. Not now. So, she simply turned. Tapping Corydon on the shoulder as she passed him. At which he began backpedaling toward the elevator—keeping his pistol toward Lex. Once aboard the elevator, Ada kicked Kimberley's body out of the doorway so that the doors could shut. Ada hit the button for the ground floor, and felt her heart sink as, together with an alive Corydon and dead Jeremiah, she ascended to 20W. Her throat was lumped. Hands cold with sweat. They said nothing. Not when the door closed. Not when the door dinged again at their destination. Not when, from deep below, they heard the haunting sound of a faint, single gunshot.

20W had regressed into primal pandemonium where all who remained either sought survival or succumbed to death. Vivian, in her parapet, bounced and danced. Every obsolete in her sight, those whose BRiDGs did not break during the recent update, mimicked her every move. Yoko and Guard 40 led the dozen forgotten to a point just outside the town square where they were concealed in an abandoned store. Yoko noticed a revolutionary poster on the ground. Then, despite its warm tone, a voice that sent shivers across her every nerve, "Yoko?" She, inhaling sharply, flinched her entire body. After seeing that the voice who spoke her name came from Oriana, she relaxed.

"What's happening out there?" Yoko asked, confused by the psychedelic celebrations, "why aren't they fighting?"

"They don't have a reason to," Oriana stated plainly. Nodding to the dozen who stood by the corner, "yet."

"Do you really think it's going to work?" Yoko asked.

"It will. Let them go. It's time." Oriana nodded, affirming her own words. Yoko relayed the same nod to Guard 40, who opened the door to the store where they hid and escorted the dozen forgotten, toward the ecstatic crowd one hundred meters away. When they were halfway to the crowd, Ada and Corydon arrived at the same store where Oriana and Yoko hid. Out of breath, Ada asked, "It's happening?" Then, after a few pants, "It's happening." All four watched breathlessly as a plan that none of them knew for certain would work was unfolding into its final moments.

The first of the forgotten bumped into an obsolete. But the obsolete was so entranced that they hadn't noticed. So the forgotten kept stumbling, weakened from years of malnourishment. In a haze of overstimulation. Mechanized beings completing the one task they understood: walk. By the time half of the forgotten made their way into the crowd of crazed obsoletes one of them noticed a forgotten. "God!" he shouted, sounding drunken, "what a stench."

And when he tapped his buddy on his shoulder his friend cried out "purgers!" The outcry turned nearby obsoletes livid. They piled atop those appalling trail of alien bodies, which had no place among obedient obsoletes. The rumor of purgers present made its way throughout the entire crowd—Vivian included—via witnesses BRiDGs. From atop the parapet, Vivian shouted joyfully, supporting the assault against the purgers. "Yes, my people! Free yourselves, fight! Fight! Fight!"

Obsoletes pummeled each forgotten to the ground, gripping their throats and pounded their disgusting faces with fists. Ed, a burly obsolete, managed one forgotten to the floor facedown. Ed's desperation to prove his adoration for 6Di caused him to grab the poor forgotten by the back of her skull, after which he began pounding the woman's forehead against the gravel pavement. He battered the skull until her body felt lifeless. An ecstatic joy erupted from nearby obsoletes. Ed, stood, and facing

Vivian, lifted his fists in victory.

Vivian registered the BRiDG ID from her position, and shouted, "Ed! My faithful servant Ed, fantastic work!" His knees jittered from joy at the sound of Vivian delivering him praise.

In his ecstasy, Ed bent over to flip the forgotten's body, so he could, like a painter reviewing their canvas, admire his work. The body was frail. Petite enough for him to lift above his head with one arm. When Ed's arm was fully extended, his face sickened. Then, he dropped the forgotten who he'd just smashed. Her head slammed against the ground one more time. Ed's eyes bulged to double their size, as he cried "Tabitha?"

"Tabitha?!" Ed shouted once more, as he pulled her tenderly against his body. Her lifeless frame flopped earthward the closer he pulled her near, as if she was part of the earth now. Nothing more than a decaying substance. His outcry gripped all nearby obsoletes, and all that neared Ed abandoned their rhapsodies. Dances halted. Pummelings seized.

A disarming middle-aged obsolete, bent over and asked, "Ed, Ed, what is it? What's the matter?" Ed could only muster to glance at his friend. His mouth was long, as if it too belonged to the earth, pulling itself beyond the edges of his face. "What, talk to me," his friend said again. And as he said this, Ed's friend reached for Tabitha. And when he pulled her face into view, he too shouted. Shuttering backward as if who he'd seen was someone he thought long passed.

Their recollections were a technical impossibility, for what they saw required an imagination to codify and this was beyond the spectrum of what their BRiDGs could override. Nearby obsoletes began querying their log to see what Ed and his befuddled friend had witnessed. Gasps unleashed among the crowd. And after what was a second, the entire crowd froze. For each had verified a thought none before dared utter: that life under 6Di was the result of countless lies, and this was the first with proof.

Ed asked, hands trembling across Tabitha's mashed face, "How Thomas, how did I do this?"

Thomas looked in disbelief, peering at Tabitha's beaten face. Observing the flesh that split above her eyes revealing her skull. He studied the dry blood that masked her face. Thomas's became ashen. As if in a single beat his heart consumed all his body's blood, emptying his veins of life. "My god," Thomas whispered, "it's really her." Then, Thomas looked across the crowd and lunged toward a nearby forgotten, who lay against the floor, tattered. Thomas straddled the downed obsolete; whose frail body and crazed eyes looked exactly like someone who had been tortured and malnourished for years. "What's your name?" Thomas asked.

Then Thomas felt a snap in the back of his brain. His vision flashed white. His skin, at first painless, became an unbearable shell he wished he could shed, as if every nerve ending had caught aflame. He cried aloud, clawing at his skin. But Thomas's shrieks delivered no relief. Before Ed could ask him what was wrong, he'd begun behaving similarly. Both retreated into a fetal position, consoling their own agony. Their cries an opportune moment for Vivian to reclaim attention.

"Do you see what happens if you don't celebrate!" she thundered. "They're cursed," looking up to the heavens, hands raised high, she emphasized again, "cursed!" What Vivian intended as a moment to win back her momentum fell flat. A few voices shouted, and just as quickly silenced. Instead, the audience remained transfixed on the two possessed men whose bodies appeared moments away from imploding. Nearby obsoletes tended to the downed men. Leaving the rest of the crowd with their shared last thoughts: we were betrayed.

Another obsolete picked up where Thomas left off, "Tell us," the obsolete wondered, "what's your name."

Finally, the forgotten man opened his lips, through which two weak words escaped, "My name?"

"Yes, you have one don't you?"

"I," the forgotten obsolete said, tilting his head, "I don't know."

"Here," the kind man said, bending over to sling the nameless, disfigured body across his. Then, staggering forward with that emaciated arm over his shoulders, the obsolete assured him that, "someone here knows your name." Then, to the crowd of obsoletes he yelled, "Who knows this man?" The forgotten man was dragged through the crowd in silence. He dragged this nameless man toward the stage. Each step eroding the bit of faith that anyone here would recognize this person. "Come on," the good samaritan whispered, "surely someone knows this man." The silence was heavier to bear than the man. So, he halted his march. Released a dissatisfying exhale, and pulled the arm of this nameless man off his neck. Before the forgotten's body was placed back to the floor, a fellow obsolete yelled, "Mark!?"

"My god, Mark?" said a faceless voice pushing her way through the crowd. When she stood before Mark her face seemed stuck in a glitch, at once expressing unadulterated joy, confusion, and sadness. Then, there was silence. The woman approached the nameless man and, with convulsing hands, reached for his face. Her hands stilled when they finally touched his skin. "Mark, sweety," she gently said, "it's Ruby." And at that moment, the man who for so long appeared divested from his surroundings jolted to life. His muscles hardened. Eyes wide. He was awakened. No longer encaged.

From the parapet, Vivian seceded to the revelations dominoing below. She had stopped dancing and exciting the crowd via mindless moves and mantras. What Vivian had always orchestrated had now happened to her; she had lost control. Yet, she did not seem distraught. She stepped down from the parapet appearing calculative and calm, as if she were already planning her next steps to regain control. Indeed, she had.

Vivian turned toward a nearby aid and ordered her to, "end this." The aid nodded, as if this were an exercise regularly rehearsed. Just another inconvenience, another hurdle, in the building of a neurocommunal society. After the aide's terse nod, she scattered her fingers across a series of keyboards and screens. And if you disconnected the consequences of the aid's actions it was pure musicality. A display of a skill so polished, its adoration precluded understanding.

Vivian stared one last time out toward the crowd. The majority of which stared back at her, their anger, their disappointment, palpable from where she stood. "Hurry," Vivian said to the aid, "they've turned." The aid, again, gave a short nod. Her hands, somehow, moved even quicker than they just were. The front row of obsoletes began to charge Vivian. Their whole world crumbled before them, and its ashes were in the hands of their leader. Vivian pursed her lips at the sight, turned from the crowd, and exiting the ridgeline, disappeared out of sight. The aid kept hammering away at the keys. Obsoletes scaled the nearby hill quickly. One was within feet from her, when the aid slammed her hand to a final button. After the last clack of her keyboard, all movement ceased. And the aid stood and walked, first past the fastest of obsoletes, then to the edge of the ridgeline, where she would witness the fruits of her labor.

What followed was an unfamiliar boom. As if a bomb had been detonated. But there was no fire. No concussive blast. Just a deafening silence, as if all sound waves were at-once grounded and no longer traversing through the air. The sensation was like that of vacuum tubes attaching to one's skull. As if the smallest of internal organs, the cochlea and slivers of the gyrus temporalis, started escaping from the ear's canals. Then, there was the flash, a blindness so sudden that the vision retains its last scene frame for a time, until whiteness fades its shape. This was the humane part. The part that numbed each obsolete to the impending agony each person would unleash. Their hands gripped the back of their heads. Obsoletes tried opening the back of the skulls, to extinguish the fire burning inside their skulls. But no one could expedite 6Di's calibration.

From afar, Ada watched alongside Yoko, Oriana, Corydon, and others a process unfold that they'd all survived. It was an assault of novel proportions. An attack that epitomized the reach of Sixth Domain Industries, a demonstration that no particle, in the sea or air, among land or in outer space, not in the cybersphere, nor in one's neurons were unreachable. It was a total assault. One that few in this crowd would survive. And of the survivors, even fewer would remember. The assault was unseen. No corresponding fire or blood. Yet its force, even its anticipation, shifted the physical world. Ada felt the air around her pressurize. She turned to Oriana, wondering if she too found it difficult to breathe. Then, another boom. This one cracked the unseen pressure. All matter was disturbed. Even particles of air were slashed and slapped aside. Nothing could detour this force. Which encroached invisibly, immediately, traced only by the obsoletes who inexplicably collapsed—like dominoes. Ada cocked her head sideways, registering that the wave was making its way toward her at a pace faster than she could escape. She exhaled briefly, eyes opening wide, and contemplated the possibility that this would be her last moment on earth. The unseeable wave slammed into her chest, her head rocked backward—skull nearly touching her spine. The last thing she saw was the popcorned ceiling of the store before she fell unconscious to the floor.

Ada fell into a dream. After how long she could not measure. But in it, Ada's whole self was swimming in Vivian's cranium aquarium. Beside Ada floated the brains of her sister, mother, and father. All that was left of them were sterile, slimy blobs. Ada knew they were her family. Not by any particular descriptor. There was nothing aesthetically different from these three brains beside her than the others floating about. It was their aura that drew Ada near. And although she was underwater, Ada could breathe and speak in this dream. She adored the minds accompanying her. Imagined the bodies they occupied, the weekly dinners they shared that predated Ada's memory. Ada tried to remember the last hug she shared with each from her family. She couldn't remember when it was. But she recalled the exact dimensions of their touch. Her father's leathery palms. Her sister's cool, smooth skin. She felt the exact contours of their bodies fitting into hers. None of their minds could speak for themselves. So, they shared no words. But she didn't want a word. She only wanted to feel what it was like to hug them here. So, she reached for her mother's mind. But when her arms encircled it, the slippery thing shot upward—as a squeezed bar of soap. Ada quickly reached for her mother's escaping mind. When Ada reached for it, she missed. A panic overtook her body. She realized now she was underwater, unable to breathe. And now that everyone was out of reach, the world was turning black, and Ada thought, *No, not here. I don't want to die alone.*

Ada awakened, springing upward as she inhaled a heavy gasp of air. The putrid smell of burning flesh sentenced her to an uncontrollable bout of coughing. Disoriented, breathless, and disgusted, she oriented herself among her surroundings. But it was dark. Silent. And then an arch of electricity shot across the sky. Though startled, she was comforted by the fact that she'd seen it before.

"Welcome back," Oriana said from a few feet away, seated behind Ada against a pole in 20W's power grid.

"Oriana," Ada sat up quickly, as if she had somewhere to be. "What happened?"

"You were dreaming."

"No. I mean—"

"What were you dreaming about?" Oriana interrupted.

Ada contemplated the meaning of her dream. Wondered how she could parse between real and fantasy. "I don't really know. My family, I guess. A life now gone."

Oriana kneeled in front of where Ada was sitting. "Ada, in you are many lives. Those lived and those unlived. The unlived lives will always outnumber the ones you choose to live. They're inescapable, those unlived lives, but you must be wary of them. Because they'll always taunt you about the idea of another occupation, home, or lover. The unlived lives are never satiated. Never content. You must learn to be content with those unlived lives—and even more so with the many you choose to live."

Ada sighed. Oriana continued, "What you did was brave. And you're welcome to stay here. To help us keep building a separatist life. But I have a feeling you need to go be to yourself for a bit. And that's okay. We'll always be here."

"How can you be so confident?" Ada asked.

"Because we always have been." Ada looked at Oriana, confused. "This isn't our first rebellion, Ada. And it won't be the last. I know we'll never win. But neither will they. Each time we fight a few more join us." Oriana looked to those sleeping nearby. Ada recognized Corydon, Yoko, and a few obsoletes from the earlier riot.

"The rest," Oriana went on, "won't remember us tomorrow. And then we'll search for another glitch. Another way to break past these awful devices that enslave the rest. And eventually we'll find a way in and a few will die, a few will be set free. And on and on we go." Oriana briefly smiled, "but you should get back to sleep."

"I can't sleep." Ada whispered, as she stood to her feet. "I need to walk."

"Before you go, did I ever tell you about the first person to eat a poisonous leaf?" Ada shook her head no. "Well," Oriana began, "They died. Or at least I imagine they died. And their death came as a shock to everyone. But more importantly it became a lesson. Everyone in the tribe gathered afterward to understand why their loved one passed so quickly. The tribe came together, and you know what eventually happened?"

Ada didn't nudge at the rhetorical question.

"They eventually discovered which leaf it was. It's the reason the rest of that tribe survived. It's the reason you or I have never eaten one. We, in a weird, round-about-way, learned from that person. And that's all any of us want to do. Each of us is finding a path to contribute to the sum of human knowledge. It's the sum of billions. One day trillions. My piece is to show people beyond the BRiDG. Just as your mother did. Just as you soon will too."

"Do you know the name of that first person, who ate the poisonous leaf?"

"No. No one does. That's not the point."

It was then that Ada noticed a drawing hanging to the right of the beam which she was about to exit. It was a drawing she hadn't thought of since her time as an obsolete. Those wonderful lines of imagination came back to her so vividly. One of Lionel's masterpieces. "You said you'll be here when I get back?" Ada asked. Oriana nodded.

Ada began walking out from the electrical frame. "Where are you headed to?" Oriana asked.

Ada pointed to Lionel's drawing hung against the wall. Smiling, Ada said, "to a life beyond reason." Ada reached into her back pocket, "I suppose you'll need this first," she said, placing her mother's manifesto onto a nearby desk.

"Go," Oriana said, "and take this with you." In battle Oriana had acquired Elena's necklace. Ada took the necklace and hugged Oriana, as if—in case—it could be their last. She left the alcove and walked across the power grid of 20W. Under the arcs of electricity that empowered life and deception throughout both of 6Di's stratums. Ada entered a nearby vehicle, started its engine, and drove to the edge of the Stratum of Reason. Before her was a myth: the Stratum of Imagination, a wild and inhabitable place. But Ada believed more existed beyond the horizon—beyond the reach of 6Di. She stood in awe of the image before her. A purple and orange sky silhouetted a mountain range that etched itself across the horizon. She'd seen these mountains before, but couldn't remember their name. Ada laughed, imagining the days when Lily would have happily transported the answer to the tip of her tongue.

Ada stepped across the border that invisibly separated the Stratum of Reason from Imagination, the point at which the wilderness overtook all surroundings. She looked back at her old stratum and reached into her pocket, twirling the necklace that guided her through all the chaos of the past few months. She kissed the necklace, and tossed it back into the Stratum of Reason. Maybe she'd find Elena again. And if not, then perhaps another part of her forgotten self.

Ada took a few steps and wondered what it was she would do next. It was winter now, and dark. Then it hit her: a thought as serendipitous as complete. Like a hummingbird buzzing by, which for the briefest of moments hovers before you and looks you in the eye as it tilts its head, before fluttering out of sight. You may not know where it went or where it's going, or even be able to recall the color of its feathers. But you feel touched by something. As Ada did when she felt the biting air. *This is good*, she thought. *Cold, but real.* Like the morning showers she once took as an obsolete. Ada couldn't help but smile. How nice it felt knowing that some things would never change, and yet, to her, nothing would ever be the same.

ACKNOWLEDGEMENTS

No book worth reading or writing is the sole work of an author. This book would not have been possible without the deliberate help of many individuals. More intriguing are those subliminal influences that have shaped this journey. Instagrammers celebrating the printed page which regularly remind me that reading is not dead, designers who have built clacky keyboards that turned my writing sessions hypnotic. Journalists writing stories across the globe which remind me, too often, that for too many dystopias are synonymous with existence. This city I now call home, Austin, for making it easy for me to hide away in a closet because your drinks have become too damn expensive. Point is, this book owes unsuspecting people a nod of appreciation.

A special thank you to my editors Elizabeth Gassman and April Kelly. It's hard to write a paragraph now and not think "stakes!" or "continuity!." If you thought this book was shit, you should have seen the drafts they had to read. Thank you both for resuscitating my love for the craft of writing.

Oh friends, if I begin with you I'm afraid I'll never end. But, I must name a special few who've been invaluable in helping me write my first book. Phil, thank you for not letting me quit on publishing that zine a decade ago. You planted the seed in me that one day I'd write something even grander. Madison, how often I remind myself that art is the process and not the product. Your words have helped me see art as inseparable from time; that an artful life is always one act away. Jordan, thank you for paving the way for how to never quit on a creative dream.

At risk of ommitting names of people who've showered me with support and love, I hope you can see the little ways you've helped shape this story. If you're in my life you have. May we each continue to encourage another to lead the most adventurous lives on and off the page.

I'd be remiss if I didn't express my gratitude for two of the closest people in my life. Kendrick, I've been inspired by your greatness since I was two. I can only hope this work allows me to return the favor, for once. Lexi, your immense love has me convinced that the greatest story I'll ever write is ours.

Thank you all, for you've each made writing and reading books not only possible - but pure pleasure.

A NOTE ABOUT THE AUTHOR

Nate Eckman regularly publishes to Speculatively, a personal site where early writings germinate into his next great novel, critique, or film. His previous works include feature scripts currently under development and nonfiction essays on military service for *The War Horse*. He graduated from Columbia University with a degree in history in 2018. Nate currently lives in Austin, Texas. This is his first book.